HU$TLER$

EDITED BY
jesse grant

HU$TLER$

erotic stories of sex for hire

alyson books
NEW YORK

© 2006 Alyson Books. Authors retain the rights to their individual pieces of work.
All rights reserved.

Manufactured in the United States of America.

This trade paperback original is published by Alyson Books,
P.O. Box 1253, Old Chelsea Station, New York, New York 10113-1251.

Distribution in the United Kingdom by Turnaround Publisher Services Ltd.,
Unit 3, Olympia Trading Estate, Coburg Road, Wood Green,
London N22 6TZ England.

First edition: August 2006

06 07 08 09 ▪a 10 9 8 7 6 5 4 3 2 1

ISBN 155583-941-X
ISBN-13 978-1-55583-941-3

Library of Congress Cataloging-in-Publication Data has been applied for.
Cover photograph: Luca DiCorso. Courtesy Chi Chi LaRue's Rascal Video.

CONTENTS

INTRODUCTION

It's tough work putting together an anthology of smut this good. I've had a hard-on for the last few weeks, and no matter how many times I drain the thing, it stiffens right up at the sight of my laptop. Though I've done my share of books for Alyson Books, I'm particularly pleased with this collection. Established geniuses like Simon Sheppard and Kirk Read sit on the page next to horny newcomers like Aaron Nielsen, and the overall effect is smoking hot. We've got hustling in just about every form you can imagine in these pages: pervy boy pro-doms, rattling preachers, cool professionals blowing businessmen, and nervous young things just trying to make a buck. Throw in a few cops and a couple of ex-cons and you've got two hundred pages of perfect jack-off material. It's good to be me.

I hope you enjoy reading this collection as much as I liked putting it together for you. Now, off to choke the chicken once more before bed.

— JESSE GRANT

STIFF

....

SIMON SHEPPARD

HOW CAN I explain what happened at the Hotel Babylon?

Let's start when I picked up my phone messages. The voice was businesslike and middle-aged. "I saw your ad. Your picture looks just right, and it says you're willing to travel. I'm going to be in Vegas, and I wondered if you could, if we could … uh.… Give me a call during East Coast business hours at …" and he gave his number. I looked up the unfamiliar area code: North Carolina. What's the matter with the guy, I thought, can't he find a hustler on the East Coast? Why get somebody from L.A.? But then it began to make sense: if he was going to pay my way—and he was—it would be a lot cheaper to catch a short-hop airline to Vegas from the City of Angels than from back east. And as far as homegrown talent … well, any cute gay boy in North Carolina would be as likely as not to get the hell out of Jesse Helms Country as soon as he could.

At that point I wasn't bright enough to ask myself why he didn't make use of the abundant local talent in Vegas. I just dialed the number. Well, actually, before I dialed the number, I stripped down, stood in front of the full-length mirror, and started jacking off. I always do that before a big-ticket call. I think that johns can hear the hard-on in my voice. In this business, a dick is a dick, even when it's as big as mine; it's merchandising that makes the crucial difference.

"Mr. Czamanske's office." He'd had to spell out his name on the message.

I pulled at my half-hard cock. "May I speak to Mr. Czamanske, please?"

"Who shall I say is calling?" The voice of a blonde with big tits.

"Um, tell him it's Mr. Dick calling."

An on-hold pause.

"Harry Czamanske here."

By this time my cock was fully erect. I admired it in the mirror, a perfect tower of thick, high-priced flesh.

I gave him the ground rules: safe sex only; money up front; I was willing to bottom in all sorts of scenes for extra cash, but I was the one to set the limits; no permanent marks.

It turned out he didn't want me to bottom. He wanted to be flogged. "I can do that," I said.

We made the final arrangements. He was to pay for a plane ticket in my name and send me another hundred for expenses, the balance to be paid upon delivery. He'd be staying at the Hotel Babylon, and he'd get me a room down the hall. The final price I named was high. He didn't argue. I didn't know what his business was, but whatever it was, he must have been doing well at it.

"Uh, are you okay?" he asked.

"Sure. Why?"

"You just sound strange is all."

"I'm fine, Mr. Czamanske. See you next week." I hung up the cellular with one hand, while the other tried to catch my come before it fell on the carpet.

. . . . .

IF CZAMANSKE HAD been a gentleman, he'd have flown me out first class. Or at least business class. But hey, I'm flexible.

I land at McCarran International. Whoever McCarran was. They should have named the airport after Bugsy Siegel. Bugsy

Siegel International. I like the sound of that. I get the shuttle to the Hotel Babylon, just a little way past the Grand and the Excalibur.

I've never seen the hotel before. It's one of the newer places in town, one of those kitsch-and-craps places devoted to convincing the mid-American tourist he's someplace foreign that he can't afford, and even if he could afford the real thing, he wouldn't bother, because they don't speak English there and the water can make you sick.

But rather than trying to reproduce Venice or Paris or some other damn place, the Hotel Babylon, like Caesar's Palace, tries to convince Mr. Retail Drone that he is really the ruler of one of those fabulously decadent ancient empires that served free Wallbangers while you lost at roulette. Which means the architecture is an amazing mishmash of stuff—the Hanging Gardens of Nebuchadrezzar, the ruins at Persepolis, some motifs from the DeMille version of Samson and Delilah. And an Emporio Armani. I probably wouldn't mind so much if I hadn't just earned a degree in art history at Oberlin.

So I'm walking through this lobby, decorated somewhere between Overblown and Utterly Tasteless, and all around me are beer-gut guys and their jowly wives, folks who have come to the Babylon to live it up. I get the usual feeling: if they knew what I was up to, wouldn't Mr. and Mrs. Kansas be shocked? After all, despite the hubby's likely cruising of the girls who work the streets, their decadence is of a safer kind. They're here to lose money at the tables and gain weight at the buffets, while I'm here to fuck a guy for money. All they'll have left to show for their expenditure is heart disease and learning never to hit a hard 17. Whereas my john, if he's lucky, will be left with whip marks, a sore butt hole, and some stains on the sheets.

I have my toy bag in hand as the queeny-but-cute guy at the check-in counter tells me Mr. Czamanske has already arrived. He gives me a significant look as he hands me my key. The bellhop who takes my bags is a curly-haired blond hunk, muscular legs shown off by a historically inappropriate kind-of-toga. When we get to the room, he turns his back to me. He bends over to put my bags down on the floor, and his little toga rides up, exposing a perfectly formed ass barely hidden by the gauzy fabric. The boy knows his business. I give him a big tip.

I freshen up, change into my tight jeans, then change back into my baggy jeans, figuring that Harry Czamanske is paying for youth. I double-check my client's room number, then head down the hall. The beginning of my honeymoon in Vegas.

Czamanske answers the door. Maybe late forties, blandly good-looking in a way that suggests he might once have been really handsome. Balding, a bit overweight, slightly paunchy. In other words, just my type.

Johns like him would probably be surprised to know that I'd have sex with businessman daddies like them for free. Hell, in another world, I might even pay for the privilege. I think it's part of the reason for my success. Some of the guys who hire me actually turn me on, so I don't have to pretend; I can just relax and enjoy myself, as long as I don't let on.

Harry Czamanske looks at me like I'm raw meat. It's flattering, but slightly scary. I extend my hand. "Sam Marlowe, Mr. Czamanske."

He doesn't shake my hand. He doesn't tell me to call him "Harry." He just says, "Come in. Take your shirt off."

It's his dime; I do as I'm told. He's gotten me a standard room, while he has a suite, a big, semi-garish suite. I pull off my T-shirt and drop it on the armchair in the sitting room.

"Fold that up!" he snaps.

This is, perhaps, not going to be fun. I do as I'm told, laying the neatly folded shirt on the side table.

"Now turn all the way around."

I turn.

"Not bad," Harry Czamanske says. "'Course, you could be leaner. If you'd cut down on your calories...."

I haven't come all the way to Las Vegas for diet tips. I cut to the chase. "You want me to take the rest of my clothes off?" I ask.

"All in good time," my client says, smiling what fiction writers describe as "an evil grin."

I stand there, wondering what comes next. Czamanske stands there, just staring at me. Finally, he speaks. "Pull your dick out."

I do. It's soft.

"Is that the best you can do?"

I start playing with myself, wishing I'd dropped a Viagra.

"Pathetic."

"Listen," I say, "maybe this isn't gonna work. How about I just take the plane ticket and traveling expenses and call it even?"

"You want more money? I'll give you more money." He pulls a big wad of bills out of his pocket. "How's this?"

So I start getting hard for him.

"Come into the bedroom. Stand in front of the mirror. And keep jacking off."

For that kind of money, I do as I'm told. I watch my reflection: a good-looking guy in his early twenties, boyish face, which some johns really like. Pretty nice build, boyish too. A boyish guy working his dick—a cute, half-hard dick jutting out from the fly of baggy jeans—while a middle-aged man sits on the bed behind him and watches. The older man doesn't play with himself, doesn't display any emotion, just watches.

Not for the first time, I wonder what a nice boy like me is doing in a place like this. And the usual answer comes: working. It's a job, a job no worse than packing up paintings for shipment at some second-rate museum, or trying to sell some rich, bored woman bad postmodern sculpture at a ritzy gallery. And the pay's better.

"Take your hand away."

I take it away. My cock, pro that I am, is now standing straight up, a wet drop of pre-come drooling from the slit.

"Come over here." The tone of a man who's used to being obeyed. I pity his blond secretary.

I walk over to him. His face is absolutely without expression. Not lust, not joy, not even contempt.

"Closer. Stick your dick right in my face."

I get so close he goes cross-eyed. He inhales deeply.

"Now get out of here. Come back in two hours."

I push my hard-on into my pants and get the hell out of there.

I'm halfway down the faux-Babylonian hall before I change my mind. I go back and knock. "What the fuck do you want?" Czamanske asks.

"My money." Truth to tell, I usually wait till it's over to get paid, but in this case trust is only going to go so far.

"And what's to keep you from just running off with it?"

I give him what I hope is a stern look. "Yeah, and what's to keep you from stiffing me?"

"Tell you what," Harry Czamanske says, "when you get back here, it'll be sitting on the table. You can count it, but you can't take it till I'm through with you."

That seems fair enough. I really don't like the guy. I begin to suspect why he's flown me out from L.A.—his reputation has probably worked its squirmy way through the boys in Vegas. Out-of-town talent is all he has left. But a deal is a deal, and the money is good.

I head down to the casino. It's the usual mix of blinking neon, clanking coins, and money-losing rubes. I kill some time cruising the place, but most of the guys there are the straight-and-you-don't-want-to-try type. I sit down to play some blackjack. The dealer's nametag says "Naomi." I usually lose, and at ten bucks a hand, you can lose a lot pretty fast. But my pal Harry has lots of cash to give me, and so I have money to burn. I've just split a pair of aces and busted on both hands when a young, thin guy sits down on the empty stool beside me. Naomi's still shuffling, so I look up at the boy. Cute, in a weasely sort of way. He looks like maybe he's a card counter, but he also looks like he can kiss.

He buys in, and play resumes. I'm trying to remember what to do with a soft 13 if the dealer has a 3 when I feel his knee brush up against mine. It pulls away for a second, and my knee follows. I make contact, and his leg presses back hard.

I'm still feeling kind of horny from incompletely jacking off upstairs, and my cock starts stirring. I'm having real trouble concentrating on the game. I keep busting when I should stand pat. Then cute boy somehow manages to drop a chip on the floor, and when he recovers it, he brushes his hand all the way up my calf.

The guy's not, truth to tell, my type—too young, too cute, not beefy enough—but I am horny, and I have some time to kill. I gather up my few remaining chips, say, "I'm done for now," and stand up from the table. Cute boy looks up at me, and I, shamelessly, wink and lick my lips. I wander a little ways off, then stand looking back. The guy is leaving the table too.

"Where's the nearest men's room?" I ask a toga-clad waitress. It's over behind the Wheel of Fortune. I walk slowly toward it. When I look back, the guy is still on my tail.

In the restroom, I stand at a sink washing my face till cute boy shows up. In the awful fluorescent lights, he looks even less my type. But the very visibly growing bulge in his pants is intriguing. I make my way to the end cubicle in the row of toilet stalls; the one next to it is empty too, but not for long.

He taps his extended foot, visible beneath the metal wall between us. I stretch my foot toward the partition and tap back. He bends over and sticks his hand out. So he wants to give me head. But I still have a client upstairs; I'm not going to spew my sperm into some stranger's mouth for free. I kneel on the floor, push his hand back, and grab at one of his ankles. Meanwhile, two drunk guys at the urinals are telling each other loud dirty jokes. Cute boy kneels on the floor and slides his bare legs under the partition. His dick, when it follows, turns out to be beautiful and huge. A cock like that can make me overlook his weaseliness. It just plain makes me hungry. I bend over, stick my tongue out, and lick at his shaft, getting the velvety young cockflesh nice and wet. Then I open wide, take the swollen dick head in my mouth, and suck, twirling my tongue around the tender skin. Cute boy groans and thrusts upward, and I take the whole stiff monster down my throat. He manages to reach under the partition and jam my head down till I almost gag. Almost, but not quite; my professional abilities stand me in good stead. You know how sometimes you do something you don't really want to do just to keep yourself from thinking about something you're going to have to do that's even worse, like washing the dishes just before you're due at the dentist's? Well, that's me, kneeling down on the tile floor, sucking that luscious but unwanted cock, while outside the stall Middle America does its business. It's better than dealing with Czamanske.

Just when I really need to come up for air, cute boy lets loose, pumping a big salty load in my mouth. I usually don't eat come, and though I'm in a weird mood, I still spit it out on the floor.

I glance at my watch. Shit, I'm going to be late. I pull my pants up, zipping my fly over my still-swollen crotch.

It's then I notice a pair of white loafers on the other side of my door. You know, the kind that were already tacky two full decades ago. The kind only clueless old tourists wear. Not the footwear for casino police checking for misbehavior in the toilets, I hope.

I take a deep breath and open the door. Bingo. There stands some paunchy guy in his sixties, his eyes still unfocused by lust. He must have been watching me through the crack in the door, standing there, obvious, despite the traffic flow. Christ, the things guys' dicks will persuade them to do. I check: wedding ring.

I rush through the casino and back upstairs. Czamanske is furious.

"You're late. Where the fuck were you, you dumb fuck?"

Enough is enough.

"Listen, Harry Czamanske," I fume, "you may treat other boys this way, but I'm a fucking professional. I don't get paid to be mistreated, and if you have a problem with that, I'm getting the hell out of here right now and catching the next flight to L.A." Or more likely, I think, hitting the casino and finding another john.

Czamanske's face softens, just a little. "Okay," he says, "but I'm not paying you to be twelve minutes late. Now go get your toybag."

"Just as long as we're clear."

"We're clear."

I look around. "The money?"

"It's over there."

I go over to the sitting-room desk. There's a big pile of twenties on it, next to the room service menu. I carefully count it out.

"All there?"

I lay the money back down.

"Yeah, Czamanske."

I go back to my room to fetch the gear he's asked me to bring to Vegas. When I get back to his suite, Czamanske is naked except for a black jockstrap, which seems to be well filled. His body turns me on—hairy, strong, big nipples, nice thighs, just a little bit of meat around his middle. Perfect. Too bad about his personality.

"Now maybe we can get down to what you fucking came here for."

"Listen, Harry." I haven't used his first name before. "You trying to make me mad?"

"And if I am?"

"If you are, you're going to be punished."

He grabs at his crotch. So now we're in the scene. My real anger at his attitude will have a constructive outlet. And a profitable one.

"You don't touch yourself unless I give you permission. Got that, Harry?" I put my best sneer into my voice.

"Yes, sir."

"Louder."

"Yes, *sir*."

"Now go into the bedroom," I say, in a tone of what I hope sounds like deadly calm, "and get on the bed on all fours."

Harry looks great with his ass in the air. When I stare down at his hairy, chunky butt, its crack revealing an eager hole, my dick ignores his miserable manners and it leaps to attention.

I lay the toybag on the bed and fetch out a bottle of lube, a pair of latex gloves, and a big, evil-looking buttplug. I glove up, lube up, and spread out his butt. For a man his age, his hole is in great shape, smooth and tight but instantly responsive to my touch. I slip two fingers inside him with no trouble, plunge deeper, and hook down to his prostate. Czamanske lets out a groan, the first nonhostile thing he's said all day. I play around inside him, withdraw, then slip three fingers inside. He's loosening up nicely. I work on his ass ring till I can slip my pinky in too. Now he's ready for the plug.

I grease up the jet-black monster and position it over his wet hole. My other hand slaps his ass. His hole tightens up, then unpuckers. An invitation. I press the plug's tip inside him, and then firmly guide its tapered body into him, stretching him ever-wider around the silicone toy. The last few inches are tricky; clearly, he's not used to taking such a big boy, but I persist. The body of the plug penetrates him, the whole big thing popping into his guts. His hole closes down around the narrow neck. Only the black base is visible against his hairy ass. I slap his butt again. Harry Czamanske shudders in pleasure.

"Now, Harry boy, that big baby stays inside your pussy whenever we play. Got that?"

"Yes, sir." He actually sounds chastened.

"Now roll over on your back."

Hotel rooms, even expensive hotel rooms, don't make great dungeons. But with a set of restraints, four lengths of rope, and a bit of practice, it's easy to gracefully tie a guy down to most any bed. The Hotel Babylon is no exception. Looking down at Czamanske lying there, bound spread-eagle, his hard-on stretching his jock, I think, damn, I'm good at my work.

I take my Bowie knife from the toybag and open it. Czamanske's eyes open wide in what I would assume is fear if he hadn't been the one to request knife-play in the first place. I hold the blade just inches from his face, pass the cold flat of the blade against his cheek, then slowly drag the sharp edge of the blade down his body: throat, hairy chest, heaving belly. My client whimpers with excitement. I slip the edge of the razor-sharp blade beneath the waistband of the jockstrap, then draw it upward, stretching the elastic, pulling at his hard-on. I notice that the pouch is thoroughly soaked with pre-come.

"Oh, fuuuck," Harry Czamanske moans.

"Shut up," I say.

And I saw the knife gently, slicing at the elastic until the waistband begins to give way. It's easy to make a second cut through the belt, and I pull the wreck of the jockstrap free of his crotch.

Harry Czamanske has a nice cock. Those poor souls who haven't seen a lot of hard-ons might not understand that each dick has a personality all its own. Some woodies are graceful, or perky, or beautiful. Others are shy, or aggressive, or blunt. Harry Czamanske's cock is manly and impressive, a masculine tree-trunk of a cock. And he has an oversize slit, something I fetishize; there's no accounting for taste.

I slap the shaft. Harry groans, and his cock grows even harder. I slap again. And harder. We've arranged a safe word, but under the circumstances I might be tempted not to use it.

"There's poppers on the bedside table," Czamanske says.

"You want some?"

"Yes."

"Yes, please, sir."

"Yes, please, *sir.*"

I unscrew the lid from the brown bottle, use a thumb to close off one of his nostrils, and stick the bottle under the other. Harry inhales deeply.

I pull out another short piece of rope, loop it around the base of his cock and balls, then tie the whole package up, rope encasing his shaft, his balls stretched out and vulnerable. Sometimes you get paid for something you'd have done for free. I feel fortunate.

I bring the palm of my hand down against his well-packed ball sac. I watch his face carefully for the signs of pleasure and surrender, then hit his balls again. Pre-come drips from his veiny, tree-trunk dick. This is going to be fun.

Then he says it: "Hit me harder, you dumb fuck."

"What?"

"My fucking grandmother could hit harder than that. I'm paying good money for a piece-of-shit whore."

"Listen, I told you before. I don't have to hang around for that sort of abuse." I start to unfasten his shackles from the bed.

"Listen, I'm sorry." He doesn't sound sorry. "Flog me, okay? Punish me. Flog me."

So is this all a game, or the real thing? And when money changes hands for sex, what does "the real thing" mean anyhow?

I finish unfastening his shackles.

"Okay, Czamanske. Kneel down on the floor. There, facing the mirror."

He does, looking for all the world like a properly repentant sinner.

I reach into my toybag and pull out my good flogger, the one Jeanette Heartwood made. It's been a while since I've used it; most of my clients aren't very kinky. When they hire an innocent-looking boy, they want him to turn out to be an innocent boy, or at least a hustler who can pass for one. But Czamanske has hired me to, I'm guessing, punish him for his desires. Or something. Anyway, the flogger feels good in my hand.

I still have my pants on, my half-hard cock hanging out of the fly. I toss the flogger on the Babylon's bed and strip down, keeping just my T-shirt on. Meanwhile, Czamanske is squirming impatiently. He'll just have to fucking wait.

"While you're over there, bring me the poppers."

"Please, sir."

"Please, sir." Czamanske's voice is dripping with sarcasm. But a job's a job. Within reason. I look over at the big wad of cash in the next room and fetch the poppers. When I hand them to him, I look down at his crotch; that nice cock of his is still real hard, jutting up from his wiry bush.

I figure I might as well enjoy myself. I lean up against the mirror, my cock just inches away from Czamanske's face.

"Now, Harry, stick out your tongue, and lick the underside of my shaft, nice and easy."

He does it, half-grudgingly, and I ease my hard-on into his mouth. He's not much of a cocksucker, but at least with my prick in his mouth he can't talk. I pump my cock into my john's throat, and it feels kind of good. I grab the back of his head and push, and I'm gratified to feel him start to gag.

But work is work. It's time to fulfill my deal.

I go stand behind Czamanske, flogger in hand, and take a deep breath. I raise the flogger above my head. He's looking in the mirror, looking at me standing there behind him. He opens his mouth, about to say something, something fucked-up no doubt, when I bring the flogger down on his back.

Now, I'm a skilled top, and I know how to warm a client up, slowly escalate the scene. But this time I just whiz the flogger's tails through the air and bring them down hard, without a second thought.

Harry Czamanske shuts his mouth, shudders a little, and takes a big hit of poppers. As soon as he's screwed the bottle cap back on, I bring the flogger down again. My left hand, meanwhile, is working my hard dick.

His face is flushed. I hit him again.

"At last we're getting somewhere," he says.

"Shut the fuck up." I see myself in the mirror, see genuine anger. I don't like it. Not professional. I hit him even harder. His muscles relax. His back invites more. I give it to him.

He takes another hit of poppers. His shoulder blades are turning bright pink.

I bring the leather flogger down again. And again.

And Harry Czamanske slumps forward, against the mirror. The poppers fall to the carpet.

I kneel down. Harry Czamanske is unconscious.

No.

Oh, no.

Harry Czamanske is dead.

Oh, Jesus Jesus Jesus.

I get him stretched out on his back and try to remember what to do—my medical education mostly consists of having watched a few episodes of *ER*. I know the first thing to do is to yell, "Call 911," but there's nobody around to yell to. Then I remember I'm supposed to do mouth-to-mouth before I pound on his chest, and I'm sorry, but I'm not going to blow into a dead guy's mouth, I don't care how much he's paid me.

So he just lies there.

I'm in big fucking trouble. He's bought a plane ticket in my name. I asked the queen at the check-in desk about him. There's a big fat trail back to me. And if it's not just the poppers, if he's also done other drugs, I'll probably be blamed for that too.

But really, I ask myself, what choice do I have? Come clean now or get busted later. I go to the phone, am about to dial 911 and try to explain everything, when, just like in some movie, there's a knock at the door.

"Honey, are you there? Harry, it's Jennifer. Surprise!"

I look closely at Harry Czamanske's left hand. The indentation of a wedding ring circles his third finger.

"You there, babe? You asleep?"

I'm standing there half-naked, a just-flogged dead guy on the floor, and his wife is at the door, or maybe his mistress. I expect the door to open any second, but it doesn't. I guess she doesn't have a key. I tiptoe over and peek through the peephole. Nobody. She's gone. Most likely downstairs, to get a second key. She'll be back.

I've got to get out, and to make it look like I wasn't involved. I've got to work fast. I start to fill the sunken tub, and drag Czamanske into the fake-Babylonian bathroom. I've played with some unresponsive bottoms in my time, but this guy takes the cake. He plops into the tub with a splash.

I hurriedly gather up my toys, shove them back into the bag, and wipe down all the hard surfaces I can find. I call room service, tell them I'm Czamanske, order a hamburger, tell them to leave it inside even if no one answers the door. I figure the bellboy will open the door, discover the body, call a doctor.

I'm ready to get the hell out of there when I remember the poppers. I get down on my hands and knees and find them under the bed, where they've been kicked in the chaos. I start to put them in my pocket when I get a brainstorm. I go into the bathroom, wipe off the bottle, press Czamanske's fingers to the brown glass, and put the poppers beside the tub. Now they'll think Czamanske was jacking off when he bought the farm.

I've thought of everything, except … oh Christ, the butt plug. I drag him around in the tub till he's on his side, wrap a towel around the slippery base of the plug, and tug. No dice. I feel like I'm going to scream. Trying not to think of what I'm doing, I pull harder. The muscles finally let loose, and the plug slides out of him. I wrap it in the towel, ready for the toybag, and tip my client's body back down so he's lying, almost relaxed, in the now-filled tub.

On the way out I pick up the wad of cash from the desk. I've not only earned it, I've earned it ten times over. Trying to hurriedly stuff it in my pocket, I fumble, and the cash flutters to the floor. Oh shit! There are a few twenties, but Czamanske has replaced most of the bills with singles. I've been ripped off, and I'm furious. Even dead, Czamanske is a really, really bad client.

There's a knock on the door. "Room service."

I hear a key in the lock. I don't know what to do. Trying my best to sound like a bad-tempered, middle-aged man, I yell, "Leave it by the door." The delivery boy's not going to get a tip, but hell, why should I be the only one who gets stiffed?

I'm crouching there, waiting for the bellboy to go away, when I hear it: slosh, slosh, slosh.

Harry Czamanske has come to.

He's alive.

Thank God I'm a better hustler than I am a doctor.

I grab up the last of the bills and make for the door.

"Come back here, fucker, and suck my cock!" I look over my shoulder. Czamanske is standing there, soaking wet, waving his big, hard cock at me. Men are such amazing pigs; even dead, they don't lose their woodies.

If I were a good businessman, I'd insist on my money. But I've been mistreated. I've been ripped off. I've witnessed a resurrection that, though maybe less miraculous than J.C.'s, actually has saved my ass. Now I'm getting the fuck out of Vegas, without delay. I open the hotel room door. My erstwhile client is yelling. "Get back here, boy, and suck my hard dick!"

And there, standing in the doorway, bleached-blonde and overdressed, is, I'm assuming, Mrs. Harry Czamanske.

"Harry?" Her voice rises to a shriek. "Har-*ryyy*?"

I figure I'll just leave the lovebirds alone.

"Excuse me, Mrs. Czamanske," I say politely. "Nice meeting you."

I push my way past the gape-mouthed woman and step right in the middle of the overpriced room-service hamburger lying in the hall.

The next hour is a blur, a blur headed straight back for L.A. I don't even stop to wipe the ketchup off my shoes until I get to McCarran International Airport. Whoever the fuck McCarran was.

SAN SEBASTIAN

MARK ORANJE

I'D NEVER HEARD of the place before my editor told me I was to go there. But I was assured that the tiny island of San Sebastian did indeed exist. A craggy outpost, nestled off Puerto Rico, where publishing magnate Chay Zane had recently opened a luxury complex, which our magazine had been invited to review.

Mind, I couldn't help but wonder why I'd been selected for the assignment, given that my boss generally had the pick of destinations and that the Caribbean was one of his favorite vacations. It was only when he revealed that San Sebastian was for gay men that I realized that the island wasn't part of his heterosexual style and that I, as the only qualified guy in the office, had won the job by default.

Still, I wasn't about to complain. Especially given that this was my first shout since God-knows-when. Who cared that it was likely to be some tacky one-star hotel in the middle of nowhere! Why, even the fact that I had to have a blood test to gain entrance to the island didn't bother me too much. The important thing was that I would be out of the office for a few days. Away from the early spring chill of New York and enjoying the heat of the tropics.

I can't deny that my reservations didn't resurface before my arrival, mainly as a result of having to catch three flights: first to Miami, then to San Juan, then finally to the small private runway that was San Sebastian International Airport.

In fact, by the time we finally touched down on the concrete, I couldn't help but wonder why any dude in his right mind would actually want to make the effort to visit this lonely garrison. Zane's project was already doomed by its geography—a point I noted mentally in preparation for my ultimate report.

To his credit the charismatic proprietor was there to meet me in person. A hefty fellow, sporting a cream suit and panama, who looked dapper for a middle-aged fart. Clearly he was keen to impress a point, emphasized by his prompt instructions to his two young, half-dressed lackeys to take my bags.

"Mr. Gardner!" he exclaimed, as if I were an old friend. "I can't tell you how pleased I am to see you...."

He shook my hand, then promptly pulled me in the direction of his jeep. "You had a good journey?" he inquired.

I nodded my head out of politeness. Fact is, I'd had enough of traveling, and the realization that I still hadn't yet made it to the complex filled me with frustration.

"In just five minutes you will have arrived at the world's greatest gay man's paradise," Zane explained, with a defiant wink. "And believe me, my boys are more than keen to impress, so I hope you've come ready to partake in the action. After all," he continued, glancing back at his skivvies, "we don't want you leaving this place without having sampled the full delights of everything and everyone that this island has to offer. Do we, guys?"

The handsome pair of grooms each gave a toothy grin in my direction but said nothing, leaving me to wonder what sort of place this was exactly and what was the precise nature and role of the workers here.

Fortunately, I didn't have to wait too long to find out.

Zane had exaggerated when he'd described it as a five-minute journey to the complex, for it was closer to ten. But it gave the man an opportunity to sell his pitch as we were driven along a one-way track, with rain forest on either side.

"I know what you're intending to say in your report," he

remarked. "That this place is too remote. Too difficult to get to."

"It has crossed my mind," I confessed.

"But that's the idea, Mr. Gardner. Besides, I don't think the authorities in the States would have appreciated me setting up shop in Palm Springs or Long Beach. They'd have said it was a male brothel and closed it down."

I was almost lost for words by his sincerity. "And is it?" I inquired.

Zane smiled. "My boys provide entertainment, that's all. You know, I had two thousand applicants when we started, which I whittled down to just seventy-five. Seventy-five of the spunkiest, hottest well-hung studs this side of the Rockies.

"And in return for providing hard cocks and willing holes for my customers," he continued, "I treat them like prize stallions and paid a fortune for them. They are my stable. My finest collection. And after a few years, most of them will be able to leave here and live like millionaires. As such, everyone wins. My clients get the vacation of their dreams. My boys get rich. And I get satisfaction from fulfilling the fantasies of gay men everywhere.

"Not that I can complain about the money either...." he wryly added.

"By the way," Zane sighed, glancing at me up and down, "I'm looking for a new blond."

I couldn't help but blush. "I don't think it's quite me," I observed.

"Really? Tell me, how much is that rag-mag paying you for this?"

I stuttered, "Well, I'm not sure...."

"Come on," he urged. "How much do you get paid a week?"

"Well, about six ... seven hundred...." I finally admitted.

"Hey, Paolo," he shouted to the lad in the front passenger seat. "Tell Mr. Gardner here what you picked up last week."

Paolo grinned. "Over three thousand," he confirmed.

"And it wasn't a busy week," Zane added. "Not by a long shot."

. . . . .

WE REACHED OUR destination. An ocean-view hotel, set into the side of a cliff, and boasting one of the largest outside pools that I had ever seen.

Not that it was the size of the lido that warranted my greatest attention. For taking a second glance, I realized that several older guys (who I assumed were visitors) appeared to be enjoying the attention of the island's young, horny residents. One fellow—who looked old enough to be my grandfather—sat on a lounger with two studs sucking him off. Another, in his thirties, was being blown at the water's edge. And meantime the water itself was filled with a bevy of naked hookers, swimming and frolicking about in the sunshine. It was, as Zane assured me, a fantasy made real.

"I take it you like the scenery?" the owner teased, noting my interest.

"The scenery?" I asked, puzzled.

He laughed. "You're right. No one notices the scenery. All this sun and sand and sea we have here—and the only thing any visitor thinks about is which guy he's gonna have sex with first! Talking of which, once you're booked in you're free to have any guy you want. Come on, I'll check you in at reception...."

Jeez, this was all just so surreal. A little island where men basically did nothing but have sex with each other day and night. Where the horny tourist could select whichever beau took his fancy and demand whatever sexual favor he craved. And where the only sound seemed to be the slurping of mouth on hard cock, or the *slap-slap-slap* of low-hanging balls against some pert, hungry rump.

Little wonder that I should have found my own shaft pulsing in my pants. I mean, for heaven's sake, what was happening here was just so debauched. Young men (many of whom were probably straight and only here for the money) being used by dirty-minded businessmen and pervy professionals. Prostituting themselves for the next easy buck and displaying not an ounce of self-respect in the process.

"Come on, Mr. Gardner!" Zane insisted, noting my hesitancy. "The sooner we book you in, the sooner you can make a start!"

So I followed him into the hotel's reception, where a curly, dark-haired, bare-chested stud waited to register my arrival.

"Simon," the proprietor began, "this is Mr. Gardner. The reviewer from New York I was telling you about. He'll be with us for the next few days, during which time I want you to make sure that he gets everything and anything that he wants."

The receptionist gave a disarming smile. The sort that makes your heart melt on the spot. "Certainly, sir," he assured Zane before checking my blood-test certificate, registering my details on the computer, and handing me the keys to (somewhat appropriately) room 69.

"Simon will show you to your room," Zane confirmed. "Just to let you know that service is available 24/7 and that you are free to roam anywhere within the compound at any time. The boys themselves work a constant shift pattern, and while they're on duty you may have sex with them anytime you like. You may also request that they have sex with each other if that is what you'd like. The use of rubbers is an entirely personal matter—hence our stringent testing policy—but I think most of the lads consider them unnecessary."

"Are they allowed to refuse sex if a visitor refuses to wear one?" I inquired.

The fellow laughed. "These guys are call-boys, Mr. Gardner. They never engage in everyday conversation. They never fall in love. And they always do exactly what the client wants. If he wants to ride bareback, then so do they. If he wants them to swallow, then so do they. My purpose is to keep the boys safe as best I can. Their only purpose is to give the customer one hundred percent satisfaction. Isn't that so, Simon?"

"Sure is, Mr. Zane," the young man brimmed.

"And like we always say here, satisfaction is never achieved until the last drop of come is drained from the client. Because the only truly happy balls are empty ones!

"Now," he concluded, "I don't think there's any need to keep you a moment longer, Mr. Gardner. I'm sure you've seen something to take your fancy."

Zane promptly disappeared, leaving me little choice but to follow young Simon, who had obligingly taken my bags and headed in the direction of the elevator.

To be honest, I was still trying to come to terms with everything that I had discovered about San Sebastian as we stepped into the lift together, and for a few moments there was an almost deathly silence as we began to ascend to the third floor. After all, I'd never in a million years imagined that a place like this could exist. Yet here I was, in a premium-rate brothel, surrounded by a batch of gorgeous young men who were being paid to provide constant relief to Zane's horny, rich customers. That realization left me wondering how morally debased some people would get to make a quick dime, but it also made me feel so fucking hot that all I wanted to do was order Simon to part his legs so that I could partake in the fun.

All the same, it was strange to think that I had this brief luxury, and I was still struggling to find something to say as we finally reached my suite.

"I take it you have your own room somewhere here....?" I quizzed the lad, who was dressed in nothing but a tight pair of shorts and sneakers.

He glanced at me with his dark eyes as he unlocked the door. "I'm sorry, Mr. Gardner. I'm not allowed to have general conversations with visitors."

"I see," I remarked lamely, following him into the luxurious room beyond. At which point he proceeded to run through the amenities on offer, including a note on the fantastic view of the ocean from the window (as if the average visitor would notice!)

"Right, sir," Simon finally concluded, looking me straight in the eye. "Is there anything you'd like from me right now....?"

I stuttered for a reply—desperate as I was to take advantage of this unexpected situation, but unable to conceal my utter inexperience. "Well—I don't know, um...."

The boy stepped forward a little. "I know perhaps I shouldn't be saying this," he began in a whisper, "but I'm very well-lubed. Another guy had me about half an hour ago, and I can still feel it oozing out of my ass even now...."

Needless to say, he didn't need to utter another word, for just the thought of his juicy, wet man-cunt was enough to stoke my confidence.

I found myself stripping down before I had a chance to think what I was doing, while Simon pulled away at his own shorts and kicked away his shoes. Seconds later we were lying on the bed together, our hot sweaty bodies pressed against each other, our cocks straining at the prospect of the hard action to come.

The boy was every inch a professional right from the very start. He promptly moved his mouth down to my hard, erect nipples, which he pulled and sucked like a baby.

Thereon, he bravely slipped even further down my frame. Lapping at my belly button before easing himself through the treasure-trail of hair that lay above my crotch. My dribbling shaft was straining and pulsing, aching to be consumed by his young, firm lips, which I knew were going to feel just fabulous on my flesh.

He rolled his tongue in anticipation, glancing up into my eyes just for the briefest of moments. Then he firmly grasped the base of my weapon like the slut he was. And it was at that point that I suddenly had the most disgusting thought that I had had so far: that this young man was debasing himself to pay his way through college—was whoring his way to academia because no other legitimate means were open to him. And that thought drove me just crazy!

"That's it, you fucking cocksucker," I demanded, pushing him down onto my rod. "You get sucking my hard cock! You hear me? You suck it real hard, you fucking cunt!"

I could hardly believe that I had said such things, but it was testimony to the cruel reality of violation that all men hide. For given the opportunity, all men will take advantage to abuse, and I for one was certainly no exception. Indeed, you could bet your last dollar that I was going to make the very most of this whole opportunity—well, let's face it, my present job here on San Sebastian demanded it of me!

. . . . .

THE YOUNG MAN showed not the slightest evidence of shock at my sudden outburst. But then, why should he? Such a tirade was surely not atypical of his clients, and I would probably have appeared no different from the guy who had fucked him earlier, or indeed any other fellow he had entertained on this island.

No, what shock that existed was mine to endure, and mine alone. Not that I allowed it to bother me for many moments, for before Simon knew it, I was again demanding his unstinting devotion to my aching shaft. I thrust it into his open mouth so that the crown of my cock slapped against the back of his throat—an act that would surely have caused the young man to gag had he not been such a professional. For life on the island had left him decidedly experienced in the art of handling cock, and it was with a deft tongue that he began to suck on my hard rod.

I still couldn't quite comprehend that San Sebastian, and all its crude depravity, existed. Or indeed that I was lying there, watching some young hussy gorge hungrily on my hard cock— and not because the fellow really wanted to, but because it was all part of his job description. The entire project was just totally unbelievable, totally outrageous, and yet at the same time so fucking hot that I was completely certain of its ultimate success.

Yes, there was absolutely no doubt about it: this was one holiday resort that every upwardly mobile gay man in the world would visit!

The hooker was slipping up and down my rod like a professional now, his fingers cupping my hairy, tight balls and his throat groaning in pleasure with every stroke of his lips.

"That's it, boy," I urged. "Earn your paycheck. Suck that cock real good!"

With that he seemed to feed even harder on my flesh. His eyes momentarily glanced up toward me as if to ensure that he was providing satisfaction. And that was something he was most certainly doing, believe me. For this dark, curly-haired stranger was clearly determined to ensure my most basic contentment and was aware that his mission would not be complete until I was suitably drained of all my sexual fluids.

By this time, however, I was beginning to think of that sweet little pucker of his, still freshly dripping from his previous engagement. I demanded that he toss himself backwards onto the bed and spread-eagle his legs into the air. After all, I wanted to know whether this guy was telling the truth in his bid to secure my business. I wanted to see for myself whether he was indeed holding a load of fresh ball cream.

Mind, I could tell at a glance that he was an honest lad. For the slight patch of coarse hair around his hole was decidedly moist, and pushing my finger to the mouth of his crack, my solid digit was sucked in with almost unimaginable ease. Yes, it had been a long time since Simon had boasted virgin ass, that was for sure, and the creamy froth that my finger promptly encountered inside was mere testimony to the fact. Cute as a spring lamb, this guy was now unashamedly brazen, and I knew it wouldn't be long before his bowels were being whitewashed by another load of cream, courtesy of myself!

I can't tell you how easy it was to slip two fingers between his crimson ring. Indeed, the cunt fed on three before either of us knew what was happening. But ultimately it was my cock that needed relief, and the fact that I sensed that Simon was enjoying himself at my expense meant that I was only too pleased to firmly mount the subject. After all, brothels aren't built for the satisfaction of the residents, only for the needs of the clientele. And as long as I was a customer, you could bet that I was gonna make the most of the opportunity, forcing my way upon him with such a thick, raging hard-on that he couldn't help but gasp as I penetrated his open rump, my balls promptly slapping against his butt as I did so.

I grabbed hold of the headboard to give myself extra weight, then demanded that he part his legs even wider. "Open up, you fucking queer!" I ordered, thinking again of that diploma he so badly wanted, and which had brought him to this tragic point. "I wanna cream your guts real bad, boy! You fucking understand me? You know what I mean?"

He finally shrieked—the stretch of his legs almost too much for him to bear. But that was enough to get me pounding his slit like a man possessed. Forcing my body down upon him, time after time. "Oh fuck, that's good!" I groaned with every deepening blow, my rod forcing a gentle flow of the stale come out of his crack as I did so. "Fuck, that's fantastic!"

I almost couldn't get deep enough by this point. But I knew I wouldn't hold off much longer anyway, for every nerve in my stake was now buzzing into overdrive. Which was surprising really, given that the thought of having sex with a rent-boy was something that had never once crossed my mind until arriving at the complex. Then again, this was a million miles away from the seedy image of a whorehouse I'd previously had in my mind. For San Sebastian was unquestionably the Monte Carlo of brothels: wonderfully expensive and yet surely worth every single penny it demanded.

I grunted my ferocious eruption deep inside him—bolt after bolt of hard-won come to add to the generous offering that his earlier client had deposited—before collapsing down onto the bed in a sweaty heap of exhaustion, gasping and spent and yet longing to go out and enjoy much of the same sort of action with the other guys on offer.

Simon, meantime, promptly rose to his feet like nothing had happened, slipping back into his pants before discreetly reminding me that he was but a mere taste of everything that this tropical oasis had to offer.

"You expect a tip?" I questioned him finally.

"A generous tip is always welcomed but never expected," he assured me. "Besides, I'll be satisfied with just a recommendation in your report, sir."

I smiled. "That's a promise," I assured him.

Simon turned to leave. "Well, if there's nothing else, sir...."

"Actually," I began, "I wonder if you could make a recommendation of your own?"

He looked puzzled.

"Of other horny fucks," I explained. "I mean, for all I know you might be the only decent lay here, and I don't want to get people visiting under false pretenses now, do I?"

"Strictly speaking, I'm not allowed to recommend...."

"Think of me as quality assurance," I teased. "I just need to take a few samples, so that I can be quite sure this place is everything your boss says it is."

"Sir, I don't think you'll find a bad fuck here—Mr. Zane makes sure of that very personally."

I was intrigued. "He's fucked you himself, then?"

Simon blushed. "I can't comment, sir," he insisted.

"In fact," I continued, "that's who'd fucked you before I arrived, wasn't it?"

"Again, I can't comment, sir. But I can tell you that the poolside is very popular. I think you'll find plenty to amuse you there."

I grinned—amused, as I was, by his embarrassment. Fact is, I wasn't at all bothered by Zane's methods—indeed, in many ways I was flattered that the guy had gone to such lengths to ensure that I was welcomed by such a wet and welcoming hole. But the power that I as a visitor now held over Simon (and all his comrades) was almost intoxicating, and I was already beginning to anticipate the next easy fuck that would be provided for my entertainment. Yes, the lifestyle on this island was one I could most definitely get used to!

I dismissed the lad, then slipped into some shorts and made for the pool. As before, several clients were enjoying the services of the local hosts, including one who was fucking some well-hung stud over a table; but my direct attention was caught again by the collection of young hunks in the water, now playing volleyball together and each one looking even more fuckable than the next. Which was a bit of a problem, given that I felt compelled to choose only one of them.

That said, by the time I'd seated myself in a lounger to observe the gang, several of the hookers had abandoned their game to offer their services to me—primed by Zane to ensure my keenest satisfaction. As a result, I found my pants being pulled away by some blond slut before I had a chance to think twice about it, while a pair of outrageously hung Russian cunts began to lick on my dark nipples like a pair of young calves.

As a consequence, I soon found myself subject to a barrage of attention from three very promising orifices, with the blond quickly taking hold of my shaft in his mouth and firming it with a gummy roll.

I couldn't begin to tell them how good such wanton attention felt, but the look of rapture on my face would surely have been enough to signal my agreement. In fact, I was beginning to feel as though I had died and gone to heaven as the bevy of beauties continued their adoration of my flesh, each one taking turns to suck on my hard shaft while fondling my balls and running their fingers around my aching crotch.

"I take it that sir is satisfied with the service…" a voice

interrupted from above. I opened my eyes to find Chay Zane glancing down on my pleasure.

"Very much so," I gasped breathlessly.

"Excellent," he replied. "A couple of big Hollywood stars came here last week and said pretty much the same thing about these guys, so I know they're hot. Like all my boys, I might add …."

"Yes, Mr. Zane," I groaned. "I'm beginning to appreciate the quality you have here!"

"Good," he grinned. "Still, I won't keep you. I can see you have quite a boner there—and these guys won't be satisfied until they've all had a ride!"

With that, he disappeared again, leaving me to express my appreciation by ordering the three lads to bend over before me and part their legs in anticipation of a forceful pounding up their love-tunnels.

Mind, it was surprisingly difficult to decide which guy I should mount first, for each one had a delicious-looking slit between his open cheeks, and all were begging for my spunky patronage. They knew that securing the favor of clients was the key to their ultimate success on the island. After all, he who fucked the best—and who drained the most balls of their precious nectar in the process—gained the greatest financial reward. And let's face it, that was the only reason any of these guys were here in the first place.

The one Russian guy, it transpired, had a sister who was suffering from leukemia; he was here to pay for her expensive operation in the West. The other needed cash to supplement his father's ailing business. While their blond companion—a cheeky-looking Dane—had discovered that working at the complex was the quickest route to obtaining that millionaire lifestyle he had always dreamed of. Quite simply, these lads needed money for a variety of reasons, and each was prepared to surrender his dignity in its pursuit. Which to a gay man with plenty of ready cash was just fucking wonderful—as I was now discovering!

In the end, I chose the blond first, though by this point another client had come across and asked whether I would mind if he joined me. As such, we were able to fuck two simultaneously, which meant that only one had to be disappointed at any given time. Switching holes every few minutes, we each slammed our pulsing weapons deep into their exposed guts, slapping our fulsome balls against their pert rumps while grasping their hips for support. The game of volleyball continued behind us in the pool, as though the sight of guys fornicating was the most natural thing in the world.

Which on San Sebastian, of course, it was.

Finally, the three guys crowded round us on their knees, watching eagerly as we jerked ourselves off above their young, pretty faces, their mouths open like a nest of chicks waiting for nourishment. Which in this instance was in the form of fresh, sticky come that burst from the pulsing ends of our meaty shafts in thick ropes, plastering their mouths and matting their hair.

Fuck, they looked hot afterwards. And I for one could not have decided which deserved any tip more than the others. But the other guest showed no such uncertainty, ordering the blond to bend over once again so that he could thrust a small wad of dollars into his moist crack. A photo for a memento—and at last the lad could collect his earnings.

"That guy is just such a ball-breaker!" the guest finally admitted. "I've had him a dozen times already this vacation, and I swear he gets hotter each time!"

I smiled in agreement, though in truth I thought all three studs were pretty faultless. In fact, I just knew there wasn't a bad fuck in the whole bunch, and I was already penning a report to that effect in my head.

Not that I was finished on the island yet. True, I was already convinced of its quality, but I still had a few days left to continue my indulgence and to investigate every single hole on offer. After all, I was only ever gonna be on San Sebastian once, and I was fucking determined to make the most of the opportunity! As such, the next few days provided me with an orgy in a sauna, a threesome in the gym, countless blow jobs pretty much everywhere, and more hot ass than I would've ever imagined before this break. It was, in every way possible, the holiday of a lifetime. My article secured such fantastic interest in San Sebastian that Zane actually rewarded me with a lifetime pass to the island. As well as the continued offer of work there should ever I choose it. Well, who knows? I might decide that writing for a New York rag-mag just ain't worth it, especially in comparison to the fortunes being earned elsewhere. For the meantime, however, I'll just relish the role of the tourist—and the all-encompassing power that it gives on that very unique Caribbean island.

SKEET HARPER AND STEVE ANDERSON

BRAD STEVENS

SKEET CHECKED THE front outer pockets of his jean jacket, first the left, then the right. Next he appraised the inside pockets. All seemed to be there, the lube, the condoms, the mouthwash, his business cards. Not necessarily in that order, of course, but then again, in about as much order as his present state of mind.

Earlier he'd removed his lone earring—a small green stone representing prosperity—and had dressed himself in clothing suitable to the occasion. Which in this case was tan jeans, a light blue cotton button-down without a tie, a black belt with brushed silver buckle, and black socks and sneakers. He'd combed his hair neat and then finger-brushed it to give a subtly unkempt appearance. Before leaving the room, he looked around one more time. The place was a mess—yet another reflection of his inner thinking, he supposed. Ever since he'd left the interview two days ago, his mind had been running on something akin to cruise control. More accurately, it was just out of control. He felt as if he'd segmented a part of his reasoning self off to the side and was living out of some other area.

The feeling of being separate from himself was somehow familiar, but he couldn't quite place how so or when he had felt this way before. It was a sensation of some part of him lurking off to the side, as if he were living out a part of his past. Like some dark, slinky event from long ago was about ready to pounce on him unexpectedly. Maybe it was payback of some kind from another lifetime, a reincarnation of mistakes made previously. He'd cheated on his wife in 1723 and now had to feel cut in two to make up for it.

But, he wondered when he actually thought about it and didn't just let it haunt him, how could it be unexpected if he expected it? Expected what? He wondered. Just it. Whatever it was.

Skeet pulled the door until it clicked shut, then double-locked it and headed down the stairs. When he hit the bottom landing, he remembered he needed his cell phone. Usually he needed it to call the agency after he was done with the trick. But since this session was going to take place right at the agency, he didn't really need the phone. Still, it wasn't a good idea for a 'scort to be cell-phone-less. Skeet stopped in his tracks, turned and ran back up the few steps of the landing, unlocked the bolts, and grabbed his phone. It was only when he was halfway out of the building again that he remembered that he didn't have the guy's phone number. It was unlikely that he'd need it, since the agency had it and could always get hold of him if necessary. Then again, better safe than sorry, Skeet thought.

It took Skeet three attempts to leave the building before he had everything he figured he required. This was nothing new really—Skeet was often a wee bit scatterbrained. When he finally got to the street, he wiped the beginnings of perspiration from his forehead as he again did a mental checklist. Cell phone, dude's number, cock ring, lube, etc., etc., blah blah blah. As an afterthought, Skeet had even grabbed a small black whip that he owned. The guy, whose name was Steve Anderson, had said he liked his boys to be submissive, and Skeet figured that maybe he'd like to use the lash on his butt or something. Then again, Skeet knew that men often mouthed one fantasy over the phone but wound up being total white bread once they got together.

Skeet had spent the last two hours preparing—douching, brushing his hair, moisturizing his skin, shaving, and all the rest. He wanted this to be a good date, his first one with this particular agency, and he tried to work out in his mind everything that needed to be done. Steve had said that the last guy he used at the agency wasn't exactly clean, so Skeet was going to be sure that wasn't a complaint with him. He'd have to look pretty hard to find a speck of dirt. Shit, Skeet had even scrubbed his ears and elbows raw.

Besides, he knew the guy—he recognized his nasal voice the minute the guy picked up the phone. This was a guy he knew from the gym, someone he'd gone on an actual date with once. At the time, he'd nixed the idea of having sex with the guy because he wasn't really Skeet's type. But this was different now. This was business. The concept always made Skeet feel simultaneously evil, adult, and boyish. But not just that, somehow the idea of being paid for doing this guy aroused him. Go figure. The funny thing was that after the date (they'd gone for burgers), the next time Skeet had seen him at the gym he'd given Skeet this little teddy bear. It was the sort that you'd see at a Hallmark card store—cheap and kind of lame. Skeet had been sort of at a loss for words. Here he was planning on not going out on another date with Steve, and Steve gives him a teddy bear. Thinking about it in retrospect, he realized that he'd never even really thanked Steve Anderson for the burger he'd bought him that night.

Since that time, whenever Skeet saw Steve at the gym, he'd make polite conversation. But always—and he meant always—Skeet would feel just a little guilty. Guilty of what, he didn't know. But guilty nonetheless.

Skeet had always wanted to be a hooker, ever since he saw the movie *Midnight Cowboy*—and that had been about twenty years ago, for crying out loud. Most of his friends had been depressed by the movie, said it was really a downer, but not Skeet. He'd always thought the life that Joe Buck and Ratzo Rizzo shared was way cool and romantic. He'd felt that way for twenty years, and now knew it to be true.

As it turned out, the guy who owned the agency was a friend of a friend. He and Skeet both went to the same massage therapist and had actually passed each other a few times in the hall between sessions. In fact, the therapist had given Skeet the guy's card when he found out Skeet was interested in working for him. Or had Skeet asked for the guy's card? He couldn't remember.

Outside, it was a miserably hot Fourth of July weekend. Thank God, thought Skeet, the heat kept the damn tourists inside where they belonged. You could say a lot of nice things about Washington, D.C., but goddamn-we-love-the-tourists wasn't one of them. Least of all Skeet Harper. Skeet had always lived in places where tourists ruled the local economy. San Francisco, Key West, the Big Apple. He guessed it was a love-hate thing, because most everyone he knew hated the damn tourists.

The night Skeet went into the agency for the interview, he was led to a small room where the operations were carried out. The owner, a man in his early fifties, sat on a couch with a dinner plate on his lap. The plate held a huge slab of rare steak and some broccoli. During the so-called interview, the owner alternately grilled Skeet about his sexual history and cut, chewed, and swallowed chunks of beef. Skeet's concern that there might be an audition where he'd have to expose himself or even have sex with the guy never happened. He'd had Skeet fill out a job application and then gave him the job. It was that simple.

He'd also shown Skeet a list of dos and don'ts that the escorts were expected to adhere to. Things like no jewelry and keeping clean and not talking about politics and stuff. The guy also explained that the escort agency gave its clients two choices of where to meet. The client could meet the escort at his house or hotel or in a special room provided by the agency.

Skeet's current client wanted to meet in the special room — which was good for Skeet, because the escort agency was only three blocks from his apartment. Even so, what with the heat and his case of jitters, Skeet arrived at his destination bathed in sweat.

Skeet stopped at the front desk and checked in. It was a weird setup, because the fantasy room was on the other side of the wall of the owner's office, and as soon as Skeet had seen the room he just knew the owner probably had a way to watch—maybe even video, the sessions that took place there. This didn't bother him much, except for the worry that videos of him might turn up somewhere public someday. But fuck that, Skeet told himself. It was part of the risk one took as a 'scort.

The guy at the desk asked Skeet if he wanted to buy a Viagra for ten bucks, and Skeet said no thanks, only slightly offended that the guy would think he needed it. Then he went into the fantasy room to wait for his client to arrive. Other house policies were that you had to arrive before the client and you couldn't offer drugs to a client or accept drugs from a client. Which was fine with Skeet, since he didn't indulge in drugs anymore anyway.

When the client arrived, Skeet was lying on the bed wondering how this would all turn out. It was sort of funny really, given that they'd already gone out on a date together and nothing had happened. Skeet found himself falling immediately into what he called hook mode—that space where the client is transformed into the most beautiful guy in the world and serving him is the main priority. For Skeet, this was way easier than going out on a regular date, where what the guy looked like and how he behaved were so important. In business, pretty much anything went, and all Skeet had to do was act as if he was having the best time in the world. But still, this felt a little odd.

The two exchanged light banter while they undressed.

"I had no idea you were an escort," said Steve.

"Well, it's not something you share with someone on a first date."

"Oh," Steve said, and then thought for a few seconds. "You mean you were doing this two years ago?"

"Yes," Skeet confessed.

Skeet could almost see the wheels grinding in Steve's brain. He was probably figuring, what the fuck, you couldn't sleep with me but you could become a hooker. To circumvent those thoughts and prevent them from destroying the mood, Skeet added, "Also, I try not to mix business with pleasure."

For a second it seemed to Skeet that Steve was weighing out that statement. Thinking maybe that there was no way Skeet could have known then that this was going to be business someday. But as usual with most men, Steve opted to stick with the simplicity of the moment—the that-was-then-and-this-is-now mode of thinking. Steve's brow and eyes revealed to Skeet that his mind had decided to accept the information favorably.

"So how long have you been with this agency?" Steve asked.

"Actually, you're my first client at this place," Skeet offered.

"I thought that might be the case," Steve said, adding, "I've been using them for a few years now and haven't ever seen you before."

Skeet just smiled, giving it as much charm as he could, choosing not to point out the fact that Steve was using hookers while they went on that date. His smile had a quality he'd honed over the years. He had learned how to use that smile to get what he wanted from his mother years ago (his father rarely fell for it). Then, in acting classes, he felt an odd sense of pride when the instructor told him his smile was "a natural, one of those that just charms the pants off people." After that, Skeet had literally practiced his smile in front of a mirror—using his film heroes, guys like Brad Pitt and James Dean, as examples of ways to smile.

"You have a beautiful smile, Skeet."

Skeet allowed his eyes to twinkle over and his mouth to naturally reach out just a bit toward his ears. Then he lowered his eyes as if he were a little embarrassed and said, in an appropriately halting, aw-shucks manner, "Thanks, Steve."

"I'm actually honored to be your first client with this agency," Steve said.

Skeet smiled a little more and took a breath. "Yeah, me too." But Skeet was actually thinking that Steve's comment was just a little lame, considering this encounter was only the luck of the draw—and Steve knew that. In reality, the initial call could have been forwarded to any one of a number of escorts on call that day. But Skeet needn't have worried about bursting Steve's balloon— he was about to burst Skeet's instead.

"Yeah," Steve offered, "I had told the guy manning the phones that I was looking for an older, more mature escort. Good thing I didn't ask for one who'd been with the agency awhile." With that, Steve chuckled.

Inwardly, Skeet winced and felt the hair on his arms rise slightly in anger. What the fuck did he mean by an older, more mature escort? I'm not older—shit, I'm only in my midforties— and people were always telling him he looked to be in his thirties. Fuck this shit!

As Skeet removed his shirt and began to pull down his designer briefs, Steve paused and reluctantly said, "But there's something you should know."

Oh great, thought Skeet, here it comes. He's got the clap or no dick or whatever. "What?" he asked.

"It's sort of embarrassing. I just had a hernia operation and have a huge scar."

Whew, Skeet thought. "That's not a problem at all," he told Steve.

Steve smiled. "That's a relief," he said as he pulled down his drawers.

The scar was huge, long, angry red, and gross enough to make Skeet's stomach turn just a little bit. "That's not so bad," he lied to his client. "I've seen worse."

Steve smiled happily. "Thanks, Skeet. I knew there was a reason I liked you." Skeet grinned back at the man with as much sincerity as he could muster. "And I thought it was just my great looks."

"That too," said Steve as he stepped toward Skeet and embraced him.

As Steve put his arms around him, Skeet smiled and forced himself to look longingly into his client's eyes. "Ummmm," he said as he allowed Steve's embrace to surround him. "Nice."

As Steve murmured a responsive sigh, he suddenly foisted his crotch toward Skeet, unexpectedly grinding it forcefully into him in what he obviously thought was a sexy move. The aggressive action surprised Skeet, and he instinctively pulled away.

"What's wrong?" Steve asked.

"Oh nothing. You just surprised me," Skeet told him.

No sooner had the words left Skeet's mouth than Steve suddenly planted his lips onto Skeet's and started grinding his lips into Skeet's. Immediately repulsed by this action, Skeet forced himself to allow Steve to continue, even going so far as to part his lips and let Steve's tongue lunge down his throat. Skeet didn't know where Steve had learned to kiss—no doubt from his wife of eighteen years—but he definitely lacked skill in that area. Immediately Skeet knew that the only way this session was going to work was if he took control of the situation.

Gently disengaging his lips from Steve's, Skeet said, "Lie down on the bed, man."

Steve dropped his butt to the side of the bed, and Skeet got on his knees. Slowly, he began removing the tangled underwear from around his client's ankles. Then he removed his socks, allowing himself to get close enough to get a whiff of the guy's feet. It was clear that Steve hadn't bathed before coming over. This, thought Skeet, is going to be work.

From his vantage point on the floor below Steve, Skeet could see the guy's entire body laid out on the bed, beginning with the feet. Skeet lowered his head near Steve's feet and slowly began to move it up his body, letting his hair fall down and massage Steve as he went along. Skeet's hair was soft and blond, and Steve slowly began to sigh—a long, continuous sigh that continued until Skeet reached his chest.

Skeet stopped just before getting to Steve's face. "Oh man, that was fucking hot," Steve told Skeet.

Skeet looked at him, allowed a sheepish smile to cross his lips, and then raised his finger to his own lips. "Shhhhh," he told Steve softly, "don't say anything. Just relax."

Slowly, Skeet pulled Steve's arms upward until he got the idea that he was supposed to move up onto the bed. Steve complied, and Skeet swung his leg over the man and straddled his cheek. Then he slowly began to feather Steve's chest and nipples with his fingertips. Steve, his eyes closed, moaned. Then Skeet lowered his face toward the man and gently blew. When Steve opened his eyes to see what the breath blowing on his face was about, the first thing he saw were Skeet's eyes. Unfocused, clear as day, slightly teary, and in love. Skeet moved in and kissed Steve the way a man is supposed to be kissed.

A minute later, when Skeet released the man's lips, Steve said one word. "Fuck!" It was obvious that this man had never been kissed properly in his entire life.

Emboldened with power now, Skeet embraced the teaching role. He laid his body down on his student and took a deep breath, slowly letting it out as the weight of his body fused the two of them together. Rubbing his cheek against Steve's, he kissed the man's face and then let the tip of his tongue flick against each of his eyelids. "Oh my God," Steve appraised, and—again—Skeet knew that this was an experience the man had never felt before.

By now Skeet was on his traditional roll—and it was a roll that he would remember for the rest of his career. Search and destroy. Divide and conquer. A good escort, Skeet knew, found a man's weaknesses, his strengths, or the experiences he was lacking, and provided the counterbalance to those areas. If a guy couldn't kiss, you taught him how. If a guy needed a man's touch, you provided that. And if a guy was afraid, you made him feel comfortable. Finally—and this was the most important—if a man wanted to feel guilt after a session, you allowed him that guilt. Allowing the man to feel his guilt and/or shame almost guaranteed repeat business. Making him feel extra guilty usually meant a fat tip. The trick was to make the trick think it was all real.

Years ago, when he was just getting started as a career call-boy, one trick's name was Troy—or it was presumably Troy. Troy was a man from the suburbs who had a pale white circle on his finger where his wedding ring normally sat. He didn't know how to kiss, barely knew how to embrace another man. Skeet, the novice, had let the entire session peter out into a morass of boring hugs and slipshod, sloppy kisses. When it was finally over, Skeet was confounded as to what had gone wrong. It took him several such trials before he came to understand that he, the escort, was in charge. It was his obligation to make everything work out. And it was up to him to teach the student how to be a good lover.

Skeet allowed himself to fall into Steve's eyes—to take a swim—to become an integral part of the inside of the man. "Whatsamatter, baby?" Skeet whispered at Steve. He reached up with his right hand, supporting his body with his left, and brushed the hair out of Steve's eyes. While simultaneously pushing his crotch firmly into his client's, he said, "Cat got your tongue."

In fact, Steve seemed mute, at a loss for words. "I— I—" he stammered.

"Shhhhhh," said Skeet. "Just lie back and enjoy it." With that, he moved his entire body downward until his face became even with Steve's substantial cock. Exhaling with his nose, he allowed the air stream to gently rustle the pubic hairs around the organ. Then, gently, he began to run the tip of his tongue around the perimeter of the man's cock. While barely touching the skin, he slid his tongue around the inside of Steve's legs, around the patch of hair on the right side of his crotch, upward over the hair on the pubic bone, down the left side, and again around the inside of his legs. Then he brushed the man's cock with the hair on his head, finally lowering his mouth to the head of his dick.

"Ummmmm," Skeet said as he gently blew and then drew in a whiff of the man's musky-smelling cock. "Nice." And with those words, Skeet lowered his entire mouth on the guy's cock, making sure that he swallowed the entire dick without so much as letting the sides of the dick actually touch his lips. The cock sat like a long sausage gently hovering inside Skeet's mouth, there within but not actually making contact.

Skeet then breathed slowly in before slowly exhaling, so that the air whisked along the length of the man's cock, the air being the only thing actually making contact. Steve let out a great sigh that was both the anticipation of the mouth he knew might grab his meat and the sense of the air brushing his cock gently. "Fuuuuuuck...." The word slowly escaped Steve's mouth as Skeet continued to entice him.

Then, almost without warning, Skeet retreated, lifting his mouth away from the man's dick. Steve let out a breath. "Jesus, Skeet—"

But Skeet was reaching up with his right hand, and when he let his fingers brush the man's right nipple, Steve broke into an even louder moan and arched his entire body upward. Using that as a cue, Skeet pinched the man's nipple hard and swallowed his entire cock—this time letting his mouth slide along the skin of the organ.

Taken by surprise, Steve actually let out a whelp. Skeet applied pressure around Steve's dick as he intently ran the cock in and out of his mouth. Then, with his other hand, he placed his fingers on the area between Steve's asshole and the base of his balls, gently feathering the area as he sucked the cock. Steve was instantaneously arching his body and moaning at the same time, taking in enormous gulps of air.

Then, without warning, Steve's big, fat cock expanded in size and began to gush—the come seeming to surprise Steve as much as it surprised Skeet. Skeet felt the first part of the load splash against the roof of his mouth, and then, because he was sliding the dick out of his mouth at that moment, the next glob of come sprayed all over his lips. Skeet, who knew a good thing when it was happening, picked up the zeal with which he was sucking and allowed the next surge of come to spill into the area just behind his teeth and on his tongue, then allowed the cock to slide through that deposit of semen and push it down his throat. As the cock pulled away from the back of his throat, it was already unleashing yet another copious spray of the delicious, loamy seed.

At this point the two men were simultaneously separate and combined entities. Each was alone in his ecstasy, but that ecstasy was contingent upon the other's presence. Without knowing it, they had become symbiotic sex machines, each feeding off the other. As Steve sprayed yet another load into Skeet's mouth and as Skeet withdrew the dick so he could feel another load spray across his face, Skeet grabbed his own dick and began to pump. As the final spasms of jizz forced their way into Skeet, he himself let off a surge of come that sprayed all over Steve's legs and onto the sheets between them.

Then, silence, except for the sound of the two men trying to catch enough oxygen to stay alive. Their breaths were short but fierce, and they were both bathed in sweat.

"Oh my God, fuck," Steve finally uttered.

Raising his body upward and then falling onto Steve, his wet sloppy dick aligned with Steve's wet, sloppy cock, Skeet looked lovingly into his eyes.

"I don't think I ever thanked you for that hamburger," he said, smiling as he ran his tongue along the man's full lips.

IF LINDA BLAIR HAD BEEN A BOY PRO-DOM, OR, HOW TO MAKE RENT AND INFLUENCE PEOPLE

KIRK READ

THE OTHER NIGHT a preacher came to my door and said, "Please whoop my ass. Please tie me down and go further than last time. Please go deep." So I blindfolded him, bull-tied him, and spanked his ass with a hairbrush so long that his butt had welts. Then I turned it over so the wires in the brush would poke holes in him until he was smeared crimson. As I bloodied his ass I read to him every passage about queers in the Bible.

I read him Romans, then ripped out the page. I read him Leviticus, then ripped out the page. I read him Paul, then ripped out the page. I balled them up and wiped them across his bloody ass. His ass jumped at each crinkled prophesy. Some of the ink traded places with his blood, until his ass was gray with scripture and the Good Book was stained with the blood of one very lonely fifty-two-year-old man who believed every word. He believed every word.

I pushed the pages into his mouth, onto his panting tongue. I fed him Jesus and the Saints. I gave him sermons and serpents.

I held his mouth shut like I was giving a dog a pill and I said, "*Chew!*"

He tasted his blood, and for the first time he resisted. He pulled away. I slapped him hard across his face and said "*Chew!*" and he did.

"*Get your molars into it! Chew, little boy! Chew for your life!*"

Tears were running out of his eyes, and when I could see he'd gotten the pages into a small wad of pulp, I led him down the hall to the bathroom. I held his face over the toilet and said, "*Now spit!*"

He shook his head violently.

I pushed down on his shoulders so he'd kneel, then leaned on him until his face was inches above the toilet water.

"This is for your own good," I said. "I promise."

Then I pushed the back of his head so hard that his face went into the water.

"*Spit it out! Spit it out! Spit out that goddamn poison!*"

And as he wailed, the wad dropped from his jaw. It was an accident. This was as far as he could go today. He tried to dunk his head into the bowl to bob for Jesus, and I held him by the hair two inches from the water, pulled the blindfold from his eyes, and flushed.

He gasped as the wad of God went spinning into the sewer. His blood mingled with cheap ink and thin, unforgiving paper. After the flush, that wad surfaced like a stubborn turd. Before I could flush again, he begged me, "Can I keep it? Can I keep it for later? I want to push it up my ass and jerk off."

"You can have anything you want, angel. Thine is the Kingdom. But I want to watch."

I took him back to bed and held him and listened to him tell me for the twentieth time how he wanted to get out of the business, how he wanted to be free, how he wanted to stop worrying about getting found out, how he wanted to find love.

And I did what I always do, which is to squeeze the sobs out of his body until he's breathing again, stroke his hair like a baby and tell him, "You're a good boy. You're such a good boy. Daddy loves you."

He'd tip if he could. I tell him I'd rather he saved up so he can get out and start over. Maybe someday he will.

Today he hands me a piece of my rent and closes his hands around mine.

"God bless you," he says. "See you next week."

BOY IN THE PICTURES

AARON NIELSEN

for Shane

I'M JERKING OFF on my Web cam with a kid who looks like my favorite porn model, Shawn. Except this kid in the grainy, twitchy image is from Antwerp, uncut, not American. Shawn is American, brown hair styled into a boyish cut, sweet but wanton blue eyes, rosy cheeks, skinny boy next door with a huge cock. My Belgium friend here isn't quite as hung as Shawn. I type into the instant messenger box: *I want to see your ass.* The kid stops pulling on his hard-on, turns around, arches his back, spreading open his pale, smooth cheeks, exposing his hole. I type: *I want to eat your ass.* And I do, I'm being sincere. I'd tongue-fuck him until my tongue went numb, then I'd ease my cock into him while he begged me to fuck him and come up his ass. When the kid finishes wagging his butt at me, he types: *Thanks.* I guess he means the compliment about his ass. Then he asks: *Ready to come?* I'm pretty close, so I tell him: *Yeah.* He angles his cam so I get a view of his cock jetting out over the top of his desk. Three strong spasms of spooge arc out of his dick. After he's finished, the camera swings back up to his face in a nauseated swirl, and then he types, *Your turn,* and licks his spunk-dripping fingers. I point my cam down at my crotch, spread a black T-shirt across my lap to catch my wad, and then unleash. *Awesome,* he tells me.

Thanks, I type back. Then the kid's image blinks off, and I stuff my wilting erection back into my briefs.

I stroll out into the kitchen and grab a bottled water from the fridge and then go plant myself on the couch. There's nothing on TV save for chat shows and soap operas, neither of which interest me at all, so I do another line of coke. There are still five lines cut on the coffee table, and I have enough Xanax to knock out a horse, so at least I'll be able to sleep at some point. I don't know what to do with myself. I'm so coked up at this point that everything is just blank and the edges of my vision are foggy. I would jack off again, but I'm too sore. I guess it's because I'm so fucking void right now that I decide to do it. I pick up the notepad with the escort agency's number scrawled on it, grab my cell phone, and dial.

"Thank you for calling Boy Toy Escort Services, hold please," a chipper female voices yaps at me. I'm about to hang up, but then she comes back on the line.

"Hello, how may I help you?"

"Yeah, hi. Uh, I'd like to schedule a date with one of your, uh, guys."

"All right, who would you like to set up a date with?"

"Shawn."

"Oh, he's very popular. Let me check his availability. One sec."

"Okay, thanks."

"Let's see here. Ah, you're in luck. There was a cancellation. How does two weeks from now sound?"

I sniff—nosebleed. Shit. "That, that, sounds great. Sure."

"All I need now is a credit card number, and your reservation'll be secured."

I fumble around in my wallet while my nose oozes. "My card number is 5534...."

After I hang up the phone, I go into the bathroom and stuff bits of tissue up my leaking nostril. Then I dig through the medicine cabinet, find the Xanax, pop a handful, and head off to bed.

. . . . .

I WAKE UP and it's dark out. I don't know what time it is, I don't care what time it is. I reach over to my nightstand, grab my cigarettes, and light one. While I smoke, I gingerly pull the congealed tissue out of my nose. Some of it sticks, and so it hurts. I hope my nose doesn't start bleeding again. I go over to my computer, make a rental car reservation, and then start looking for hotels. The agency that Shawn works for is located in, of all places, Washington, D.C. I haven't been to D.C. in a decade. I went my sophomore year of high school on a field trip. We stayed there for a week, saw all the monuments, went to the Smithsonian, and I also gave my first blow job. I was sharing a hotel room with a freshman, his name was … Ian … I think … anyway, we were up late our first night there, watching scrambled porn. We couldn't see anything, but the prospect that there was sex going on behind those wavy, sepia-colored lines was enough to get us hard. We were both in our tighty-whities, so our erections were really obvious. I ended up pulling my dick out, while he rubbed himself over his underwear. I remember he was so nervous and/or excited that he was shaking when I finally bent down, took out his cock, and put my lips around it. I wish I could remember what the name of that hotel was. I'd like to stay there again, for nostalgia's sake. I mean, I've never hired an escort before, and it'd be kinda cool to do my first hooker the same place I did my first blow job. Whatever, I'm sure a Motel 6 will be fine.…

I've been infatuated with Shawn for about seven months now. His pictures keep popping up on various message boards and Yahoo groups. The vast majority of his photo sets are just him going from fully clothed to coming on his chest. I did, however, track down a video of him getting fucked. Which was hot—just thinking about me or anyone else fucking this guy is a turn-on—but the video was poorly lit, horrible camera angles, and just really amateurish. I don't think the camera guy had any previous experience before filming Shawn getting plowed. The lighting was so dim, I couldn't tell if they were using condoms or if it was bareback. I actually hope that it was bareback, I'm kinda twisted, I guess. And the worst part of it all—it was a foot fetish film! Over half the scene Shawn is licking the other guy's toes, rubbing his feet on his dick, etc. Not my thing at all. Feet are just boring, I don't get the appeal. I just wanted to watch some incredibly cute guy get fucked by some other really cute guy. But no, I get an obscured toe-sucking video. I'd have been pissed if I'd actually paid for it. Luckily, I was able to download the clip from a bittorrent site. Shawn has also done some other fetish modeling. There are a few series of him getting pissed on by other guys. I think that's pretty gross, but it's obvious this kid is into being humiliated, which is hot. I'm still not into those pictures, however.

Despite all the kinky stuff he's done, this kid couldn't break his spell over me. I'm still totally into him, even after seeing him piss on himself while some other dude was peeing into his open mouth. Anyway, I was reading through a thread devoted to Shawn on the onlytwinkshere.com message boards, and lo and behold someone posted info on how he's an escort now, the poster even included a link to the agency's Web site. I checked out the site, found his profile on it, and then scribbled down the number. It sat on my coffee table for over a week. It was just a fantasy, I couldn't actually see myself really calling and getting a date with this guy. It still doesn't seem real that I'm going to be meeting him, in the flesh, in fourteen days.

. . . . .

I PREPARE MYSELF for the meeting by going to the gym twice a day. It's not that I'm out of shape or anything, it's just that you can always be more cut, more fit. I really want to impress this guy. I mean I want Shawn to think I'm fucking hot. I do Pilates for an hour in the morning, and then run six miles. When I go back to the gym in the evening, I weight-train for two hours and then go swimming. Since I've been working out so much, I've virtually stopped doing coke. I'm not insane; I don't want my heart to explode. Who the fuck gets all coked up and goes to work out anyway? That's just sick. I do need to get more for the trip, though. This is what I think about as I jog on the treadmill, encroaching upon my fourth mile. One of the TVs in the gym is tuned to CNN. Some commercial is on advertising some news show; there's a montage of Washington, D.C., which gets me excited, makes me think of Shawn and what's going to happen there in a few days, and then they show Karl Rove's face, and the moment is ruined. Yuck, who would want to fuck that fat fuck?

Shawn. Shawn. Shawn. I repeat his name over and over to myself, it keeps me going, I say it over and over so the beat of his name synchs up with the beat of my heart, my pulse, my now-throbbing cock. Shawn. Shawn. Shawn.

In the locker room I strip out of my sweaty workout clothes, but I leave my jockstrap on. I want the other guys in the room to see me in it, so I rummage around in my locker for longer than necessary looking for my towel, shampoo, etc....

There's only one other guy in the showers, and he's pretty hot. Older than me, early thirties, dirty blond hair, tight chest, lean stomach … my abs are better, but he's got a good cock, a nice pair of pink low-hangers. I soap myself up and let my hand linger around my cock for longer than it should, but not long enough to look like an outright perv. Out of the corner of my eye, I catch him looking over at me, so I stop fluffing myself.

"Hey." He nods in my direction.

"Hey." I nod back.

I wonder where this is going. Then he asks, "So you're the guy who wears the Speedo in the pool, yeah?"

"I'm one of the guys, yeah."

"Why do you do that?" He asks, slightly disgusted.

"I played water polo in high school; we had to wear Speedos

for that, so force of habit, I guess."

"Oh."

Despite the fact that this isn't going the way I want it to, I remain undeterred. "So that's what that's all about," I tell him to keep the conversation going.

"I guess I've always been curious...." He trails off, soaps up his crotch.

"About Speedos?" I finish.

"Yeah, Speedos." He smiles.

. . . . .

THE BLOND GUY from the gym is lying facedown, spread-eagle on my bed. I've been rimming him for what seems like hours now. My cock is so hard it's aching, pre-come dripping. His hole is as pink as his balls, and it's driving me crazy, I just can't seem to get deep enough in there. He's moaning, thrusting his ass in my face, wiggling his hips, and then I start fingering him. I slide one finger in effortlessly, work it around inside his slick ass, feel its textures, try to find his prostate. Is that it? Wait, no. Maybe. Then I work in another finger, and then another. I wonder if he's into fisting. I've never done that, but I guess there's a first time for everything. I pop a fourth finger in. I'm just about to figure out how to get my thumb in him when he starts whining, "Fuck me," in this breathy way that I suppose could be sexy but instead comes across as desperate and a little slutty. My fingers make a slight slurping sound as I pull them out of his ass. I yank his hips close to my crotch and spread his cheeks. His asshole is wet and red now; I rub my cock up and down his crack, he goes wild. I push the head of my dick against his pucker, and it slides into the warmth of his ass with no effort. Then he freezes, stops moaning, wiggling, etc....

"Dude, are you wearing a condom?"

"No, shit, sorry, it's just the tip. Sorry, I got carried away."

"Okay, just put one on, all right? You're neg, right?"

"Yeah, totally," I tell him as I go over to the nightstand, grab a condom, and unroll it over my fading hard-on. Then I lube up and start fucking him. I watch, almost mesmerized as my dick slips in and out of his ass. After I get bored with that, I flip him onto his back so I can watch him jerk himself off. I love watching guys jack themselves while they get fucked, it makes them look so submissive and sad. It's great. Anytime a guy looks pathetic in bed, the better the sex is going to be.

I fuck him for what seems like an eternity. Maybe I loosened him up too much or maybe he's just a huge bottom whore who's had his ass torn up too many times, but no matter what position I stick him in, I can't seem to get enough friction to come. He shoots before me, so I pull my cock out of him, take off the condom, and masturbate onto his chest.

After it's all over, we take a shower together, pretend to be sweet to each other, pretend that it was more than it was, and then he tells me to call him, like that's going to happen. Like either one of us really wants that.

Once the trick's finally gone, I bust into my emergency stash. I have two grams that I've been saving for an occasion like this. Basically I feel like shit, and it's either do coke or spend the afternoon crying. At least if I do enough coke I'll be motivated to clean my bathroom. I don't think I'd be motivated to do anything if I gave in to this stupid self-pity. I have to choke back the tears as I cut lines. Then I snort one, and it's instantly better. Three more days until I meet Shawn, my heart's all aflutter, and it's not all on account of the coke.

. . . . .

I'M HASTILY THROWING T-shirts, pants, and socks into my suitcase. I got hold of my dealer after lunch and bought an eight ball and some Valium off him, then picked up the rental car. Now I'm packing. As soon as I'm finished, I'm out the door. I

Mapquested the drive, and it should only take four hours to get to D.C. from here, from New York.

I try not to speed, but I'm anxious. That and I have to make up for lost time. I've been pulling over a lot to do coke. So that means every half-hour or so I have to find some place to stop to do a few rails off the dashboard. I should have flown, but there's no way I was going to smuggle this much blow onto an airplane. Shit ... I should do another line....

· · · · ·

THE HOTEL I ended up making reservations at is much nicer than a Motel 6. What good is a trust fund if you don't use it? Besides, it's only for two nights. Were I staying longer, I would have found a cheaper place.

D.C. is a lot like I remember it being. I think that before I leave I'll check out some of the sights. Yeah, right, who am I kidding. I can see a good chunk of the city from my hotel window right now, why do I need to go and see it up close? Besides, the Washington Monument isn't the reason I'm here. I flop down on the bed, take off my shoes, turn on the TV, and start flipping through the channels. I wonder if they have any of those pay-per-view sex movies. I'd feel weird about ordering one, though, so I do another line instead and page Shawn. Our "date" isn't until tomorrow, but I wanted to touch base with him. I e-mailed him the address of the hotel, but I didn't tell him what time to meet me. I can't find anything to watch, so I keep clicking through the channels over and over again. I stop at the Food Network, but that bores me, so I change the channel again, and again, and ... I should do another line. I'm really anxious, and it's not all because of the coke. How long has it been since I paged Shawn? Only ten minutes. I cut another line on the top of the nightstand, snort it, gag, then go into the bathroom and pour myself a cup of water. I start to get worried, so I count how many Xanax I have left. I have thirty-two, so I should be good.

I contemplate doing another line, just because there's nothing else to do, but then my cell phone starts to ring.

"Hello?" I ask.

"Someone page me?"

He's not queeny-sounding at all. I'm relieved. I hate femme guys.

"Yeah, Shawn, it's Mark, we have a date for tomorrow night...."

"Right, right, okay. Hi."

"Hey," I tell him.

"So, what's up?"

"Oh, I think I forgot to tell you what time to meet me."

"All right, so what time do you want to hook up?"

"Is ... um, what about seven? Is that cool?"

"Yeah, cool," he parrots back to me.

"So, do you want to know what I look like, so you can find me?"

"Uh, sure."

"Well, I look like Edward Norton."

"Uh-huh."

"And I'll be wearing a black blazer with gray pinstripes, a gray button-down shirt, and blue jeans."

"All right. And we're still meeting at the bar in your hotel?"

"Yes. At seven."

"Got it."

"So, Shawn, can you get any coke?" I blurt out, and I'm not sure why.

He's quiet for a minute, then says, "No, but I can probably get 'tina."

I don't get it. "No, I don't want a threesome, I'm not bi."

"No, no, no ... 'tina is meth, crystal—christina, get it?" He chuckles.

"Oh. I only do coke. But, you know, bring whatever you want for yourself."

"So you're into pnp?"

"What's pnp?"

"Never mind. Do you need anything else?" he coyly asks.

"This might sound weird, but do you own a jockstrap?"

"Um, no. Why? Are we going to play football or something?" he asks, laughing.

"No. I just think it'd be really hot to see your ass in a jock."

"Ohhh ...."

"Can you pick one up? I can reimburse you when you get here."

"Sure, I can probably swing that."

"Great. See you tomorrow then."

"Later."

After I hang up with Shawn, I do another line and click through the TV channels again.

. . . . .

I'M SITTING AT the bar waiting for Shawn. Last night, after our conversation, I downed a bunch of Xanax and passed out with the TV on. I've only been awake for an hour or so. I finish what's left of my Stoli and tonic, signal to the bartender for another, and wish I had done more coke before I came down here. It's only a quarter till seven, so Shawn's not late yet. Even so, I keep obsessively checking my watch, as if that'll make him materialize. Some Muzak version of a Barry Manilow song drifts through the bar, and I think I'm going to throw up, but then the bartender brings me my drink, and that makes things slightly better. Shawn. Shawn. Shawn. I whisper to myself as I stare into my vodka, at the small tonic bubbles popping up between melting ice cubes....

At seven o'clock, I order myself another drink. At five past seven, Shawn enters into my peripheral vision. I see him walk up to the bar, and my heart freezes—this is like real. I wonder how or why the gravity of the situation eluded me before. If I hadn't paid in advance, I would have bolted back up to my room, packed my shit, and been in the car heading home before he even realized I stood him up. I don't think I can do this. Luckily I don't have to—he approaches me.

"Mark?" he asks.

"Yeah, Shawn?" I question back.

"Yeah. You weren't lying, were you?"

"About what?"

"Looking like Edward Norton," he tells me.

"No. I guess I wasn't."

I don't think we can fuck. I've built you up too much in my head, and now it's never going to work.

"So ..." he wonders out loud.

"Do you want a drink? Or should we just ...?"

"I wouldn't mind a drink." He smiles, and I just melt.

"Ohhkay ... so what's your poison?" I stammer.

"Rum and Coke," he tells me, with a polite chuckle.

After getting thoroughly fortified, Shawn and I stumble up to my room. If it weren't for the alcohol, I would have chickened out. It never would have gotten this far. I slip the card key into the lock. The little green light blinks on, giving me the okay, and so I open the door, turn on the lights, and sit down on the bed. Shawn sits across from me, and he's really baby-faced. I figured that he'd show up looking haggard, worn out from drugs and extreme sex. But his features are still blissfully free of that hardened look some porn stars and hookers cultivate after a few too many years in the business.

"So, do you want to know what I do?" I ask, because I can't think of anything else to say.

"No, not really," is his reply.

"Well, I go to film school, at NYU."

"So, does that mean you're going to videotape us? 'Cause that's going to cost extra."

"No. No. I'm not going to tape us." I actually hadn't even thought about doing that.

"Okay, cool. So what are you into?"

"That's abrupt."

"Well, it's best to get it all out on the table," he explains.

"I was kinda hoping it would just happen organically."

"You're nervous," he tells me, while staring into my eyes.

I turn away, light a cigarette. "Yeah. I am."

"You know, I'm an escort, not a hooker. You paid to spend time with me. Sex doesn't have to happen."

For some reason, him saying that relaxes me. "I guess I never looked at it that way. I would like to, you know … if you want to." Jesus, why can't I say "fuck"—what's wrong with me?

"Sure, I'd like to. You're pretty hot."

That gets me hard. "Great." I smile.

Shawn leans in close to me, bites my bottom lip, and then sucks it into his mouth. We kiss violently for what seems like an eternity. I have to pull away to catch my breath and ask, "So, do you bareback?"

He hesitates. That means yes.

SWEET DICK

SHANE ALLISON

THEY LITTER PARK Avenue, cruising down Martin Luther King Boulevard where the streetlights kiss the asphalt with a peach hue. Spanish moss sways in the southern Saturday night breeze above them. I have to be careful considering it's rumored that men are getting busted by cops and mugged by the crackheads from Frenchtown. The porn videos and magazines filled with big dick white boys are getting boring. I'm too horny for porn mags and skin flicks. There's something stirring in my blood, surging in my crotch. I don't want to spend the night getting off by my own hand with a bottle of baby oil. I want to be touched, teased and pleased, pinched and kissed tonight.

I slow to almost a standstill with only my parking lights on to light my way. They're everywhere. Beautiful boys of all colors, creeds, and cock sizes. They stand leaning against parking meters, sitting on the porches of privately owned law offices, all waving their dicks in my view as if they were Confederate flags. Some men are in jeans with T-shirts cut off at pierced belly buttons. Others are shirtless with tattoos of all sorts strewn like graffiti across tight torsos. There are ghetto trannies in sequins and stilettos working the johns for a date. I'm envious of the hot breeze blowing across the buxom behinds of the buff Latino boys.

I'm looking for a grungy boy, someone who doesn't look so much like a hustler, a man like the stud I had last night who damn near sucked the skin off my dick for twenty bucks. I want myself a take-no-shit kind of young thing who knows how to party serious.

When I see Sweet Dick sitting on the bench in front of the library steps, I know I've found what I've been looking for. His hair is slicked back and black as the licorice I hate. He has cute, Cuban boy features and biceps covered in large tattoos. I park beneath an oak tree and stare at him from the passenger's window. I watch him suspiciously as he gets up and walks behind my car, playfully tapping his fingers against the roof. He stands in front of my window in a faded Led Zeppelin T-shirt, wearing bleach-blotched jeans. Sweet Dick's crotch comes straight to my face. I think since these guys are in the business of selling their asses, then it must be mandatory to sport a rock-hard cock 24/7, and Sweet Dick has a boner that's itching for some attention, a dick that looks as if it's exclusively for me. He taps on the glass with inked knuckles. I notice the letters L-O-V-E tattooed on the fingers of his dirty left hand. I roll down my power window to get a better look at this hottie.

"What's up?" he asks.

Sweet Dick smells of cigarettes and English Musk. His full cherry blossom lips are as hot as the rest of him, just as gorgeous as his bulging tattooed biceps. He's the one I have to have, and I'm hell-bent on paying whatever it takes to get him back to my place.

"How's it going?" I ask.

"I'm just out looking for a hot guy who's out looking for a hot time tonight." I like that he's quirky and clever that way. I breathe in his spearmint-sweet breath.

"So, are you looking for a hot time tonight, hot guy?" he asks, caressing my forearm.

"What's your name?" I reply.

"I go by a lot of names round here," he says. "Miss Christmas, 'cause with me it's Christmas year-round. Thunderbottoms for obvious reasons." He turns to show me his ass, which is the roundest, firmest bubble butt I've ever seen on a prostitute. The bleached jeans he wears droop a bit below his booty, exposing tighty-whities. "But my friends call me Sweet Dick, and if you're nice to me, you just might find out why." He runs his hand lovingly across my face.

"How much?" I ask.

"Fifty for head, a hundred to fuck, baby," he replies.

"I live over in Jefferson Commons. Apartment 4B. Think you can come over around midnight? I'll pay you double."

"Sure, daddy." Sweet Dick reaches down into my seat, between my legs, and squeezes the hard-on that's straining against my pants.

"Mmm, nice," he moans, smiling and smacking gum.

When I get home, I realize that my apartment is in shambles. It's 11:35, and I have only a few minutes to take a shower and get ready. My heart feels like it's trying to claw its way out of my chest. As I check myself in the mirror for the umpteenth time, the doorbell rings. He's right on time.

"Come on in, it's open." I sit on the sofa in a seductive pose. I dim the lights a little so it's not too bright. The last thing I want is for Sweet Dick to feel like a wild deer caught in headlights.

"Come on in," I tell him. The door quietly clicks closed behind him.

He stands in the middle of the living room and looks me over.

"What the hell is this? Look, man," he says, "if you want me to do some freaky shit, it's gonna cost you extra."

"On the table," I tell him. He turns around and sees the stack of hundreds. Sweet Dick takes the cash and pushes it down in a tattered pocket of his jeans.

"So who are you supposed to be?"

"Monica Lewinsky," I reply. I searched for weeks to find a navy blue dress that's similar to the infamous one Bill shot his load on.

"Have a seat." I pull the tail end of the dress over my nylon-covered knee.

Sweet Dick sits down, cocking his foot on the edge of the coffee table.

"You want something to drink? I've got bottled water, juice, beer...."

"Beer's cool!" Sweet Dick yells from the living room.

I grab two cold ones from the fridge and sit them on the countertop. I take a bottle opener from the dish rack and pry the tops off the long necks of Bud. My heels click across the tile of the kitchen floor, coming to a hush as they meet taupe-colored carpet in the living room.

I hand Sweet Dick his beer and take a seat next to him. "Let's make a toast," I say. "To a night both of us will enjoy. Cheers." Our bottles clank. We both take a swig from our beers. The alcoholic carbonation burns my throat.

"So, um, you dress like this all the time?" Sweet Dick queries.

"On occasion I do, yeah. Last week I was Linda Tripp." Sweet Dick takes another drink nervously and says, "That's ... cool." I look at him and laugh. "I'm kidding." He musters up a smile and takes another swig.

"Just relax, man," I say, sliding my hand beneath his Zeppelin tee, running my polished nails of Golden Red up along his stomach and across his pierced nipples. As I move in closer and tongue those pierced teats of his, he shoves my head away.

"Oh, sorry, did I hurt you?"

"No, they're just real sensitive, that's all. I just got 'em done." Sweet Dick fingers the right stainless steel barbell that sticks through his perky pink flesh. I start to wonder what else is pierced, or even tattooed.

"I promise I'll be gentle." I lean into his torso once more and run my tongue gently across his nipples as I caress his belly. I kiss his neck. It's coarse with stubble. He pulls away when I draw close to his lips.

"I don't kiss."

"That's cool." I'm sure he doesn't want to kiss me because of the Playful Plum lipstick.

"So can I ask you something?"

"Yeah, what?" replies Sweet Dick.

"When did you start …."

"What? Sucking dick for money?"

"I hope I'm not out of line?"

Sweet Dick takes a sip from his beer.

"Whatcha got cameras set up in this bitch or something?"

"No, I promise, nothing like that. I'm just curious."

"I was fourteen when I sucked my first cock," he explains. "Older guys mostly, but they didn't know how old I was. In the beginning I didn't do it for money. I was just a regular horny little motherfucker. I don't remember ever having sex with dudes my own age 'cept for this guy I went to high school with. I was a sophomore, and he was a senior I think. We used to sit behind these desk cubicles in the corner of the library and jack our dicks. His name was Mark. He would never let me suck him off. He had a big, pretty freckled boner."

My dick pulsates in my panties as Sweet Dick shares his experience with me.

"When I was sixteen, I used to stand in front of urinals in the bathrooms of movie theaters and malls and look at guys' dicks while they took a piss. I didn't start doing it for dough until I was eighteen, when a friend of mine told me how much money I could make. I wasn't real sure at first, but I figured, since I like sex, I might as well make a buck or two. There were plenty of horny truckers and middle-aged married men lined up with fat dicks. But all I gave a shit about was the bulge in their pocket. My first night I was scared shitless, but all the guys were cool and didn't give me any shit about being the newbie."

"So what was your first john like?" I ask.

"There was this one guy who wanted me to spit on him while

he sucked me off. So we did it behind the dumpster of that place ... the Blonde Iguana I think it's called. I charged him a hundred bucks. He didn't even let me get my dick out before he started pulling at my zipper. He sucked at sucking dick. Gave teeth, but I endured it anyway."

"So how long have you been hustling?" I ask.

"Started at eighteen, I'm twenty-three now, so I guess ... five years."

"Not that long."

"So, enough about me, what about you? Are you one of these freaky heteros who get blow jobs from guys because your wife won't suck you off?" Sweet Dick asks with an abrasive tone of sarcasm.

"Uh-uh, I'm gay."

"I pegged you for one of them straighties who comes out and complains about his lady not giving him head," he states with an accent. "I get a lot of johns like that. So, um, you got a boyfriend?"

"I had a lover, but we broke up. He was like your first john— couldn't suck dick either. But that's not why we broke it off. He liked giving head, but never really enjoyed getting sucked off."

"That's fucking weird," Sweet Dick declares.

"Yeah, I know."

"So, what are you in the mood for tonight?" Sweet Dick asks.

I slide my hand up my nylon thighs, hooking my thumb in the elastic waistband. Past the hose and the panties, I finger my dick.

"I like to get fucked and eat ass."

"I'm down with that. My ass could use a good cleaning."

"So why do they call you that?" I ask.

"What? Sweet Dick?"

"Yeah."

"Why don't I show you instead?" He unfastens the copper rivet of his jeans and slides his filthy fingers down past the elastic into the hothouse of his undies. I stroke my dick beneath the pantyhose with sheer anticipation, waiting to see what I have to work with. Sweet Dick pulls the underwear below his hips, unfurling a pretty, honey bun–brown cock with a mushroom helmet. It curls up thick like a banana.

"Fuck, you're huge," I pronounce, surprised.

"You like this, baby?" Sweet Dick asks.

"Can I suck it?"

"You're paying for it, baby."

I hold his fat fruit at the base and tongue the crown, smearing it across glossed lips, leaving behind traces of pre-come. The musky stench from his pubic forest is intoxicating.

"Suck my boner," he orders, scooting up close to my face. As I suckle his crown, Sweet Dick starts to work inch after inch of his dick into my mouth until all eight inches of this hot Cuban stud is down my tender pipe.

"Swallow this dick, dude," he tells me, lifting his faded Zeppelin tee above sable crotch hair. I stare at his stomach of tats with naked little men holding their cocks in their hands as if they're gearshifts.

"Move your hand," Sweet Dick says.

I hold onto his hips as he face-fucks me forcefully. I gag when his shaft grazes against my tonsils.

"Take it slow," he says. I don't want him to come just yet. As much as I want to work this hustler's hard-on till dawn, I stop and swirl off his dick. It falls limp from my lips, drenched with saliva.

"Why'd you stop? That feels hot."

"I want you to fuck me, baby." My pucker's wet with perspiration and hungry for something thick with veins. "I want you to fuck me. I want you to fuck me with a cigar."

"With a what?" he asks.

"A cigar. There's some extra cash in it for you if you can handle it."

"So let me get this shit straight. You want me to fuck you up the butt with a … a cigar?"

"Not just any cigar," I tell him, "but with a thick Cuban one."

"So that's why you're dressed like that."

My dick grows stiff just thinking about Sweet Dick running it through my asshole.

"So, are you down? The cigars are in a box on the kitchen table."

"Your time, your money," he pronounces.

Sweet Dick takes the cash lying on top of the entertainment center and stuffs it in his pocket.

"Where'd you get these things anyways?"

"I have my ways," I tell him. I can taste the chemicals from the cologne after I give his dick a work over. He walks over to the kitchen table, where a pencil box sits. When Sweet Dick opens it, the cigars are lined up in perfect rows like cinnamon sticks.

"Bring the whole box over," I say.

He sits them on the coffee table next to the beers, which are surely warm by now.

"Assume the position," Sweet Dick orders.

I lie on my back. My dress cinches at my stocking thighs as I kick up my heels to the ceiling fan that swirls steady above us. Sweet Dick stands on his knees between my legs and begins to rip off my stockings, desperate to get past the nylon to the manly parts of me. He pulls off the panties I purchased from a plus-size women's shop and throws them above my head.

Sweet Dick sucks his middle finger, getting it wet with spit. I watch him reach between me and slowly work his tattooed finger past my cheeks and into my ass. I wince at the sharp pain that surges through my hole.

"What end would you like me to fuck you with?" he asks.

"Surprise me." I look into his autumn eyes while he sucks at the cigar. I rest my legs on his sinewy shoulders for comfort. I can feel him making a passageway to my scut.

"Give it to me, man," I say, bracing myself.

I can feel the grainy tip being worked through my sphincter. My dick thumps against my navel as Sweet Dick runs the cigar along my ball sac and the starting line of my crack. He glides the cigar beneath his nose, taking a deep whiff of my booty's ripeness.

"Fuck me!" I say.

I'm not sure if my asshole will take it, but to my surprise the cigar goes in easily. I spit into my right palm and smear it on my dick for lubricant and beat off while Sweet Dick fucks me in and out again with the thick end of the Cuban stogie.

"Kiss me," I whisper.

Sweet Dick reaches up and wipes off the Playful Plum lipstick with the collar of my dress and kisses me hard. His tongue tastes minty.

"You like this cigar up your butt, boy?"

"Fuck, yeah, man! Fuck me!" I can feel my right ass cheek being pried ajar; the stogie slides in deep.

"I'm gonna come!" I yell.

Sweet Dick fucks me faster.

"Yes, that's good, like that. Punish me."

"You're bad, boy," Sweet Dick says.

He looks me in the eyes sadistically as he drives the cigar deep within.

"I'm coming, oh … uh!… Fuck me! Fuck … uh!" I squeeze my nipples through the stuffed bra.

"Yeah, shoot that juice for me, man." And I do just that as come bubbles up, oozing over Sweet Dick's dirty fingers. He wipes my semen on his grimy jeans while I ease my skewered ass down into the cool cushions of the couch. Sweet Dick sits the cigar in an ashtray on the table.

"How was that?" he asks me. "You liked it?"

"That was awesome, man."

"You hungry for my ass now, baby?" he asks.

"Oh, yeah!" I imagine Sweet Dick's hole is just as filthy as the streets he walks, just as dirty as all the mouths of johns that swallow his sweet meat nightly. I've wanted his ass ever since I saw those bleached jeans hanging from it. I lie down with one leg hanging off the end of the sofa and my other straight, with the toes of my right foot touching the armrest. Sweet Dick pulls off his jeans and underwear, tossing them in a wicker chair in the corner. The odor of sweat and ass fills my apartment while he stands over me and lowers his plump rump upon the throne of my face. His left ass cheek has a tattoo of a heart with a dagger through it. A tat I've seen on dozens of arms, shoulders, and upper backs. Sweet Dick's ass is lightly dusted with dark fur. The ripeness of his shitter grows stronger as he draws in closer to my mug. I wedge my eager tongue between his globes.

His hole tastes soapy and clean. But I'm prepared for anything and feast upon his crack as if it's my last meal. The louder Sweet Dick gets, the harder I drill through his cherry-red core. Who knew a five-year veteran of street whoring was such a tight ass? I reach back and with my fingers I pry his cheeks farther apart to make room for my butt taster. I hold on to his hips and maneuver him down onto me. With a mouth full of butt, I breathe through my nose, smearing Sweet Dick's booty across my face. I can tell he's beating off while I eat him.

"I'm about to come," he says as I eat his scrumptious scut. I'm hard again. I want him to shoot off on my dress, for it's only fitting. His body tenses, his sphincter tightens on my licker. I wish my tongue was a fat porno pecker up his pucker.

"Oh, damn, I'm gonna fucking come, dude!"

I can feel his cock porridge dissolving into the silk of my dress.

"Yeah, that's nice," he whispers. "Eat my butt."

I feed upon his sloppy booty like a pig. Then he stands up and it's over. I don't want to turn him loose, but he steps over me with his slobber-covered ass. Sweet Dick grabs his clothes off the wicker chair and gets dressed. His spent dick swings between his legs. I stare at him, soaked with sweat and sex, as he pulls the neck of his Zeppelin tee over his head, over a tattooed torso of Celia Cruz.

"Can we make this a regular thing?" I ask, with my arm snaked around his shoulder.

"Sure, man, anytime you like." He hugs me and gives me a kiss on the cheek. "You know where to find me."

COCKED AND LOADED

SHANE ALLISON

THE STENCH OF piss reeks from unflushed urinals. I pull the neck of my shirt over my nose to avoid the smell while I fondle my dick between fat fingers. It aches for the vacancy of a warm mouth. I've been told that this bathroom is the best cruise spot on campus where some serious money can be made. I'm here to find out if the rumors are true about all the trust fund college cock that frequents this place, or if smoke is just being blown up my hot-pink pucker. I peek through the slit of the occupied stall in an attempt to get a look at the guy next to me. The glory hole between us has "Make this hole bigger" scrawled in black ink above it. I pull out my purple Sharpie and scribble my cell number for "blow job $ervice" in bubble penmanship. It isn't much, but it's large enough to catch a glimpse of the horny piece of trade giving himself an afternoon hand job. I can see him piercing back at me. I turn in his direction to give him a better look at my brown sugar stick. A drop of pre-come forms at the piss slit as I tip it up to my belly. I slide my left hand beneath my tender sac, massaging my low-hangers.

I stand up off the commode and spread my dark chocolate globes so he can see my hot goods. It turns me on to hear his dick meat slap against his palm. I run my finger along my shitter to show him my ass. I like being watched; I'll put on a show for anyone for the right price. I sit on my toilet and tap my foot to let him know that I'm up for anything. He slides his index finger along the bottom of the partition. I lift my sleeveless shirt up above my gut. My dick is thick and throbbing, hungry for a stranger's mouth, starving for a man's butt. I think, who knows where that finger has been—caressing the supple helmet of a dick uncut, perhaps? Maybe up a scut big enough to shove a watermelon through? I hope his dick is enough to make my prostate purr. I stand off my toilet again with my underwear and jeans down below thighs and knees, roped around ankles, and glide my eight inches of grade A meat beneath the divider. I'll give 'em a taste, I think to myself. His hand is hot and tight around the shaft as he jacks me off.

"Suck it," I whisper below my breath.

His clothes rustle along the tiles; his belt buckle of heavy metal clangs against the floor of dried come. I look down at his face. He's a gorgeous, b-boy thug with a shaven head. His hairline is neatly trimmed, as if he's just come from the barber. His skin is a color of sunshine that mixes nicely with my tender sheath as it skims along voluptuous lips, darting in and out of his mouth. Damn, you can suck a dick, I think. My legs ache as I shove them further beneath his stall. I pop my pierced pecker out of his yapper, stand off my skinned knees, and pull back the latch to my door.

"Come into my stall," I murmur.

He ducks in, holding baggy shorts up over his ass; his dick, peeking from the slit of his zipper, curves up slightly instead of sticking straight out like most of the cocks I've had. My mouth is already watering for his meat.

"You can suck me," I tell him. "But this dick ain't free."

"How much?" he asks.

"Fifty," I reply.

He pulls two twenties and a ten out of his jean pocket and hands it to me.

The trick sits on my toilet and runs his hand under my shirt, caressing my belly before taking my dick, tilting it up to his lips. I lift my T-shirt out of his face as he blows me.

"Suck it," I order as I ram his head deep within my stinking musky forest of pubes. He gags, and it is music to my ears. I shove his hand away so he can't control how much cock gets rammed down his throat.

"C'mon, dude, show me you can take it."

When we hear the door open, it startles our lusting hearts. We pause and our blood slows. We hear boot steps tramp across the gritty floor strewn with tufts of tissue and paper towels.

"You two in the first stall, I need you to open up, let me talk to you."

"It's a cop," I whisper with wide-eyed shock to the cocksucking cruiser. The last thing I need is to get arrested again, being that I'm on six months' probation for whorin'. We both freeze. The slurps from the cruiser's blow job have fallen silent.

"We're just talking," the cruiser says, looking at me.

"Open up … now," he orders.

We fasten, button, and buckle our clothes as quick as we can. I slip the latch out of the metal hole of the door of my stall.

The policeman, dressed in a brown polyester uniform, is built and buff with black, greased braids protruding from beneath the rim of his hat. He's big, and towers over us. Officer Will Gray is etched in white letters on the nametag that's pinned on the right side of his breast.

"Let's see some identification."

We both reach for our wallets in the back pockets of our pants. I pull out my driver's license that's snug between my voter registration card and a business card that was given to me by my public defender.

"Derrick and Carlton," he says. I think to myself, so that's your name?

"So what were you two doin' in here?"

"We're jus' talkin'," says Derrick.

"It didn't look like you were talkin' to me. We've been gettin' complaints from the staff about suspicious behavior in this bathroom. Are you both students here?"

"I'm a junior," says Derrick.

I lie and tell him I'm a senior.

"All right, both of you turn around."

"C'mon, man, we weren't doin' nothing," says Derrick.

"Shut up and do what I tell ya, and there won't be any problems. Now put your hands on the wall."

Thick pearls of sweat trickle down our cold panicking faces.

Officer Gray pads us down for weapons. He looks at me with dark, suspicious eyes.

"You look familiar. Where do I know you from?" he asks.

"No place," I reply.

"You don't have a weapon, do you?"

"No," I say.

My dick gets slightly hard as his hands slither between my inner thighs. His fingers are inches away from my crotch.

I look over at Derrick when I feel something being poked in my spine.

"You ... lock your fingers," the officer says in a snide tone.

"Are you arrestin' us?" Derrick queries, looking over his shoulder.

"Turn around." He forces Derrick's head back toward the wall.

"Bro, what is this?" I ask.

"Keep your hands up, and I ain'tcha bro." Officer Gray runs his nightstick under my shirt.

"Man, what are you doin'?" asks Derrick.

"Shut up and keep your hands on the wall."

I knew I should have gone home, I think to myself.

"Spread your legs." He pushes my feet apart.

He runs his nightstick between my legs, sliding it beneath my balls.

"Both of you ... strip."

"What?" I say.

"Take your clothes off."

We disrobe, leaving nothing on but our socks. I'm terrified, thinking that this guy is some homophobic fag basher out to beat us both to a bloody pulp.

"Nice," Officer Gray says, poking at our cold booties with his nightstick. I'm not sure about Derrick, but my dick is good and hard, pressed between the wall and my belly.

"Turn around," he says.

With our hands in the air, we turn our backs to Officer Gray. I'm unembarrassed by my boner.

He looks at me and says, "I looked under and saw you two engaged in a lewd act."

"I swear we weren't …"

"Hey, hey, hey," he says. "Don't lie to me. I saw him givin' you head."

I'm shocked by the way he speaks. Officer Gray looks to Derrick.

"If you lie to me, I'll take your ass to jail. Were you performin' oral sex on him?"

Derrick drops his head, looks to the floor, and says, "Yeah."

"He's lying, I …"

"Shut your mouth!" he yells. "Now listen up. There's a way you two fags can get outta this shit storm you're in."

"Yeah, what? Anything," Derrick says.

"I wantcha to show me how you suck dick."

"What? No fuckin' way!" I tell him. "How do we know you still won't arrest us?"

Officer Gray shoves me down on the toilet against its metal pipes.

"You don't," he replies, forcing my thighs apart.

Derrick places his hand calmly on his arm.

"If we do this, will you let us go, man?" he asks.

Officer Gray doesn't take his eyes off me.

"Maybe," he replies. "If you suck it real good."

Derrick looks to me and says, "Let's just do what he wants."

"Listen to your boyfriend," he says to me.

"He's not my boyfriend."

Officer Gray presses the nightstick harder against my Adam's apple.

"You know you've got some mouth on ..."

"Okay, man, I'm doin' it, look," says Derrick, as he tilts my dick to his voluptuous lips. He opens his mouth and impales it with all nine inches of black dick.

"How does his mouth feel?" Officer Gray asks, tweaking my nipples. "You like gettin' your cock sucked?"

My contempt for him fades as I enjoy the blow job that Derrick is giving. I take a chance and grope the cop's bulge.

"You wanna suck me, boy?" he asks.

I bend over and lick his polyester crotch.

"Take it out," he tells me. "Take my dick out."

I unzip the zipper and ease my hand down into its copper gape. His meat is firm; my adrenaline is running through me like volcanic lava knowing that I would soon have a policeman's wang in my mouth.

Derrick reaches around and pinches my cheeks that flow over the black rim of the commode, steadily slurping upon me.

I hook three fingers into the elastic of Officer Gray's Fruit of the Looms, tugging them down past a bushel of pubes. Veined ridges run down the middle of his shaft. The rest of his dick pops from the waistband with a meaty mushroom crown.

"Think you can handle this?" Officer Gray looks down and gives me a shit-grinning smile. His dick is musky with sweat. I'm scared that he'll crack my skull, but ready, willing, and hopefully able to work the slab that hangs between his thighs. I slowly work the head into my mouth. The ridges rub against my lips. I work up more spit to lube it up as I slide down, devouring two, three, four more inches. The muscles in my mouth begin to ache a bit as he overpowers me. I go in deeper—five, six, seven, eight more inches of dick disappear.

"Whata mouth," Officer Gray says. "Whata … mouth."

I swirl down and up, down and up, noticing in the mirror the slobber that runs along the underside of his penis. Derrick is still at me, trying to get me to blow my load. I damn near forgot that he was between my legs, being that Officer Gray was hard at work knocking his dick against my poor old tonsils. I gag a few times but keep at it.

"Don'tcha puke, punk," he says, gyrating his hips into my face.

"Squeeze my ass," he tells me. I take my right hand and pinch the cop's chocolate ass cheeks.

"Hard," he demands. In order to keep with the pace of my blow jobs, I squeeze his booty when I go balls deep. My own hole is wet with sweat, anxious for plowing.

When I back off Officer Gray's dick, a web of spit runs from my lips to his chunked cock. I'm dying to feel this cop's cock skewing my butt. He plays with my chocolate chip nipples. The scent of sex hovers above our naked brown bodies.

"You get fucked?" the cop asks.

I slide off his dick and say, "Sometimes."

I usually charge two hundred for anal, but what could I do? He was a cop.

"Well, you gettin' fucked today. Get up," he says, tapping Derrick on the shoulder. A trail of spit trickles down Derrick's chin and neck of stubble.

My asshole is ready to swallow that porno star prick. I stand up and move to the sink. I bend over and spread my legs. Officer Gray hangs the nightstick on the metal rail screwed to the handicapped-accessible wall of the stall. He unbuckles his belt that holds his pistol. I don't doubt that it's loaded. He unfastens the copper rivet of his pants. They drop to his feet. The buckle clangs on the tile floor.

"Don't move or I'll have to stick my gun up your ass," he tells me.

"Or maybe you like that shit."

He scoots up behind me. His dick is warm as he smears the head of it from one butt cheek to the next.

"I hope ya'll got rubbers," Officer Gray says.

Derrick pulls a red packet out of his tattered jean pocket and hands it to him. The big dick cop tears across the edge with his teeth. His meat rests upon my ass as he pulls out the lubed latex.

"This betta not be that cheap sheepskin shit," he says to Derrick.

Get that thing in me, I think to myself.

I can feel Officer Gray's angry fingers creep in, prying my cheeks ajar. Derrick sits on the toilet and whacks what looks to be nine inches of light-skinned dick. I brace the edge of the sink for the cop's cock. My rectum pulls and stretches as he works it in me slowly. It hurts like hell, and I try to relax all my muscles. My eyes are red and watery as Officer Gray's dick devours my ass. I'd give anything to see his cock explore my middle.

"Let him blow you," he says to Derrick. He walks over and stands at my open mouth while Officer Gray pounds me hard from behind. Derrick parks his dick in my yapper, fucking my face while the cop impales my booty. His pre-come is salty on my palate. The two of them laugh, knowing that both ends of my body are getting poked.

"You got a fat hole, man," Officer Gray sighs.

He says he hasn't jacked off all day, that he usually finds a secluded place to park to blow off a wad, but hasn't had the time since he's been busy patrolling the campus.

"Damn, I been bonin' for an ass like yours all day," he says as he thrusts his honey bun–brown dick through me.

Derrick continues to snake his prick down my gullet, holding it there until I gag.

"I'm 'bout to come," he says as he rapes my mouth. He pulls

out; a thick string of semen shoots across the side of my face, into my hair. I take his dick and pump the rest of his cream off into the sink.

"I'm gettin' close to shootin' off," the cop warns as he pushes and bucks through the remnants of my insides.

"Oh, shit, I'm comin'! I'm gonna shoot, dude!" he yells.

"Shootcha juice," Derrick says.

"Ah, shit!" the cop hollers.

His face grimaces, eyes squint shut.

"Ah ... shit!" he yells, steady pumping his white fire into the rubber that slides along the sore walls of my ass.

When he's done using me, Officer Gray slips out. I collapse into the sink.

"Jesus, you can fuck," I say.

He unrolls the come-filled condom off his meat and slings it in a trash can of wet brown paper towels.

"That was hot," the cop says, pulling his pants up over his booty. I try to get dressed, but every muscle in my body screams.

"So, are you going to take us to jail?" Derrick asks.

"Well ... you're free to go." He looks over at me as I pull my jeans over my spent ass. "But you ... you stay."

Derrick takes one last look at me and walks out of the bathroom.

"I knew you looked familiar. I busted you last month for sellin' your ass over in Frenchtown.

"I'm takin' you in. The guys at the station are gonna love you."

THE GIFT

WHIZZER CRAFTON

CHRISTMAS EVE, MY twentieth year, the worst day of the worst year of my life, I hopped the F to Midtown to suck some lonely rich man's cock. It had snowed, and everyone in the city smelled like wet dog. The train was full of Christmas people. The bags and the kids and the hideous hats and the very stupid-looking oversized coats. People from places like Tenafly and Poughkeepsie and Nanuet on their way to stand on line for about eighty hours so they could ice skate and buy fake antique clocks and cognac for family members who didn't love them anymore. What I remember most about being young and living in the city was not so much my young hungry cock or my young hungry belly or my young hungry mind, but the degree of hatred I had for folks from Poughkeepsie. None of them understood how to stand on the subway. They took over the place like herds of rhinos, and I felt like the Invisible Faggot squished between them.

The problem with turning wealthy tricks was this: if they called you to have their asses rimmed or rammed, if they needed to pay someone to have their dicks licked or balls sucked, if they needed to shell out cash in order to penetrate fresh asshole, if they couldn't accomplish the exchange of fluids via more respectable avenues, say, asking a guy out for sushi or a movie or a light beer, you knew it was because they were suffering somehow. By this, I mean they were ugly. It was different if the john had saved up for you, if he had stayed at home for two weeks so he could blow his wages on a special Friday. That made you feel like you were some kind of treat, and usually he treated you like a total queen or total shit (your choice), but whatever he did was full of intention and hot, so hot. So when I got the message to meet some guy named Cassidy at an old building on West Fifty-seventh, caddy-corner Carnegie Hall, I knew it was going to be a night of unfair hard labor, of kissing the bad-breathed, of holding in my arms the fat or sick or small and crooked cock, of pretending to love the universally unloved. It was literally dry work. There was sweat involved, but only the emotional kind. I would go home from turning this specimen of trick with a lacerated ass and a wad of cash, feeling like I'd been through a war, unsure of who I was or what I'd been up to, and very, very tired.

I had nothing against ugly people. I'd lived on the streets for three years in three different cities, and I'd had many ugly friends. That's the worst thing—sleeping outdoors does for people: it makes them impossible to look at. That's why you don't want them in your neighborhood. Hunger doesn't bug the eyes. But gaping pores and skin diseases and black corroding toenails—you don't want to see that on your way to work. Ugly people had been my friends and lovers. I'd once had a boyfriend who was ugly by most people's standards. He'd been in a bicycle accident and had a cratered scar on his face that looked like a map of Utah. It was inches deep and hard to look at and impossible not to at the same time. You saw it and you wanted to slide two fingers in it, there's no other way to say it.

Still, nobody understood how to fuck me the way Billy fucked me. He could turn my ass into a puddle and have me lying on the linoleum wincing for his cock. He made me hard, but mostly that guy made me wet, like I was a giant cunt needing to be fucked in order to exist. He was the one who taught me to take dick. To swallow it with my anus. After every fuck I died a little. The more I fell for him, the more fuckable he grew. An ugly trick's an ugly trick, but if you really love a guy, you just think he's got sex dripping out of his nostrils, no matter what he looks like. He was a nice guy. I'd never been more pissed at anyone. We once spent six weeks throwing kitchen utensils at each other and fucking in his basement apartment in Minneapolis, only leaving the house to buy frozen pizza-bagels, Sunny Delight, and drugs. I was fifteen then. One day he got arrested and became very sick. I don't know where he is or what he looks like now.

What's crazy about the West Fifties is you can hear the clop-clop-clopping of Central Park horses like you're in a time warp. I always thought I'd entered a portal coming up onto Fifth Avenue. There I was, a twenty-year-old kid from the future in a leather jacket on his way to suck some melancholy Christmas dick, and I was surrounded by lights and taxis and old horse-drawn buggies.

It was one of those two-thousand-year-old marble-and-stone lobbies with not one but two doormen. One operated the elevator, a pretty foxy young uniformed guy named Ernest. He was so nice to me, like I was this Cassidy gentleman's long-lost nephew coming home to surprise him for the holiday. He just kept smiling and nodding, and the way he did this made my cock wake up. The city was mean, and nothing made me want to bone like sweet people.

My trick lived on the top floor. There was a large wooden knocker on the door, no doorbell, and I felt a little like Dorothy knocking dumbly at the doors of Oz. In the hallway was a very bedraggled Christmas tree with tinsel weeping all over it. Looking at it brought tears to my eyes. I was about to turn around and just go back home, maybe go to my only friend in New York's "Christmas for Lonely Jews" party, when some clown answered the door.

I'm speaking here of a literal clown. The man wore an orange polka-dot shirt, white clown makeup, the cheap sweating kind, and on his head he had donned a plastic crown.

Even now I do not understand the faction inside our greater

community of sexual outcasts that fetishizes clowns. I'll take pain, I'll take ponies, I'll take Saint Bernards. One time a john dressed up in a diaper and shoved a grape popsicle up my ass, and I came, dutifully, on his chest. Once I even put my mouth on a woman's cunt, and it tasted like vinegar and I liked it. But nothing will make my dick wilt like the sight of a clown. Clowns are scary. They do not belong in parks, at birthday parties, or anywhere near children. They aren't sexy-scary like vampires or witches. They do not belong in the vicinity of sexual activities or even near places where sexual thoughts might inadvertently take place. I normally oppose capital punishment, but I do believe the guillotine should be reinstated for the reprobate freaks who are turned on by clowns. This includes those who get off wearing clown makeup, which was right then melting off the man's face, I think because he had been crying.

"Welcome to Cassidy's Castle," he said, like this was the merriest fucking Christmas of his whole entire life. "Would you like a glass of eggnog?"

"Yes please," I said, and he slipped into the kitchen.

To tell you the truth, the apartment was grimy. It was dark. There was the congealing smell of cigarettes that had been smoked long ago. Liquor that had been drunk long ago. The furniture was the furniture of a rich man, but I had a feeling when I walked into the living room that everything in it was greasy with film.

Evidently this clown was a cock collector. There were dicks everywhere in his house. Sculptures of dicks, paintings of dicks, books about dicks, framed photographs of pierced dicks, squirmy dicks, stealthy dicks sliding out of corners like salamanders, what looked like a cake the shape of a dick presented festively on the coffee table, a pencil-thin dick statuette on a pile of sheet music on the piano, an enormous dick that lit up as a lamp next to a globe. The clown himself was tall and fat and sort of sausage-shaped. He was bald under the crown, and there was something vaguely penile about the shape of his head and nose. He came out with the drinks, and we sat on the couch surrounded by all those dicks. At first it was quiet, and we sipped eggnog and looked out the window at the snow. The eggnog was warm, and I drank it up. It had a filling effect, like a hot meal. Those years were a little hungry, I must admit. And not always because I was broke. I forgot to eat a lot. My friend Lucille joked that I was manorexic, but I think I just had a hard time feeling anything.

"Well," I said. "Should we, like, start?"

He stroked my cheek with his fingers and the back of his hand. I looked down at his shoes to see if they were clown shoes, but they were just a dusty pair of cowboy boots. Then I looked at his crotch. This clown was stiff already. Two fingers rested on his fly. He smiled, and I noticed his incisors. They were rabid with the clown makeup, and the way he calmly sat there smiling, lightly touching his own penis, I thought for a moment he might suddenly take my head off with his teeth. With his thumb, he wiped away the eggnog mustache that had formed above my lip.

"You aren't for me," he said, sucking the eggnog off his thumb. "You're for my boy."

I don't know why, but when he said "boy," I immediately assumed he was talking about a little boy. It could have been the clown makeup. I imagined he might have been loitering around the tot stops in Central Park earlier, maybe hanging out by the Alice in Wonderland statue, and lured some curious boy, maybe with balloon animals, to come with him to his house to see more tricks. Some terrible visions went through my head of what he could do to a boy with all these phalluses around. I understand now that this assumption said more about me than it did about him. When I was young, it felt like the whole world was a playground for pedophiles.

I stood up.

"I don't do kids," I said defiantly, but my voice cracked. I put my hands in the pockets of my jacket and turned around to leave.

But then the kid walked from the light of the kitchen into the living room. He was a boy, but only a couple of years younger than me. He was maybe seventeen, or else eighteen, and private-schooled. He wore no shirt, and his hairless chest glistened a little. He had broad shoulders, like he swam or fenced, and a very hard-looking stomach, but there was also something gawky about the way he stood, as though he had this body on loan for the night and wasn't quite sure how its limbs worked. He wore reading glasses, and at first this seemed strange, but I realized that the combination of this and his awkward buffness made him even more handsome. He sat on the floor next to the clown almost like a cat. The clown stroked the boy's thick head of hair. He leaned down and whispered something in his ear.

"You're his gift," the clown explained to me.

"Well, this is going to cost more," I said. "Plus a bonus. It's Christmas."

The boy said nothing. He just smiled and came close to me. I took my jacket off and threw it on the couch, where the clown still sat. The kid was bigger than me, but so were most people then. To be honest, even though I'd been getting naked on a regular basis for most of Manhattan and some of the outer boroughs, and some of northern New Jersey, I felt a little embarrassed in front of this kid about the size of my shoulders. I put my hands on his chest. He was warm. I played with his nipples with my thumbs and he kissed me. He tasted like water. His tongue searched the inside of my mouth. This boy was sweet, I could tell by his tongue. Once again, the safety of that sweetness made me hard. I tried to forget about the repulsive clown who watched us. If my dick wasn't so hard I might have wondered what the hell this kid was doing with him. But the kid unbuttoned my jeans, reached in, and pulled out my cock.

"That's nice, Melvin," the clown said. "That's playing nice."

The kid got down on his knees and started massaging my shaft. He looked over to the clown, maybe to see if he was doing it right.

He got the nod of approval from the guy, who was full on rubbing his cock under his pants. The Melvin kid had grown-up hands. He leaned in and kissed the underside of my fresh-shaved balls. I felt his glasses on my scrotum. He took them off and put them on the coffee table next to the dick cake. My cock was rock-hard and almost flat against my stomach now. He licked it up and down, not quite taking it into his mouth yet. He flicked his tongue over my dick head really fast, then slowly, pulling back my foreskin and sort of fucking my piss hole with his tongue. This was making me crazy. He reached behind and pulled down my jeans so I was standing there stupidly with my whalebone purple and upright and my BVDs and pants at my ankles. I was still in my boots. My socks were wet from the snow. The kid slurped at my dick, then slowly took it in his mouth. I held his head and fucked his face a little. I tugged at his ear and gave him a little slap on the cheek, just to tease him. Cassidy laughed, the dumb clown. The kid smiled a little, and it broke my heart with my fat dick poking from the inside of his cheek.

"That's sweet," Cassidy said. "Now rip him apart."

I didn't want to come in the kid's mouth, it didn't seem right. So I pulled my dick out and made him stand up. He got behind me, and I immediately felt his cock pulse on the crack of my ass. He held my dick, which was wet with his spit, and began to lick my ear. He went crazy on my ear, biting it, sucking at it like it was a pussy, lining the folds and nooks with wetness, flicking the cartilage like it was a giant clit. He whispered little things in my ear. I was so overstimulated I could barely hear. But I know he said something about how he was going to fuck my ass so deep I was going to feel his dick come up my lung. I had to concentrate not to jizz all over Cassidy, who was still sitting on the couch in front of us, revolting, with his pants down, tugging at his cock very slowly.

"You're feeling a little lonely this Christmas, aren't you?" he said. And the way he said it, he reminded me of Billy. Like he was accusing me and taking care of me at the same time.

"It's the season of sorrows," he said. "But at least we have each other."

As the kid licked my ear he lubed my anus with his finger. The kid's dick penetrated my asshole slowly. I hadn't seen his cock yet, but I could tell it was enormous, bigger than mine, bigger than the clown's, maybe bigger than anyone I'd ever taken.

The clown produced a dildo and started to lick it as he watched us. He pulled his own hard dick out of his pants and stroked himself with his left hand as he shoved the dildo in his mouth with his right. I have to say I was surprised by this guy's girth, and I had a hard time not looking at him getting himself off. His cock looked young and fresh. There were no gray hairs on it. It was thick and meaty. He just kept stroking it, this old hand stroking it, the palm of his hand pumping it up and down, and with his young lover ramming my ass and the trickle of pre-come on the clown's dick, and the way he was stuffing the dildo down his throat and pulling it out and licking the tip, like it tasted so good, like he could never get enough, it just made my own cock a little crazy. I pushed myself toward him with my dick in my hand. I was jealous of the dildo. I wanted his tongue on my dick as I was getting reamed. I didn't want to look at him, at his makeup and those teeth, but I did want him to slobber all over my cock.

He got the hint and took the dildo out of his mouth and fucked his asshole with it. He left it up there, his pants at his ankles, his dick still raging hard, slid off the couch, and came toward me on the floor with his mouth. Those teeth. I had to close my eyes. I felt his makeup and his whiskers on my cock. They burned. Then his tongue. It was hot too. I mean, his tongue was like a hot razor. It almost hurt. He just ran it up and down my shaft in long, hard licks. All I could feel was the roughness of his whiskers under the paint and the sharp heat of his tongue and his breath. The boy behind me held my ready-to-burst balls firmly and guided my cock into the clown's mouth. That was crazy. The ass fuck and then the boy forcing my cock in with his hands. He squeezed the base of my dick, and every time he shoved his prick farther up my hole he let out a soft moan in my ear.

"Yes, feed him to me, Melvin. Feed me cock," the clown said, coming up for air, and then going back for more of my cock, which was taking the white tint of his face paint. "That's my boy," he kept saying. "Fuck him like you hate him."

"But I don't even know him," the kid let out sweetly as he fucked me hard.

"Fuck the blue out of his face," the clown ordered. "Fuck the sadness out of him."

I was close to coming into the clown's throat. It was so warm, and I kept thinking, if I could just fuck his face a little harder, if I could just reach his stomach with the tip of my dick. If I could turn this clown's throat to pulp … then what? I could get rid of my head. Oh God, I kept thinking, I just wanted to fuck face and be fucked. There was the sound of cock-in-cheek slurp. My ass was breaking, bleeding a little, wet with blood and come and shit. I'd taken so much in my life, but this was like a fucking freight train. It hurt, it opened, everything destroyed. My eyes turned to water, not from sadness but from breaking. How could a kid be so young and fuck so hard? And who was the kid? And was he really younger than me? And was the clown a real clown? Was that his job? And who was I to mock someone's job? My mother didn't raise me that way. And it wasn't enough. I reached behind and spread my ass cheeks wider so I could feel even more.

"Shit," I said. "Shit."

The boy up my ass came, in one fluid movement, pulled his dick out, and shot come on the small of my back, wailing a little. He immediately started rubbing the hot come on my ass like a lotion with his hands and licked it up, now and then sliding his tongue into my tattered anus. I still had my legs spread, and the clown kept gobbling my dick, and so now I had two tongues working me.

I could tell the story right now of what I was thinking then, make something up about what I was contemplating as I was getting fucked: the phalluses, the lighting of that weird apartment, the eggnog on my breath, the blue quality of this perverted Christmas Eve in my twenty-first year (where was my family, wasn't I afraid of diseases, who were my friends?), the choice of curtains, the clown (why a clown?). I could pretend it really hurt, that it was kind of empty, that there were needs unmet and promises broken and ghosts inside this fuck, and Billy could reappear, making my mentioning of him in the earlier part of this story significant, his ugliness could resonate—I'll include all of that in another version, the next time I tell it; but at that moment I was just a piece of Christmas meat. I was all dick, ass, balls, and breath. I had no brains, no eyes to roll, no dreams, and it was fucking great. I just had two tongues servicing my organs, eating me up. The tongues did not ask questions, they were not lonely or conscious tongues. They didn't care it was Christmas. They did not have issues. They weren't beautiful or ugly or young or old or bitter. They licked and ate. And I was sort of breathing. That was it. This was the best job I was ever going to have.

I shot my load in the clown's throat. He swallowed, and I pulled out of him. My chest tightened a little, the way it does when I come sometimes. The boy who'd been fucking me kissed me. He licked my lips before slipping his tongue into my mouth. Water again. But now I could taste my own asshole on his tongue. I'll never forget the scent of that kiss. It was like I had stepped outside of my own body and fucked myself. There were a couple of minutes of the three of us lying on the floor, and I fell asleep. Against my rules, but I was tired. It was quiet when I woke up. I could hear horses. And then the clown went into the kitchen.

"He didn't even come," I said to the boy, who was sharing a pillow with me.

"He hardly ever does," he said. "He's a giver in a world of takers."

"It's Christmas. He should at least have a fucking orgasm."

"I think it keeps his heart ticking," he said.

The kid pulled his jeans on, put his glasses back on his face, paid me five hundred dollars in crisp twenties at the door, and I shook his hand and left. The streets were empty. Church bells rang. I walked, clutching the bills all the way home like a crazy person, counting my blessings out loud.

REVERSAL

....

JASON KIMBLE

SOMETIMES EVAN HATED the way his mind worked. Everything was overcomplicated, full of extra associations. Like now, his thinking went around this loop: he flashed on a memory of reading something by a writer who loved the fresh, clean scent after a rain. Obviously, Evan grumbled in his head, said writer didn't live in a city, especially not in a crap neighborhood with crap garbage collection in the middle of summer. Because the rain that had just stopped here? It just made the air heavy and wet, and that wetness soaked up all the stenches that had been content to hide in the uncollected garbage piles. Then all that garbage-soaked air clung to Evan, stuck his T-shirt to him, and made him sweat—just what the current smell needed, surely.

Luckily, that wasn't the impediment to picking up a john you'd think it was. Half the guys out cruising the strip were into the dirty street kid look. Evan didn't pull off the "kid" part quite as well as he used to, but he was still fresh enough meat to get attention. Plenty of older guys still considered him boyish; plenty of younger ones wanted someone a little more seasoned to play with. Usually, anyway. Maybe it was the muggy stink in the air, but the cars kept their windows up, buzzed on by without giving him the chance to catch a ride. If there was anything worse than standing in the stink-soaked after-rain, it was standing around in it without a prospect.

The kid shuffled into view from down the street, hands stuffed in his tight jean pockets. He wore a less-than-white wife-beater that showed off the cut of his arms. Something curvy and tribal tattooed on the left shoulder. Evan figured that floppy black hair wasn't the wet look but the real thing.

Evan leaned up against the lamppost, doing his best nonchalance. He crossed his arms, pulled out his butchest voice, and rumbled an "evening" as the kid got closer. Nah, he wasn't really a kid either. More the TV version—the kind of smooth-faced twenty-something you'd see on a whiny high school drama. Evan let a sly grin fall into place.

The kid looked around a second, like maybe Evan was talking to the invisible someone behind him, then returned the smile.

"Nice night, yeah?" Evan lied, pushing off from the lamppost and taking a few steps forward. The game started now, and for Evan that was often the best part.

"Rain's stopped at least," shrugged the other, shuffling a touch closer.

"True 'nough." Evan finished bringing them intimately close, but didn't initiate contact. "Looks like we both forgot to come in out of it … what was your name?"

"Mark."

"Should have known." Evan chuckled. "So, maybe it's better late than, and we should, you know, come inside now? I'll even give you a rainy day special."

Mark snagged Evan by the belt loops and pulled him in. Their crotches bumped against each other. Warm breath added to the moist after-rain heat.

"Run," whispered Mark.

"Wha—?"

"Shut up," Mark hissed, one hand sweeping up behind Evan's head. His mouth dropped down to feign kissing Evan's neck, but he kept whispering, "I'm a cop. Run. Now. Because they're already on their way."

Evan pushed free, and Mark let him go. There, near the corner, a straight couple taking a stroll. At night, in this neighborhood? Made more sense if they were other plainclothes. He tried not to stare but still keep them in his peripheral vision. Fast but not desperate, Evan, he thought, backing away from the street. The woman in the couple giggled, loud. Forced. Evan felt a shadow fall across him. He was in the alley.

Run.

He didn't pace himself. He sprinted all out down the dark, echoey space between civilized buildings. His feet pounded down in a puddle of he didn't know what, but the splash no doubt soaked his jeans, so he'd have the pleasure of identifying it later. The noise would call out his position.

Push more. Faster.

The wet air seemed to thicken around him as he tried to slip through it. It clung inside his mouth, raked along his throat.

Turn here. And again.

His legs burned. His heart beat its desperation strong. Evan swore it had grown to fill his entire, shaking chest.

Left. Right. Right again. Don't stop. Can't stop.

Then there was nothing left. No more push. Evan fell forward at the wall, barely managing to get his hands up to catch himself. Uneven brick dug into his palms, though his nerves only registered it as vague pressure; they didn't have the energy to codify discomfort beyond that. Sound was just layers of noise behind the pounding of blood in his ears. The air too had lost its pervasive odor. It burned its way into his nostrils and down to his chest.

Slowly Evan's senses came back to him. The brick gained a sharp texture. Tires and horns and splashes distinguished themselves again. And there was the lovely smell of whatever he'd splashed his way through in the first alley. He welcomed it, though, as it came with muscles regaining their stamina, a pulse that didn't threaten to explode. When he trusted himself to move again, Evan crossed the street. One of his hotels of choice lay across the slowly dwindling traffic.

The shower was just what he needed. Everything opened up and relaxed. Until, that is, Evan started replaying the night in his overthinking brain. Okay, marks turning out to be cops wasn't exactly new, but having one of those cops warn a guy? It was a new twist to the game, a potential threat that put them both at risk. Evan remembered that, remembered his heart ramming against his insides, and hell if he wasn't hard by the time he was toweling off. He decided to air-dry then. Turn down the AC and cool off, in more ways than one.

"Wondered how long you'd be in there. Any hot water left?"

Mark sat on the bed, leaning backward on his hands, eyes shining. Evan looked to the nightstand where metal flickered under the dim bulb of the lamp.

"That badge will get a guy a lot of things, I guess," Evan announced.

"Folks in this part of town want to keep the law happy."

"Suppose so."

Mark slinked his wife-beater up over his head and flung it across the room. Evan didn't figure he'd ever seen a cop on the force in that kind of shape. He could count those abs in the shadowy light of the room. He tried not to stare, but moving his gaze only brought him to the hard curve of the equally chiseled pecs.

"So, you … want the shower, then?" The chintzy towel wasn't hiding anything. His erection would have stood out to blind men looking the other direction.

Mark chuckled, rose from the bed, confidently closed the gap between them. His nose hovering in front of Evan's, he said, "Eventually."

Mark dislodged Evan's hand on the towel. The hustler watched it fall, and when their eyes met again, Mark reached up, caught Evan's face between his hands, and pulled him in for a deep kiss.

All the overthinking crumbled. Evan's tongue played along Mark's lips until they opened and let him in. As the men's tongues slipped across each other, their hands groped. Four sets worked at Mark's belt, his zipper. Then Evan's worked their way up, thumbs ticking over the abs, fingers playing in the light dusting of chest hair. As they curved around those too-perfect pecs, Evan leaned in, overbalancing them, forcing Mark backwards, onto the bed. Mark's breath rushed into Evan's mouth, just the slightest bit sweeter than he'd expected.

Evan disengaged. He shifted his weight to his knees, drew free hands down Mark's sides, to the undone but still-in-place jeans. Mark's own hands worked through Evan's thicker chest hair, found the nipples, and tweaked. At the belt, Evan gripped strong and pulled down fast, yanking jeans and boxers to the knees. He pulled up a foot, snagged the waistband with his toes, and pushed everything down into a puddle of fabric beside the bed.

Mark's legs swept up, ankles meeting in the small of Evan's back. His hands moved from nipples to shoulders. Evan followed the pressure to move closer. Their tongues played along each other's necks, up to trace the ears. Mark arched upward, groaning, then suddenly shifted his weight, toppling Evan to one side and straddling him.

Evan's breath caught, and he moved to reach up to Mark, but the other pushed down on his chest, straightened himself so he sat atop him. He smiled, his hand slinking around behind him to slowly begin jerking Evan off. Evan, forced flat but desperate to move, reached for Mark's own erection and matched his stroking.

The AC blared on. A chill washed across the sweat Evan had built up. He grabbed Mark around the waist, angled his legs off the bed, and stood. It was awkward, the weight off-center, but Mark's hard-working stomach lifted him up. He looped his arms behind Evan's neck, fingers holding at the shoulder blades, ankles pressing hard into Evan's ass. Another strong, deep kiss, forcing them back.

Evan spun as they fell, and Mark was beneath him again.

Evan moved the kiss downward, over the Adam's apple, tongue making a wet path through thin chest hair, then flicking across Mark's nipple. The man on the bottom groaned, his hands on Evan's shoulders now. Evan tongue-circled the nipple, then fluttered at its tip again. One hand felt its way to Mark's other nipple, working that one hard as well.

Mark pushed at Evan's shoulders, and Evan moved down. His hands firmly gripping the other man's sides, Evan kissed his way from nipples to stomach, stomach to thighs. Then his tongue traced its way up the shaft of Mark's solid, pulsing cock, fluttering again at the cut tip. The groan this time was louder, and Mark arched upward off the mattress, his fingers digging into Evan's shoulders.

But as Evan had his mouth open and poised, Mark grabbed him by the ears. He forced Evan up as he sat up himself. Another kiss. More groping. And in the end, once again Evan wound up with his back on the mattress. Mark's turn to trace his way across Evan's body with his tongue, hands working up and down his sides, reaching in to tweak nipples at the apex of their travel.

The sudden stop timed with the AC kicking off, and Evan felt deaf, his nerves somehow lost to him for the second time that night. Gasping for breath, he craned his neck to see Mark tear open the condom wrapper with his teeth. He grabbed Evan's hand and put the latex into it, twisting the lid off a small bottle of lube as he said, "Put it on me."

Evan's fingers quaked a moment, but he fumbled the condom in place, rolled it slowly down the length of Mark's endowment. He squeezed it just a touch between thumb and forefinger, massaging as he went. Mark's hand followed, lube sliding along the latex surface. As Evan continued jerking, Mark's lubed fingers moved across Evan's ass, traced his rim, flitted in, retreated. Mark added more lube to his sheathed cock as Evan shifted in the bed, throwing his feet up over Mark's shoulders. Hands gripped his knees. Evan closed his eyes and relaxed, sucked in his breath as Mark eased up inside him.

He started slow, soft, shallow. His hands whispered along the length of Evan's body. Evan mirrored, his own hands exploring Mark's sides, his arms, his chest. Mark leaned closer as he pushed in deeper, though still slow. His ripped stomach brushed against Evan's cock. Evan's fingers spasmed, clamping tighter on Mark's nipples, and the man atop him hissed, "Yeah. Like that."

Deeper, harder. Evan shifted his legs to wrap around Mark's body. Mark's torso fell across Evan's, their stomachs pressed together to stroke Evan as firmly as any grip or mouth. Mark's thighs churned, raising and lowering Evan's ass, and neither one of them could form words anymore. They gasped and groaned and growled, gaining speed, plunging further, matching each other's rhythm. Evan couldn't tell if the heartbeat crashing against his ribcage was his own trying to escape or Mark's pounding to get in.

Mark slowed, just a moment, and Evan opened his eyes. Mark was biting his lip, breathing long and deliberately. A different kind of warning this time. Wordless but just as understandable. He was holding off. Evan worked a hand between them and clamped down on Mark's nipple.

It was like he'd flipped a switch, and Mark sped back up. He bucked up inside Evan as he came, a long, loud groan breaking out from deep in his throat. His back arched him off Evan's chest. He substituted his hand for his stomach, jerking Evan in rhythm with his orgasm. Before he'd gotten to five, Evan was losing count, gasping for his own breath, rising with the building tension that started in his cock and gathered the rest of him with it. One deep, steady breath, and when he could inhale no longer, his groan echoed Mark's. All the tension raced from one end of him to the other, spraying out the tip of his cock. He heard the wet drops of come landing on his chest; his nerves were too busy firing in unison to actually feel it.

They held there, gasping for a moment. Then, just as the

euphoria started falling away, Mark shifted. Slowly, he pulled out, his hand sliding tight up along Evan's cock, matching the retreat. He exited as his thumb rubbed along Evan's tip, initiating one last, shuddery gasp.

Evan lay there, trying to find his breath, until he heard the shower start. Carefully, he lifted himself up, found his balance, and moved for the bathroom. The air was already wet from steam, scented with the musky combination of the soap Evan had left in the shower and the sweat Mark was covered in before he began to clean. If this had been what after-rain smelled like, Evan could understand a person enjoying it.

He grabbed a clean washcloth, doused it with hot water, and lathered with a hotel soap. As his heart slowed back down and his breathing steadied, Evan cleaned the come off his chest, wiped off the extra lube, then rinsed clean with water from the sink. He toweled off on his way back into the room. Mark took his time in the shower. Evan was dressed by the time he came out, hair wild and dripping water down his front.

"Leaving already?" Mark asked, catching one of his stray drips with a towel, then draping it over his neck.

"Duty calls," Evan returned, buttoning his collar.

Mark walked over to the nightstand and picked up the badge, then pinned it in place on Evan's chest.

"Wouldn't want to forget this," he quipped.

"Suppose not," Evan said. "Time to go back to playing my side again."

Mark laughed and flopped onto the bed. "No worries. You know I'll be your bad cop anytime you want."

"Damn right," Evan growled, straddling the hustler again, this time in his uniform rather than the ratty street clothes he'd brought for the game. "You don't want to be on my shit list."

Mark took it in stride, grabbing Evan by the collar and pulling him in for one last kiss. "You're so butch when you suit up, officer." He reached into Evan's pocket to pull out the roll of bills they both knew was waiting. Then he shoved the cop backward, onto his feet.

"I can keep the room for the night, yeah?"

Evan chuckled as he opened the front door to make his way to patrol.

"Anything to keep you hookers off the street."

PERSONAL SERVICE PROVIDER

TROY STORM

THE BAR WAS so thunderously noisy—being contact central—
and its hyper-energized darkness so blindingly shattered by
flashing disco lights, I couldn't believe the big muscular guy and
the sloe-eyed twink could possibly be communicating—except by
feeling each other up.

Duh.

A flash of greenbacks between them flushed the adrenaline
through my system, and my buzzing, inquiring crotch suddenly
wanted to know why I hadn't had the guts to move in earlier for
some heavy-duty negotiating myself.

A cash transaction had been made. There would be no more
pussyfooting from prospect to prospect sweating over what buttons would get me some action and which ones might set off a
nuclear nelly blast. I would now get in line, waving my bills, and
get some. From either one—since I wasn't that sure in what direction the transaction had flowed. I wasn't proud.

I was horny.

I headed through the mob, plowing after the beef and the
twink. Over the heads of the bright-eyed bimbos desperately
buffing their egos, I saw my guys disappear through the back door
into the alley.

An even beefier type stood guard. "Go out the front," he yelled.

"But I just saw …"

"It's closed. Fire regulations. Go out the fucking front." I noticed a folded bill in the breast pocket of his tight dark dress shirt—and the press of a prominent nipple through the two layers of fabric. At a different time I wouldn't have minded tangling with the dude. I grunted, turned, and charged back through the crowd.

It was half a block around to the entrance of the alleyway that led to the back of the bar. The two heavy-breathing shadows were outside the back door, humping against bare brick walls, the surrounding security lights creating pockets of obscuring darkness from overgrown scrub trees and piled-up boxes.

I sidled up to a nearby utility pole and watched. There was grunting and gagging but also snorts and sighs of satisfaction. At least one or the other was getting his money's worth. Cash wasn't the only thing burning in my pants.

A ray of light glinted on a shaft of bare flesh that connected the two black, shape-changing forms, but it was hard to tell if the impressive length was real or wished for and whether it was going or coming.

I snickered and reached for my dick, ready to do a little coming myself, but suddenly the big shape extricated itself from the lumpen mass and vanished through the open-and-shut shaft of disco-throbbing light back inside the bar.

The kid was left alone. He slowly slid to the ground. I lurched forward, my chest swelling, broad shoulders back, a prince among rescuers.

"Aaagh," he yelled, scrambling backwards on his haunches. "You scared the shit out of me, dude." He stood, his light body tensed, ready to bolt if need be, clear eyes cutting around to be sure I wasn't setting him up for half-hidden buddies to pounce. He wasn't as young as I had thought.

"No, sorry." I held out my palms, placating. "I, uh, just wanted to check that you were all right."

He focused on me as well as he could in the murky alleyway. "Why, you been watching?" He glanced around again.

In the bar his golden head had been mostly down; now it was up, firm chin high. A goddamned, fucking piece of gorgeous Calvin god-head meat. I wondered why he needed to sell himself. I would have thought rich dudes would be fighting to pay him to open those pretty lips.

"How much?" I stammered.

It took him a moment to catch my drift. He laughed. No ordinary mortal likes to be laughed at, even by godheads. That's why there are no more gods.

"I'm sorry," he calmed me down. "It's not you. It's just that I've had a really shitty day and the last thing I expected ..."

"Things weren't looking so shitty a few minutes ago." I marveled at how the mean light sculpted his perfect features.

"I got what I paid for. It was the best I could do. Now I've got to go. I've got a big day tomorrow." He started down the alley.

It took me longer, and I still wasn't sure what his drift was. He paid? The muscular dude was the hustler? The one who was back inside now, hustling? And here I was outside with—what? Another loser? A beautiful loser, but nonetheless a loser who had to pay? For what?

I hurried after him. "I ... I ..."

He stopped and eyed me more carefully, his fat-free lean body still ... unsatisfied.

"What do you want? You were in the bar, weren't you? Watching. What are you doing out here?"

"I ... wasn't sure what was going on. But ... now ... maybe ..."

"Okay, I can't dig that. You're looking for action. And you're willing to sling the shekels." His slim, muscular arm shot out to grab my pecs. I jumped.

"Not bad. Turn around." I did. He felt up my ass. Thoroughly.

"I could use another fuck. I thought I was … okay. I was wrong. How about it? I'll make it worth your while."

He unzipped his pants and pulled it out. It was the impressive column of flesh I had seen illuminated by the streetlight. Obscenely lengthy, semi-firm, not yet committed. Pale blue veins circled the creamy shaft, waiting to engorge, the deeply colored knob at the end smoothly rounded, the piss slit gaping. It would slide in easily.

I nodded. We moved into the shadow of a large dumpster. I dropped my pants and shoved the seat of my jockeys off my ass. He rubbered up, and I braced my hands against the metal, still warm from the heat of the day. He stepped in close, nuzzled the damp nose around, and, finding its target, shoved it in.

Fucking bliss. His fuck pole was made to fit inside me. Solidly. The tissues of my shit chute seemed to galvanize it. The pulpy column thickened and solidified, satisfied, digging deep, lunging deeper, stretching my sphincter and plowing through the forgiving, enfolding tissues.

It was interminable. It kept advancing, filling me up, tingling my pits, tickling my throat. My navel twitched, my tits electrified.

His breath came hard and fast. The front of his tight, sculpted body melded against my backside as he climbed higher and higher inside me, his solid arms locking tight around my pounding chest. His cheek pressed against my ear, and the words hissed out. "Jeez, man. Holy fuck portal, your ass is amazing. So fucking tight. Yet so fucking … fuckable. Ungh."

He gave a final shove, and his tight balls slapped against my ass cheeks. I grappled for my dick as I fought to hold my balance with the other hand. I was almost at the point of exploding into the damp cotton. I freed my furious bone, choking the come back, gripping hard to hold back the boiling, liquid fire. Pre-come slung out in long mucousy tendrils. I slammed both hands back onto the side of the dumpster and tilted my hips to aim my rigid fuck pole at the asphalt.

He pulled out. Grunting, tenuous, maybe feeling the same as me. Why not just stay perched on the point of perfection? Live there awhile. Die. Could it get better? His throbbing hot meat retreated inch by inch, allowing my gorged insides to fill in after him, stuffing the emptied space, to grapple after his goodness.

He sighed. I imagined his bare ass high in the fetid night air, high to have extracted such a length of skewering meat from my doggy-arched body, his butt up, my pants down around my ankles, arms stretched, biceps hard. Only his amazing dick's arrowhead remained inside me, locking us together, nuzzling at the liquid, meaty entranceway, constrained by the encircling band of clutching sphincter muscle.

"You are beautiful, man," he murmured, hot breath to my ear straight to my packed nuts. "Thank you for finding me. I'm going to fuck your brains out now. Okay? Shit, and to think I paid …"

I opened my mouth to speak as he rammed his pole back in and all speech left me. Please, my thrilled asshole begged, please, my packed insides begged as he extracted the crammed meat from the crammed hole and then crammed it in again, over and over, his fat nuts slapping hard against my butt, setting fire to the outer mounds to match the building blaze inside.

He shoved his hands up inside my shirt, grabbing my nipples, grinding them to white hot steel points until I was dancing on my toes, pleading incoherently through gritted teeth.

"Where's—your—dick?" he muttered, fucking my ass like fury, dragging his hands down my front searching for my flapping dong. A fist curled around my swaying low-hangers, another fist choked the base of my throbbing pole. He used his double grip to lever his body harder into me, to shove my hips back as he slammed forward. I felt his pre-come on the back of my tongue.

"I'm coming." A pleading, grateful, plaintive announcement. "Oh my, Miz Scarlet, I'm coming home."

His dick swelled obscenely inside me and released its load and then swelled and deflated again and again, repeating the shotgun blasts. My come rocketed out through the barrel of his clutching fingers, matching him splat for splat, arcing up into the dappled night air, painting the side of the dumpster, filling the cracks of the ancient asphalt that lay between it and my dancing feet.

We finished, the both of us, barely able to stand, gasping for breath. My wet palms struggled to stick to the metal box, as my shaking thighs struggled to support us with his dead weight glued to my back. Head down, I was amazed at the coverage of the drizzling coat and the clotted rivulets of spunk. My shrink would have a field day deciding why this, in these stupid circumstances, had been the best butt fuck of my life, producing the most astounding wad I had ever jettisoned.

"Please, sir, may I have some more?" I grunted.

He laughed out loud, pushing himself off my back, easing his engorged, condom-covered fuck pole from my annoyed hole. He stuck a finger into the imploding, puckery tissues and stirred. "I'll be back." Stripping his still-thick meat of its sagging plastic cover, he o-ringed his thumb and forefinger down its still-fat length to flush the tube clean, tossing the knotted plastic sack unceremoniously into the dumpster. No matter, there was plenty more where that came from.

"I've got a proposition for you, pretty butt." He pulled his pants up, carefully stashed himself away, zipped up, and modishly partially tucked his logoed polo shirt into his waistband. "Will you spend the night with me?" He ran his fingers through his tousled blond hair and, satisfied with the result of his grooming, waited for my answer.

"Sure." I envisioned not being able to walk in the morning. No problem. No fucking problem whatsoever. I could always crawl.

"Well, it's nice to be appreciated." He threw a quirky grin at me. "You wanna know why?"

"Are you serious? Look at you. Look at me. Do I care why? Just so long as you don't leave scars that show."

He chuckled and started out of the alleyway with me hobbling along zipping up beside him. "I've got this really important gig in the morning. If I don't blow it, I might have a shot at a really big campaign. Billboards, runway, print, who the fuck knows where it might lead."

We came to a swell-looking spiffy little roadster. No honking hulks for this sleek dude. He beeped something from his pocket, the doors unlocked, and we climbed in.

"I get so fucking nervous—and horny, God, so fucking horny—when something like this happens—it must be haywire hormones or something—that I've just got to get my nuts calmed. You're the best butt fuck I've had in a coon's age. The muscle whore, he wasn't bad, but, man ..." He reached over and squeezed my crotch. I was instantly hard.

He stroked my chin. "Yeah. Just like me." The engine yawned and stretched, and we shot out onto the avenue. "I'll pay. You'll be available to get me through the night. Okay?" He pushed a couple of buttons, and the whole fucking top of the car folded itself into its ass.

"If you pay, does that make me a whore too?" I yelled, standing and leaning into the wind, pulling a DiCaprio *Titanic* moment.

He laughed. "When I hustled, I called myself a 'professional service provider.' You can call yourself anything you want, just let me know that ass is mine whenever I need it tonight."

"It's all yours, whenever, however," I yelled, shoving my pants off. I swiveled around to spread-eagle into his lap, my throbbing dick in his face, my bare butt against his bulging crotch.

"You fucking horse-hung nut," he grinned, steering looking around my body, sucking on the end of my meat for a couple of seconds. "If I'm gonna die, I want to die with your butt skewered on my dick."

I crawled off and settled back down in my seat, a leg hooked over the side-view mirror, a hand jammed into his pants, caressing his poundage. He reached over and jacked me off, driving with one hand. "Shit, man, you're as big as I am. I may have to do a little lap-dancing myself."

I blasted a load onto the windshield, howling, "Fuck, yeah!" as his hips twitched and he emptied a load into my sweat-soaked palm.

We never even made it to his bedroom. We barely got into the foyer of his fancy high-rise downtown digs before he was all over me, tongue digging for my tonsils, hands clawing at my duds. I was naked and on my back, ass up, hole hollering, before he could get out of his clothes. He dropped, mouth suctioning my anus, as he struggled to rip off his pants.

His naked ass rose above his broad back, the twin mounds so perfectly sculpted and tanned it was hard to believe they would ever be punctured by my outsized, skinned meat.

In the blazing light of his pad, the mirrored walls reflecting perfection everywhere, he made quick work of perfecting my ass for his perfect entry. His slim, beautifully manicured fingers stretched and prodded, vying with his tongue to loosen my hole. When he reared up to shod his rampant ramrod, his handsome face intent and serious, I silently begged for him to ram me deep, scramble my brain pan.

Blissfully, it took longer this time. He fucked with deliberate determination, evenly, steadily, lost in the masculine physicality of plugging himself in and pulling himself out of the meaty masticator. The tension flowed out of him, was pounded into me, slapped and shaped with his beating balls, pumping my meat up to phenomenal proportions.

He looked down, heavy eyes dreamy, and grinned. "I have a special aptitude. Prepare to lose your fucking eyeballs." He slowly bent his head and sucked my dick into his pretty mouth as he continued to pulverize my prostate.

Unbefuckinglievable. I thought my nuts were going to drop off when I came, pumping another fantastically fulsome load down his throat. He pulled off me grimacing, the fine features flickering between passion and pain. "Your ass does amazing things when you come. You may have broke my dick." He continued to pump. It didn't feel broke to me.

His rhythm became like the beating of my heart. Ka-thump-slap, ka-thump-slap, as his meat gagged my hole and his balls reddened my ass. I dozed. Impaled on a huge phallus, Greek vase–like, his noble body supporting me, fine thighs planted wide, as I slid up and down the massive pole, the perfect dick head popping out of my mouth to squirt a carton-load of manmilk with each prod of his perfect butt.

"This'll wake you up, pretty bastard." I heard the grunt through my daze. He came, and instantly I was back on the floor on my back, trying to keep from being skidded across the hardwood as he fired volley after volley up my ass.

We hit the thick living room rug, and he fell on top of me, thick spongy tube still connecting us. He chortled, "Gooder and gooder. Can I keep 'im, pa? Fer m' own? M' perfect ass. My sweet dick'll never go hongry no … more." And he was sound asleep.

When I woke, his dick was hard, hooked deep inside my surprisingly contented anus. Every other bone and organ in my body ached. He seemed blissfully content, breathing deeply, his lightly stubbled cheek resting on my hairy chest.

I slowly extracted the meat hook and rolled him gently onto the carpet. His dick was rock, arched up off his flat belly, drizzling pre-come into a pool surrounding his inny. I pulled the meat lever back and let it go. It slapped forward with such force the hard column left a fiery imprint on his golden, salon-tanned skin. The pre-come splatted and scattered over his hips and abs.

He sighed in his sleep, his trim body settling into the deep pile of the carpet, his face angelic. I crawled over him and sucked him off.

His dick slid into my mouth and down my throat, foreordained, as it had into my ass. He was a perfectly sized fuck-and-suck mate.

I took my time, enjoying the throb of the stretched tissues as I slid my lips up and down the endless length. My tongue explored every ridge and ripple. He was cut, no obscuring foreskin like me, his dick always unleashed and ready to ride. I rode him with my mouth. Pressing my face deep into his sparse, trimmed bush, my nose filled with his expensive scent, the sweat of his crotch, the simmering hormones on the brink of boiling over.

I tightened my fingers around his nut sack and cuddled it as my mouth moved up and down the curved length of his dick. I scratched at his pebbled flesh, I prodded between the tight butt cheeks to find his butt hole, and lightly poked to unbutton the puckered entrance.

His breath came faster. His body began to respond to the inevitable. I upped my tempo. He moaned in his sleep, bleating contentedly, incoherently. His fine musculature froze, and he blasted out a load of pure man cream, his body shook, then another and another blast of male goodness careened down my throat. I pulled my lips up to get the next few globs in my mouth, spilling over my tongue, drizzling against the backside of my teeth. I pushed my head down, dragging my molars into the swollen root of his come tube and was rewarded with another three or four blobs.

My mouth cleaned out the final drops, sucking out his sweet milk, siphoning every last bit of thick male liquid from his exhausted hose onto my curling, lavishing mouth snake before letting it slide down my coated throat deep into my gut, where it joined the other fruits of my labors.

I snuggled against him and slept.

He woke me with his dick pumping my contented rump, tousled hair damp, smelling newly showered. "One last time?" he asked, unnecessarily. I nodded, and he quickly emptied his morning load into my gulping butt.

I lay on the rug watching him efficiently move about the apartment, dressing, last-minute primping. He grabbed a script and stuffed it into a fucking logoed leather messenger pouch.

"I left you an envelope." He knelt to give me a quick kiss and briefly searched for more words, but his mind was elsewhere. "Thanks." And he was gone.

I was in the same place on the floor when he got back. He looked stunned to see me. The place was filled with flowers. Champagne was in a bucket nearby.

"How'd you do?" I asked from the floor, legs wide, ankles up, hole ready.

He unzipped his pants and pulled out his dick, and by the time he had dropped to the floor and thrust himself between my legs, it was hard and ready. He buried the bone up my ass and bent down to suck on my stalk.

"I ... got ... the account," he happily sang between guzzles, pounding my hole. "I can ... afford to keep you ... until your ass falls off." He slammed into me, and my teeth rattled. "And then I can buy you a new one."

"Damn," I grinned, "and I was so looking forward to becoming a public whore."

"Personal service provider." He licked my nose. "Maybe I'll rent you out."

Maybe.

BUS STOP

STEPHEN OSBORNE

IT WAS LATE.

I stood at the corner of Tenth and Meridian by the Metro Bus sign and wondered if the buses even ran that late at night. It didn't matter. If one didn't arrive soon, I'd take a cab. I needed the reflection time in any case.

To say I was having a shitty night would be an understatement.

Although it was late in May, there was just enough breeze blowing to make me shiver. It didn't help that I was wearing a flimsy mesh tank top and very tight and small jean shorts. Of course, when I dressed for the evening it hadn't occurred to me that I'd be spending a good portion of the night standing at a street corner waiting for a bus that probably wasn't coming.

It hadn't occurred to me that after dancing with my boyfriend for only ten minutes I'd be having the worst fight of our relationship, one bad enough to make me storm out of the bar, leaving him behind.

Note to self: next time there's even the slightest possibility of this happening, make sure you drive.

A small dark car drove slowly past me. For a fraction of a second I thought about trying to thumb a ride but quickly shelved that idea. Indianapolis may not be a huge city, but it's big enough to have its share of crazies, and the guy in the dark car could well be one of them.

I watched the taillights disappear around the corner, and my mind drifted back to the previous hour. I relived those final moments of bumping and grinding with Keith. If only I'd known what was coming I'd have kept my big mouth shut.

Talking loudly over the Cher remix, I'd asked Keith if anything was wrong. "You seem a little out of sorts tonight," I told him.

He shook his head but continued to dance like a straight boy, as if his hips couldn't move. "Nothing," he said.

It was one of those nothings that mean something, so I pressed the point. "Something is bothering you. You might as well tell me. You know this bitch doesn't give up."

Keith stopped dancing and looked stonily at me. "It's just not working."

It seemed like the dance floor suddenly became very quiet, but I'm sure that was just my perception. I knew what he meant, but I still thought I'd make a joke and pray I was wrong. "You mean this remix?"

He sighed. "With us. It's not working."

. . . . .

A CAR DRIVING by brought me out of my reverie. Surely that was the same dark car that had just passed me moments ago? Was the guy just cruising around the block? Maybe it was one of my buddies from the bar, wondering if he should offer me a ride home or not. Offhand, though, I couldn't think of anyone I knew who drove a Kia.

The car turned the corner, and I could see the driver looking back at me. It was hard to see any details since he was mostly in shadow, but it appeared to be a guy in his midtwenties with a mop of longish blond hair.

The car vanished around the corner yet again, and just as quickly left my thoughts. I looked at my watch for about the hundredth time. I tapped the crystal just to make sure the second hand was still working. It was.

I hugged myself as another breeze raised goose bumps on my arms. I leaned out and gazed down Meridian. There was no sign of a bus, and very little traffic period.

. . . . .

THE CHER SONG had been finishing and morphing into the old disco chestnut "It's Raining Men," but it could have been the funeral march as far as I was concerned.

"What are you talking about?" I demanded. "I thought things were going great."

Keith looked at me sadly. "That's just the trouble, Michael. You're so wrapped up in yourself you never stop to think about how I'm feeling or what I want."

. . . . .

WRAPPED UP IN myself, indeed, I thought as I tightened my arms across my chest. Did he think I wore this mesh top because it's fun to count gooseflesh? I wore it to look good for him, and if he can't appreciate that …

The same black car was approaching, even slower than before. In the light from the streetlamp, I could finally get a good look at the driver. My earlier guess was probably correct. He looked to be a few years older than me and was definitely not someone I knew. He didn't have the look of a club kid. He looked more like an armchair jock. Just some closet case looking at the fag waiting at the bus stop. I didn't give him another thought.

Until the car stopped just a few feet away from me, that is.

Puzzled, I looked in at the driver. He was looking back at me with a strange look on his face. He seemed nervous and expectant at the same time, as if the ball was now in my court and it depended on me to make the next move.

I frowned at him and gazed down the street, the universal signal for "Hey, I'm waiting for the bus, dude."

I glanced quickly back at the car. The guy was giving me a stare-down something fierce. Finally he leaned over and rolled down the passenger side window.

"How's it going?" he asked.

Oh, fine. I was standing there freezing my balls off, and, oh yeah, my boyfriend had just told me to fuck off, but other than that, everything was hunky-dory. Somehow that didn't seem the response that was called for, so instead I told him, "Everything's going good here."

He smiled and gave me a sort of half-shrug. "Need a ride?"

The breeze had picked up enough that my nipples could now cut glass and there was no sign of a bus or a knight in shining armor, so I said, "Sure."

He leaned over further and unlatched the door. I got in quickly and rubbed my hands together. "Thanks," I said. "It was getting a bit nippy out there."

He laughed nervously and pulled away from the curb. "I don't do this often, believe it or not."

I wasn't sure what to say to that, but I guessed that, if he didn't give rides to guys often, it was some sort of compliment, so I replied, "No problem."

"I guess you know that I have to ask the big question. Are you a cop?"

My first thought was, dressed like this? but then it clicked. He thought I was a hooker! I had to chuckle. "No," I told him, "I'm definitely not a cop."

Closet Case smiled at me, revealing a rather nice dimple on his chin. Although he wasn't the type I normally go for, he definitely wasn't bad. I wondered why he was trying to pick up hustlers off the street when all he had to do was show up at the bars and the boys would be all over him. They could smell new meat a mile away.

It was then that I noticed the ring on his left hand.

Mystery solved. Not only was he a closet case, he was a married closet case.

"I guess I have another question to ask," he said, interrupting my ruminations. "How much?"

It was on my lips to tell him I wasn't a hustler, I swear, when I heard myself say, "That depends."

I'm not sure why I said it. Perhaps the memory of Keith in the bar was clouding my judgment. I nearly asked him to stop the car and let me out. All I'd have had to do was reveal to him that he'd made a mistake. All I'd have had to do was tell him I wasn't a hustler, despite standing on a street corner in a mesh tank top.

Closet Case looked at me shyly. "I'm Adam, by the way."

Adam. The first man. Of course that wasn't his real name. I didn't see any reason not to give him mine, though. "I'm Michael."

"Nice to meet you, Michael," he replied. "I guess I'm looking for something kind of special." He told me what he wanted. I raised an eyebrow. He looked at me questioningly. "So what do you think?"

"I think I'm not who you think I am" was what I should have said. Instead, what came out of my mouth was, "For three hundred bucks, sure."

. . . . .

WE WENT TO his apartment. It was nicely furnished. You could tell wifey had a lot to do with the decorating. Apparently she was out of town or out with the girls tonight. I didn't ask and he didn't elucidate.

He turned to me after he'd closed the door behind us. "I don't kiss, if that's okay."

I was slightly disappointed, mainly because he had very kissable lips, but also because I was hoping for a little foreplay to get me psyched up for what was to come. "Works for me," I said, thinking that was what he wanted to hear. After all, the guy was paying. It was his show.

He pointed down the short hall presumably leading to the bedroom. "Shall we?"

Once there, he turned on a single lamp on the dresser, barely illuminating the room. Maybe he thought it was mood lighting. He kicked off his shoes and smiled at me. "I guess we can just get started, huh?"

Taking his lead, I started pulling off clothes. His eyes never left me. I disrobed slowly, letting him drink in each revelation, such as it was.

"Nice," he said when I stood in front of him naked.

"Thanks," I replied. Tell him you're not a hustler, my brain said. It's not too late to back out.

He reached out and stroked my stomach softly. "The stuff you'll need is on the floor on the other side of the bed," he said.

"Cool," I said.

The neatly made bed had two pairs of soccer socks laid out on it, perfectly folded and placed as if they were on an altar, which I suppose in a way they were. He grabbed the blue ones, sat down on the edge of the bed, and started to pull them on. That left me the red ones, which I was sort of happy about since red was my favorite color. I sat next to him and put mine on. I'm not a sock fetishist myself, but I have to admit they felt pretty comfortable. As when I'd stripped, he watched every move I made while I pulled the socks up to my knees.

His voice was barely a whisper. "Beautiful."

I stood up and faced him. My cock was starting to stiffen in anticipation. Surely I wasn't finding this hot or sexy? I mean ...

But I knew I was only fooling myself. Part of me—a big part— was really digging the whole thing.

"Ready?" I asked.

He nodded. Before I could even think about it, I plowed into him, knocking him back onto the bed. The bedsprings screamed in protest as we began to wrestle. Surprisingly, he was putting up one hell of a struggle. I'd figured that since this was his fantasy he'd want to get to the "meat" fairly quickly, but I couldn't have been more wrong. I was still on top of him, but he grabbed my head and started squeezing hard.

Even though I could feel my face flushing with the exertion, I was thoroughly enjoying myself. I could feel his rather large erection poking into my abdomen, which made my own cock stand up at attention.

Somehow I got my knees up and managed to free my head from his grip. I pinned his right arm under my knee and grabbed his remaining hand with both of mine. He tried unsuccessfully to buck me off him.

"It's all over, Adam," I said, somewhat out of breath. "Might as well give up now."

"Never!" he growled.

I forced his arm down and pinned it under my other knee. I darted a glance over to the side of the bed, and sure enough, just as he'd said there would be, there was a pile of white tube socks. I grabbed one and tied it around his wrist. I used another one and tied that to the end that dangled from his wrist, and then tied the other end to the bedpost. I repeated this for his left hand until long socks tied him to his own bed.

I straddled his chest, my dick mere inches from those kissable lips. "How do you like that?" I asked, totally in character.

He looked up at me nervously, which was part of the game obviously. "What are you going to do?" he asked.

He'd already told me the character he wanted me to take on, so I replied, "You're going to find out, faggot."

Also by the bed were some condoms and lube. The guy was prepared, I'll say that for him. I opened a pack with my teeth and slowly slid the condom over my now achingly hard dick, watching his eyes bulge as I did so. I hoped he was still acting and not having second thoughts.

I squeezed a generous amount of lube over my cock. "You know what I'm going to do, don't you?" I asked.

He strained, but the tied socks and my straddling body held him in place. "Please," he said softly, "don't." There was a look in his eyes of intense anticipation, however.

I slid myself down his body until I was between his legs. I yanked them up and placed one socked foot on each of my shoulders. This was my moment of truth. Could I actually go through with this? Sex with Keith had always been so gentle and loving. I mean, the guy was a closet case and he was wanting— hell, paying—for this, but I wasn't sure about it myself. This could hurt.

I must have hesitated too long, because he looked up at me questioningly.

Sighing inwardly, I gripped him hard by his pelvis and positioned him so his ass was ready to be entered. I breathed in and thrust forward, my hand guiding the way.

The head of my dick actually got in a little ways before meeting heavy resistance, surprisingly. I'd figured it would be much more difficult. (Hell, I had to finger Keith's ass for ages to loosen him up.) Adam's head jerked back, and he let out a moan. As per instructions, I let go of him for a moment and grabbed another tube sock. This I tied around his head across his mouth as a makeshift gag. I couldn't actually knot it behind his head, but it was secure enough for playacting.

With that done, I returned my attention to his ass, which was quite a nice one. I hoped wifey appreciated the hot man she had. I got his legs back on my shoulders and once again guided my dick to his waiting hole.

This time I was able to slide more in. He pretended to whimper through the gag, but I kept working until I felt his muscles relax. Finally I was in to the hilt.

I stroked his legs as I began to pump my cock into him. "You like that, don't you?" I asked in character.

In response, he bugged his eyes out, but he was starting to drop the whole rape scene at this point. He was moaning like mad through the tied sock.

Hearing the muffled moans had an effect on me as well. I was pumping like crazy, slamming my hips into his ass, my lips emitting a few moans of their own. I turned my head and muzzled his socked calf as I tensed and shot my load into him.

I was giving him the last few thrusts when I looked down and saw his own large erection pointing up to his stomach. It didn't occur to me until that point that he hadn't told me how he wanted to get off, or even if he wanted to.

While I was still in him, I reached down and began to pump his hard cock. It didn't take much. A few strokes and he shot hot, sticky globs all over his stomach and chest.

I pulled my dick out and removed the condom. I glanced at his face and saw the most amazing look in his eyes. He was happy. He was thankful.

I untied him, and we got cleaned up in silence. It really seemed that words weren't needed. It wasn't until I'd gotten dressed and he'd handed me two Franklins that he held his hand out for me to shake.

"That was perfect," he said. "Thanks."

I smiled. "Anytime."

He smiled too. "I don't suppose you have a cell number or some way for me to get in touch with you?"

When I left I had an extra three hundred dollars in my pocket. He had my cell number and maybe some temporary respite from whatever demons made him want this rape scenario. He really seemed happy, that's all I know.

Back out on the street I hailed a cab, and my thoughts went back to Keith and the bar and his last words to me.

"You're just too predictable," he had said. "There's just no adventure in you."

WOOF

....

JORDAN LEWIS

I'VE BEEN WORKING this street for eight years now. I know every whore, hustler, and dealer from here to Saint Catherine's Cathedral, ten blocks over. If someone needs a hit of something, I know where to get the best. If they need a place to stay, I got an extra room. If they want a fresh piece of tail, I take them to my place. I'm the papa of these few blocks, it gets me respect, and it also gets me shitloads of cash. There's nothing I won't do, and I'm good at it.

I thought I had seen everything, threesomes, orgies, death, murder, hell, I've even seen a whore give birth in an alley. Like I said, I thought I had seen it all, but I was wrong.

Two weeks ago I was out for an early morning stroll, cruising the johns, when I saw him walking out of Laurie's place. He was like a god, six-three, about 250 pounds, and he looked like pure steel. I could literally see his abs through his muscle shirt. Tufts of fur were sticking out of his neckline. I could see his leg muscles twitching with each step through his tight Wrangler jeans, and the cuffs were tightly pulled over the top of a pair of biker boots. A bear in his finest form.

He was walking out of the bar with a girl on each side, and I thought to myself, I wonder if I could turn him. It was an instant challenge. I had done it before, convinced this married guy to let me fuck him. He called out his wife's name, but I just smiled. I thought, maybe I can do it again.

I crossed the street and casually followed them. When they got to a liquor store, the girls went in and he stayed outside to light up a stogie. I hadn't gotten a hard-on like this since I was fourteen, just from looking at the guy. As I walked closer he caught sight of me. He asked me if I had the time, so I gave it to him.

"It's 1:12," I said as I slowly looked him up and down. He was a walking boulder—my God, he was gorgeous.

"Thanks, bud," he responded in his growl.

"Woof," I said under my breath as he took a long drag off his cigar and I wished it was my cock.

"What was that?" he asked.

"Nothing. Just wondering if you were in the area looking for some fun," I said. Most people would think me bold to say this to an obvious breeder that was twice my size and could bend me in half. But eighteen years out here will change your comfort zone.

He responded to my query with a low chuckle and said, "Thanks, bud, but I've got a couple ladies I'm taking home tonight. Usually I don't mind a little cock action every now and then to shake things up, but there are two of them, and I'm thinking that's going to be more fun."

I was in shock. I would never have thought this guy would be both a carpet muncher and an ass bandit. My cock throbbed harder, and I saw him glance down at it. The pressure in my crotch was unbearable. When I'm on the job, I always wear tight blue jeans with an unbuttoned, sleeveless shirt. So there isn't much left to the imagination.

As I reached down to readjust myself, because the pressure itself was going to make me shoot my load, he grabbed my arm.

"Leave it like that. It's starting to make me reconsider. How big is it anyway?"

"Eight and a half inches. Uncut. Thick as a beer bottle."

"Sounds tasty. Look, let me have my way with these ladies. I live about five blocks from here, over on Madison, in the

Henderson complex, you know it?" I nodded my head because words were gone. I'd never been tongue-tied before. "Good. I live in 425. Be there in a couple hours. Then we can have us some fun. What's the cost?"

"What do you want?" I asked, since my services were a wide range of things.

"Everything you have to offer."

My jaw just dropped. As I slowly realized he was smiling at my shock, I stammered out a price, and about that time the two ladies walked out, and he started walking away. I realized I hadn't gotten his name, so I quickly asked him before he left.

"Just call me ... Woof," he said with a wink, and walked off with an arm around each lady.

The next few hours were the longest of my life. I had never looked forward to a job more. This wasn't even a job; this was just downright sex. I haven't just had sex in a long time. When you work the streets, you learn to separate your job from your personal life. It's hard to do, but you get used to it.

Finally, after a few drinks and a piss, it was time to meet Woof. I walked over to his building and hit the buzzer for 425. A moment of silence passed, and I worried he wasn't there, but then I heard his rough voice over the intercom and got hard instantly.

"Yeah?"

"Woof," I said. I figured he would get the message. I opened the door and walked through the foyer, passing the two ladies he'd been with earlier. They were giggling and sated. My cock rubbed against my denim jeans as I walked up the stairs, and I moaned at each step. As I reached the third flight Woof was standing right there, waiting for me in the stairwell.

He was wearing only jeans. I could have ironed a shirt on his stomach, but I figured that night I'd just be shooting all over it. Woof stared at me.

As I got closer I could feel his breath and smell his sweat. I reached for his chest to run my hands through his thick curly hair, but he grabbed my arm and said in a raspy whisper, "If we are doing this here, then we are doing this my way, fucker."

At first I thought, I'm in trouble. But the smirk on his face told me otherwise. So I replied, "Yes, sir, anything you want, sir."

"Good. That's what I like to hear. What I want you to do first is get on your knees and suck my cock."

"Right here, sir? In the stairwell?"

"Yes, right here. Are you afraid, boy?"

"No, sir, not afraid," I said as I slowly got to my slightly trembling knees.

Eye to eye, his bulge was even more impressive. I slowly rubbed his cock through his jeans before roughly unzipping them. His cock flopped out in all its glory. I was in awe. I stared for just a moment at the eleven-inch, uncut anaconda ready to strike.

I rolled back the foreskin and licked the throbbing mushroom head before slowly deep-throating all eleven inches of his monster. He grabbed my hair and pulled my head up and down over his meat.

"Oh God, that feels so fucking good, boy. You like sucking my cock, don't you?"

Since I couldn't answer, I just moaned loudly. He got the message.

"Yeah, I knew you would suck my dick. From the moment I saw your mouth, I wanted those lips on my dick. I'm gonna wear them out tonight, fucker."

The dirty talk was doing me in. I couldn't take it anymore— I wanted more than just to blow this guy off. I needed it all. I stopped sucking, just to see how far he would take the game. I knelt there in front of him with my lips stretched around his shaft, waiting to be told what to do.

"Stand up, boy. Good. Now take off all your clothes," he said.

I took off my shirt and threw it on the ground, no longer caring that we were in the stairwell and the whole damn building could hear us. As I reached down to unzip my pants he grabbed my arm and told me to stop. Then he slowly unzipped me and roughly pulled my pants off, tearing them in the process.

So there I was, completely nude except for my boots and a smile, in the middle of a stairwell with the sexiest guy I'd ever seen. I didn't know what I was going to wear out of there, and I didn't care. My cock was at attention and wasn't going to be at ease for several hours.

Woof kissed me. His tongue roughly examined every part of my mouth, and I thought about how it would feel for his tongue to explore other orifices. Then he pulled away, got down on his knees, and took my dick in his mouth. I moaned so loudly I felt sure someone would come out to see what all the noise was.

"Oh God! That feels so damn good. Please don't stop."

He devoured my meat for at least ten minutes. I was breathing heavy and moaning, and he could tell I was close to shooting. But he stopped right as I was about to blow and turned around and pushed his pants down over his gorgeous ass. I knew what he wanted, so I gave it to him. I got on my knees with his beautiful butt right in my face. I grabbed his cheeks and spread them wide so I got a nice view of his hole. My God, it was glorious. I knew exactly what I wanted to do to that hole. I stuck out my tongue and just barely flicked the tip of it to his rim. I heard him moan slightly.

I stood up, and he looked over his shoulder and said, "Did I tell you to stop?"

"No, sir, but I want your cock in my ass."

"And why do you think you get to make the decisions, boy?" he said as he stood up and turned toward me. His cock was sticking out. I needed that huge dick slamming into my ass.

"Well, since you think you can make the decisions yourself, I think it's time for a little punishment." He grabbed my nipples and twisted them so hard I thought I would scream. It felt great. No one had been able to make me feel like that in a long time. My nipples were so large and swollen they were basically desensitized. I tilted my head back and moaned. And as I looked up I saw a face peering over a railing one floor above us.

The boy watching us looked shocked and quickly disappeared. I whispered to Woof, "We have an audience. Should we ask him to join? One floor up, looks about nineteen. Young blood is fun to break in."

"Hey, kid!" Woof yelled up the stairs. We heard footsteps, and a young voice answered, "I'm so sorry, I didn't mean to watch. But I have never seen two guys have sex before, and I've always wondered what it was like."

"Well, then join in," I said. "What's your name?"

"Dan."

"Well, Dan, let's see what you're bringing to this party." As I said this I unbuttoned his shirt and pulled it off, revealing a nice runner's build and not a hair on his chest.

"Damn," Woof and I said at the same time. Dan started taking his pants off, and as he unzipped his dick flopped out. I can happily say that this was one of the few times I've ever been the smallest in a group. The kid had a cock at least nine inches long and as thick as mine, if not thicker.

"Fuck!" Woof and I said at the same time. I instantly knew what role I would be playing in this orgy, and I was happy to do it. I looked at Woof and said, "Let him loosen me up for your gigantic dick. He's probably not going to last more than two minutes without blowing his load, and I want it."

"No problem," Woof replied as he turned me around toward the stairs and pushed me to my knees. Woof barked out instructions to Dan. "Okay, kid, get on your knees behind him. There you go. Now take the lube, spread it on your cock, don't stroke it too much, it looks like you're going to blow anyway. Nice, kid, real nice. Now put some lube on his hole. Use your finger … there you go … now you got it. Now two fingers, kid. How does he feel?"

"It feels kind of tight. Should I stick my cock in now?"

"Yeah, kid, go ahead, just take it kind of slow—I haven't had a big one like that in a while," I said to him. I felt the head of his cock touch my hole, and it was damn good. Then his young hands grabbed my hips and pulled me onto his cock.

"Mmm, slow it down a bit, kid. Damn, you're thick." As I looked up I saw another beautiful sight. Woof was standing in front of me, and he grabbed my hair and stuffed his cock down my throat. Gagging and smiling, I thought what could possibly make this better, and as I felt the kid get all the way inside me I knew it was as good as it was ever going to get. Dan slowly got a pace going, and so did Woof, and I've never felt more fulfilled in my life.

Dan started breathing heavier, and I knew he was getting close. I wanted that come all over my face and chest. I let Woof's dick flop out of my mouth and I got off Dan's cock. I lay on my back and told Dan to shoot all over me. As soon as he got a leg on each side of my head he started to spurt. I tasted his sweet come and shot my own load all over his back. Woof licked him clean and said, "Kid, you're too young to come once and leave. I know you got another one in there for us. So I want you to watch me fuck this bitch and have him suck your cock—you'll be good and hard again by the time I come. With that show you two put on, I'm gonna shoot faster than Billy the Kid. Now get back on your knees, bitch."

I did what he told me, wishing I hadn't shot my load yet. It's always easier to get fucked by a big dick when you have a load to shoot. But with the way this night was going I figured I'd get off again.

Woof lubed his cock and my hole, stretching me with his thick fingers. I felt his paws grab my hips and pull me until I was just touching the uncut tip of his dick. Then I braced myself for the best fuck of my life. I couldn't hide the fact that I was scared of his size. Woof noticed and leaned over, wrapping his big arms around me so I could feel his coarse chest hair rubbing into my back. He whispered in my ear, "It's okay. I know I've got a big dick. But I promise you, I'll be gentle. Just tell me exactly when it's too much and I'll wait."

My hole relaxed, and he slowly pushed into me. He stopped for a moment to let me relax, then slowly worked his huge cock in and out, each time getting a little bit farther in. I wanted to scream, but I didn't want to scare the kid off. Dan was hard again, and so was I. Woof was a fine piece of work. Dan saw me look at him, and he put his dick in my face, and I took advantage of it. It momentarily took my mind off the giant cock in my ass. Woof was all the way in. I couldn't believe it. It felt so damn good. I let go of Dan's dick just so I could relax a moment. We all stayed still — Woof so as not to ruin the sensation, me because moving was painful, and Dan because otherwise he'd probably blow again. Finally I looked back at Woof and said, "Can I do it, sir?"

"Go ahead, boy, go ahead," he responded. And I slowly fucked his cock with my ass. With each stroke, I loosened up a little more and was able to move a little faster until finally I was fucking him so hard he was moaning louder than I was. Dan was jacking off just as hard as I was fucking Woof, and the kid finally blew his load all over my back. Some of it must have hit Woof in the face because I heard him yell, "Oh God, Dan, that tastes so fucking good."

I looked back at Woof, and I could tell he was past that point of no return, so I mouthed the words, "Come in me." He nodded. I fucked his dick harder and harder until he growled through clenched teeth and I felt his dick spasm. He was still shooting when he pulled out, so I got on my knees as he continued to jack off and he shot all over my face. Dan joined him, jacking off his young cock again, and I was covered in come. Then I pushed Woof to his knees and jacked off right over him, shooting my second load all over his face and chest.

We were all dripping come, and I knew it wasn't over. Dan

picked up his shirt and wiped himself off and threw it to me to do the same. Then when Woof took it, Dan and I both grabbed his hand and said, "No, let us." We led him up to his apartment, where we all showered and proceeded to come all over again.

Dan left after a couple more hours, but I stayed the night, and then the next day, and then the following night again.

When I finally said to Woof, "I need to at least look at my place, make sure everything is okay," he responded with, "So how much does the total come to?"

"It's on the house," I said with a grin.

And as he kissed me and grinned back he said with a wink, "Well, you know where I live, if you ever need a place to stay." And I took him up on that offer many times.

CONFESSIONS OF
A STUDENT

ANDREW WARBURTON

*A return to oral and glottal pleasure combats the superego
and its linear language.... Suction or expulsion ... seem to
be at the root of this erotization of the vocal apparatus and,
through it, the introduction into the linguistic order of an
excess of pleasure.*

—Julia Kristeva, *Revolution in
Poetic Language*, 1974

I

I'M ONLY TELLING you my story because the editor of this
anthology has agreed to pay me. I'm not gay; I want to make that
clear. I've never touched a man for any other reason than I need
to get on in the world, and if I don't do this how else am I going
to afford my degree? It's tough being an academic. Academics
are out for themselves—that next award, that next enviable
assistantship, the favor of this or that tutor. No, it's not easy being
a student. But more than anything, it's expensive. It's easier when
your parents are supportive; mine would rather see me stacking
vegetable crates in the local supermarket. I'd rather die.

It's not like I don't have money. I do. But I've had to find alternative ways to make my attributes pay. I'm not talking about my brains; if you're interested in those, take a look at my grade point average. I'm talking about my body. My body is well defined. Every muscle can be seen through my clothes. My cock is long and fat. It sits, curled up in my pants, visible to anyone who wants to take a look. I don't have a problem with people checking me out in the street; it makes me smile. The sight of my bubble butt straining through my jeans is a mouth-watering prospect for anyone. I only get annoyed when they stare too long. I feel naked, as if my fly is being undone by invisible hands, my cock flopped out for anyone to see. I get embarrassingly hard.

The amount of studying I do, I could easily get out of shape. So every morning I jog around the park. When I get back, hot and sweaty, I strip off my tracksuit and step into an ice-cold shower. I wash all over with cream soap. Then I lather up my balls, massaging them till my cock grows long and hard. I move my uncut foreskin up and down, up and down, till my skin feels like it's bursting and my head's about to explode. Sometimes I place the showerhead under my butt and let jets of water invade my ass with a warm, delicious fullness. When I've emptied my balls across the tiles, I step out of the shower and pat my hard body all over with a towel. I dress and sit down at the computer. With my hands placed either side of the keyboard, I rest my head on the back of the chair and gaze at the picture of Mary that hangs above the monitor. She leans toward me as if praying for my soul. Her unblemished features represent spiritual purity. Her petal-pink lips, which never tasted semen, are pressed softly together. I tingle. Must I forever vacillate between the abject and the sublime?

The phone rings. I search the room. The receiver is perched on some dirty magazines. A client's voice drips with saliva. He wants buggery, but he doesn't say it right away. I sense his anality in the pauses between words.

.   .   .   .   .

IF THERE'S A deadline for tuition fees approaching, I work
hard to raise cash by visiting the "alleyway." The guys there pay
thirty dollars just for a five-minute suck on my cock. Others want
to stick their fingers up my ass or put me over their knee and give
me a good spanking. I charge accordingly. The guys there are so
disgusting they make me want to heave. There's one who's old
and overweight; he comes in a pinstripe suit—a stockbroker, I
imagine. He takes me back to his room and puts me over his
knee, tipping my body so my head hangs down and my butt sticks
up in the air, right in his face. With his bare hand, he slaps my
buttocks till they sting. Then he rubs them all over with oil and
pats them dry, watching the shivers run through me. He pulls my
cock back between my thighs and spits on it. He doesn't jerk me
off straight away, but fiddles with it and pinches it till I'm properly
swollen and begging him to end it. Then he takes the head in his
mouth, just the head, and slurps disgustingly, circling the bloated
tip with his tongue. My orgasm is tortuously slow. Another guy—
this one even older and fatter—likes to rub his asshole across my
body, leaving not an inch of my skin untouched. Starting with
my chest, he strips off his clothes, spreads his buttocks wide, and
clamps his tight, puckered hole over my nipple. Sticky, it pulls at
my chest hairs. From there, he works his way down my chest to
my navel, where he again performs the squatting operation and I
feel his wrinkled sphincter on my skin. He smears the sticky juice
of his asshole all down my arms and my legs. Then he goes to
work on my face. This time he puts pressure on his bowels so they
emit a vile-smelling gas. He presses down on my cheeks, my eyes,
and my mouth. Finally, he squats down till my nose pushes half
an inch up his ass. His pungent come sprays my face. Afterwards,
I climb the steps to my apartment and sit under the picture of
Mary. Her cheeks are as white as snow. I thought, in the end, I'd
resent her demeanor. I thought, because I kept disappointing her,

that I'd stop wanting what she offered. But I never do. I'd follow her through the gates of heaven if I could, kissing the hem of her robe. White roses would flower around us. But I can't. I slip into bed where fat men pollute my dreams, dripping their cocks on my face. I wake. I stare at the picture of Mary—mother "par excellence." The cleanest vagina in town.

II

THE HEAD OF Philosophy fixes me with his big blue eyes and spreads his legs on the desk's wooden surface. I sit opposite.

Gerry looks young for a head of department. His cheekbones blush when he speaks, and every so often he fumbles in his crotch as if rearranging something of grand proportions. I've seen him do this before, in class, but here it seems different. His smart black trousers bulge enormously, and I am the only witness.

He wants to know how I'm getting on with Julia Kristeva. I'm writing a paper on her notion of "the abject." The complexity of her paragraphs drains me.

She's great, I say. He frowns. Obviously she's too French for his liking. They have to be awkward, the French. It gets on his nerves. Things must be explicated, he says. I have my own way of explicating, I reply.

Gerry raises an eyebrow. Oh really?

The thing he'll never understand is how much Kristeva's notion of abjection haunts me. Not only do I spend most of my time writing about it, I try to live on the edge of it. Some people say academics live in ivory towers, but I like to get down and dirty with the theory, to smear it all over my body in order to know it intimately. Kristeva talks about the nausea we feel when confronted by a skin of milk on the surface of our tea; I'm reminded of the shit smell of a client sitting on my face. Freud thought that much of our disgust with sex was olfactory, linked to our genesis as upright beings. When the ape began to stand, it was as if his nether regions became an extension of the earth: the pungency of decaying bacteria on the balls and under the foreskin; the fishy, unwashed vagina. It is only in the act of sex that we fully confront the abject, the thing we once were. I turn this conundrum around. I "eroticize the abject."

Gerry coughs—my signal that he's finished with me. As I get up to go I can feel his eyes on my buttocks, exploring the crack with an imaginary tongue. He hasn't been very helpful with my paper. Isn't it always the way? Established academics, who you thought might want to help you, sit behind their desks, smiling smugly and offering nothing, because they know you're more talented than they are. It makes you wonder if they're bitter, or just insanely insecure. At the door, I turn around. Gerry watches me with a melancholy expression. His hand moves up and down in his crotch. I wonder if he'd waive my fees if I swallowed his come. What would it be like to fuck him? He'd lack imagination, I'm sure (the inheritance of his Anglo-American tradition), but it might be worth a try. Without warning, I go down on my knees in front of him and unzip his fly. Taken by surprise, a light dances in his eyes. How I could have been so stupid? All those times in lecture hall, the way he looked at me with that strange light in his eyes. He'd always paid more attention to me. I thought it was my brains, but evidently not. It was my lips he was after! My mouth sucking on his fat cock!

His hand moves to his crotch. The head of his prick is purple and engorged. The shaft ripples, thick with veins. He grabs hold of my head and pulls it toward him. My mouth opens, his cock slides across my tongue to the back of my throat, and he rocks his hips back and forth, fucking my mouth like an asshole. His thrusts become more frantic, beating my tonsils till I gag. He doesn't stop. His cock is made for my mouth. I suck because I have no choice. His rough hands threaten to choke me. I suck hard and rhythmically because it's the best way to get him off. I want this to be quick because his cock tastes of piss and I'm ready to heave.

His breath comes heavy. He grunts like a dog.

Bitter semen explodes in my mouth. I gulp it up and fall back on the floor, grinning inanely and swaying like a drunkard. He reaches down with one hand and tweaks my nipple. It hurts.

I wipe at my lips. So how about a waiver on my fees?

No chance, kiddo, he says.

III

AT HOME, IN front of my monitor, I rest my eyes on the soothing, whitewashed walls. Obsessively I repeat the O vowels from the first chapters of *Ulysses* and wonder what they mean. "Untonsured, ouns, Chrysostomos, omphalos": a more "oral" sound, that's for sure, but wrapped in consonants like miniature muffled explosions you might hear from behind the toilet door. Joyce preferred the use of his lips and his tongue, but he never scoffed at a good roasting. I picture his clear-skinned face, his flat cap and stance. He stands in front of the sea and watches the gulls dance on the fishy wind. Their wings are close, suddenly, to his face. They have the Furies' features. Their assholes open like small, puckered mouths, and a white, sticky substance splashes his lenses. He mutters clumsily, stutters, and unfolds a handkerchief. He wipes the glass. When it's clear, he brings it to his nose and sniffs it. He thinks of shit. Semen. Salmonella.

Kristeva's echolalia exhausts me. Her self-referential layers of thought. I envision the lines pouring from my eyes, cascading against the keys—a fine Times New Roman on a white, ruffled sea. I look up at the picture of Mary, the sublime folds of her ultramarine robe. What is this transfixing magic? It isn't godly, that's for sure. It's more like Circe. There's a definite pagan quality. It draws me in, and then it's too late; I'm stuck at her feet, adoring her. I get into bed. I lie (wet, musky, and cocooned) in a place between sleep and wakefulness, moistening my fingertips with the head of my cock. Undecipherable noises, half-word, half-slurp, ripple from the picture on the wall. I dream (is it a dream?) that she's alive. She spreads her arms and her robe unwinds. It falls. She spreads her fleshy thighs. Her vagina is an orchid, composed of flaps and folds like her royal robe. Her clitoris is a tiny penis. I push my finger into the tight canal. One finger becomes two, three, four. My whole hand disappears, then my arm, up to the elbow. The spongy flesh presses my face and sucks at my head. The smell intoxicates me. My jaws ache, watering as I squeeze my way inside. In the dark, tight pink walls of her womb, I curl up my arms and legs. I sleep. Only the phone can break the spell, which it does. Now.

The line is clear, the voice stentorious. He's phallic, heterosexually configured, as rigid as brick. The thought of him thrills me: another example of my phallus worship. I arrange a time and place and hang up the phone. I slip into my classic boxers, pull my pale blue jeans (just tight enough to accentuate my thighs and my calves) around my ass, and wrap a tight, white T-shirt around my chest. With my hands in my pants arranging my cock more comfortably, I look in the mirror. My breath is sucked out of me like a sylph's kiss. I part the waves of my hair. Narcissi flower on the wall.

. . . . .

I MEET HIM on the street. He's tall; his chest is powerfully built beneath a silk shirt and tie, just as I expected. He runs his fingers through his black raven hair, eyeing my body from my Adam's apple to my crotch. You've got the prettiest mouth, he says, tracing my bottom lip with the tip of his finger. Then he slides it into my mouth, staring at my lips as if fascinated by my passive response. I try not to think where it's been. He's a headmaster, he says. He wants to fuck me in his office.

For a whole two days he pays me to sit naked under his desk while colleagues and students, oblivious to my presence, march in and out. He brings me my food in a dog bowl. I have to bend over and put my face in the bowl. My backside is forced in the air and my balls hang between my thighs. He watches from a big, leather armchair and masturbates his enormous prick. If I use my hands or get up off the floor, he kicks me in the rump. Occasionally, he leans forward and slaps my ass, forcing my face into the food.

I get tired of sitting curled up at his feet. Sheer boredom makes me long for the metallic zing of his zip and the faint, musty smell of his cock as he pulls it out and feeds it to me with his legs spread wide. Through the scratchy pinstripe material, I clasp the muscles of his thighs. I relax my throat and take him deep, deep down. I never get used to the volume of his come. It fills up my mouth like an endless tap. He pinches my nostrils and holds the back of my head till I've swallowed it all. When he's not there, I climb out from under the desk and walk naked to the window, which overlooks the sports pitch, and watch the seniors sprinting around the track. With each running motion of their legs, their thighs wobble and their bulges swing from side to side, straining their satin shorts. In the corner of my eye, the doorknob turns. The door creaks. The headmaster fixes me with his beady eyes. He leaps across the room, grabs me by the arm, and pushes me to the floor. Did I say you could get up? I look up at him with all the insolence I can muster. Inside I cower. He undoes his belt and drops his pants around his ankles. His cock is stiff, upright. I've never seen it so big. As he bends over me, his shirt and tie brush my chest and my nipples stand erect; in one swift motion, he lifts my legs above my head and guides his cock toward my ass. The first stab takes my breath away. He pushes himself inside me, right to the hilt, and rocks back and forth, his cock making a wet, sticky sound. His thighs slap my buttocks. He's ready to shoot. His face is a rich scarlet, and from between his lips, sharp whistles are released. Suddenly he withdraws, panting madly and exclaiming, Quick, I wanna come in your mouth! He climbs on top of me and directs his cock, now the size of a large beer bottle, toward my lips. My mouth opens involuntarily, his cock slides across my tongue and stuffs the back of my throat. His hands cradle my head. I'm coming, he hollers. I splutter. My mouth fills with salty liquid. I drink it down. It coats my throat and sinks into the pit of my stomach. His cock rocks back and forth across my tongue, though it's lessened in size and there's nothing left to give. Only then does he withdraw, laughing as he wipes the flaccid member across my face.

IV

THE HEADMASTER DROPS me off at the "alleyway." He hands me the cash and pats me on the backside. I put my hand in his crotch for the last time and squeeze the heavy, wormlike member. He grins and pushes me away. Through drizzle I peer at the deserted alleyway, reminded of a dream that comes recurrently. I try not to think about it, but it won't go away. It's making me hard. At home in my white-walled room, I lie back against white sheets. I pound my fist into a big white pillow. I scrunch it up and melt around it. Mary watches me, judging me; I refuse to look at her. Over by the window is what I call my "throne," a leather armchair on which I like to sit naked (there's nothing better than leather on the back of the thigh). Pale light from the window falls across the seat. Its dimpled skin glistens and the room wavers. It's dusk.

There's something about that dream that won't go away. It seems like I'm already there. The alleyway at night—

… an engine hums. Puddles flash, blue and red. Car doors slam, and footsteps clap against stone. "Shit, it's the cops," my client whispers. He pulls on his jeans, throws his leather jacket over his shoulder. I watch him hurry off down the alleyway, splashing rainwater beneath his boots.

Two cops pull me roughly to my feet. Pistols hang from their wide leather belts. They shove me against the wall, knocking me breathless. One of them puts his face next to mine. I can feel his prickly stubble, his lips grazing mine. When he speaks, his breath tickles my cheek. Hot and sour-smelling, presumably from too much coffee and doughnuts.

We've been watching you, sonny, he says. We're gonna arrest you, how's that? My body goes limp. I sag against the wall. Metal cuffs bite my wrists. They take me in their arms and lead me toward the car. I sit on the leather seat and stare out through the rain-lashed window at the concrete jungle where only minutes before I'd been earning my keep. These goddamn cops think they're so big and strong, like they can do anything—rob me of my cash, my dreams. I throw myself against the door. It doesn't budge.

The cops watch me from the front seat. One is young and fresh-faced, perhaps a few years older than me, possibly new to the job. He's cute with big blue eyes. He looks almost scared. The older one's face is frozen into a cruel mask. An ugly scar runs from his forehead halfway down his nose. He glances at the boy, speaking to him. Ever seen a young hustler spray his load?

They get out of the car, come round to the side, and open the door. I turn my face away from the rain. The young guy pushes the driver's seat forward and gets down on his knees between my legs. The old guy gets in beside us and shuts the door. His hands go straight to my buckle. You guys better stop this or I'll make a formal complaint, I say. The young one laughs nervously. I catch his eye. He stops laughing and looks away. The old guy tells him to get on with it. Look, kid, he says, no one's gonna believe you anyway; we're respected officers. The protest dies on my lips.

The young guy undoes my belt and opens the buttons of my fly. He pulls my jeans around my ankles, revealing the classic white boxers. It's humiliating to be stripped like this, my arms behind my back, my thighs rising up for both of them to see; I feel a hot shame. At least when I'm stripping for a client I'm in control. At least I get paid. But this is torment. I've never been so helpless. My legs are shoved against the seat in front of me. I cannot move.

The young guy peels my boxer shorts around my waist and tugs them under my ass. My cock is fully erect. Look at him, what a picture, says the old guy. His leather-gloved hand encircles my cock. Get off me, you fucker, I shout. His hand stays locked to my manhood. I thrash around in the seat. He grabs me by the shoulders. The young guy takes my cock and moves his hand up and down it. Why don't you suck it? says the old guy to the young one, I bet it tastes good. The words fill me with dismay. I don't want this guy's lips on my cock! I want to go home and go to bed and forget this ever happened. I'd give it all up just for that. I'd forget this whole goddamn business of pimping myself nightly if I could just go home.

His lips pucker around the head. His fingers reach for the shaft, directing it inside—into the warm enclosure of his mouth. He sucks it like a goddamn Hoover as I lie back against the seat. He's going to give me a blow job whether I like it or not. His head, covered in dark brown hair, moves up and down on my cock till it feels like the inside is being drawn out through the end. His fingers circle the downy hairs on my thigh. He plays with my balls, which are swollen and tight. For a moment he stops sucking and works the shaft up and down, lubricated by glistening saliva. He bends down and squashes his lips against my balls. He flicks out his tongue. He reaches behind me and rubs my ass.

The tingling begins in my balls. My cock feels unbelievably long. I shut my eyes and arch my back. A jolt runs through my entire body. Groaning, I explode in his mouth. He sucks energetically. The old guy chuckles.

I'm emptied. Exhausted. The young guy's lips close over mine. His tongue slips into my mouth. He kisses me, long and slow and wet. I'm weak and unresisting. Liquid spills across my tongue. Salty, gloopy, unpleasant. My come! His eyes sparkle as he lets it flow from his mouth into mine. I struggle, but the old guy holds my head in place. I'm forced to swallow it—thick and nasty. The young guy grins. There you go, beautiful, he whispers.

Shall we get rid of him? says the old guy.

The young guy nods. Yeah, let's go somewhere dark.

The old guy opens the door and thrusts me out. I fall on the cold sidewalk, my pants still loose around my ankles. The rain soaks my skin.

IV

I WAKE UP with a sticky cock, my fingers smelling of semen. I grab a towel from beside the bed and wipe my stomach clean. I look at the clock; I've slept right through the night. The scenes from my dream flash through my head. There's something poetical about it, the shame I feel at being forced to drink my own come. It's utterly pornographic. I make coffee in the kitchen, then sink my ass into the soft leather seat, spooning cornflakes into my mouth. Who's to say pornography can't be poetic? Isn't poetic language, by its very nature, a form of gratuitousness? It's hardly necessary or practical to say things musically—Plato wanted to ban language that did anything other than communicate truth. Kristeva says poetic language arouses the oral and anal drives; doesn't pornography act similarly when it depicts scenes for our arousal? If poetry is the expulsion of drives into language, is it not, in fact, the pornography of language? Its utterance a form of masturbation? Perhaps we've found the meaning of "jouissance"; perhaps I'm merely a sophist.

. . . . .

IN THE EVENING I finish my paper. The last smooth, crisp page, covered in smart, black lines, shoots from the printer. Above the computer, Mary's eyes are half in shadow. A glass pane shimmers in front of her face. It's all I know of her, this shimmering veil, though I search in the crevices of unveiled bodies, in the sweat between legs, in gallons of come—disgusting or beautiful, but always male. My homosexuality is an elaborate displacement. A substitute for her. Paradoxically, I fly from her, hoping to recover her. Now it's time to go where I've always feared to go; the unveiled woman freezes my blood.

RENT-A-STUD

BEARMUFFIN

I'D NEVER SUCKED cock before, but when I laid eyes on Jason, a gorgeous, blond, blue-eyed, heavy-hung hunk, I was hooked. I had to blow him.

Last summer I was on my lunch break when I walked into Dusties, a neighborhood bar.

I pulled up a stool and ordered a beer. That's when I noticed Jason. Tony Sanchez, one of our mail clerks, was sitting next to him.

I couldn't keep my eyes off Jason. A red baseball cap was turned backwards over his long, flowing blond hair. His clear blue eyes sparkled. His powerful, buffed body was sun-bronzed to perfection. His dazzling smile was so appealing.

He wore a colorful Hawaiian shirt. It was unbuttoned, so I could see his massive pecs and etched abs. Faded cutoffs exposed his smooth, muscular thighs. Golden hairs swirled over his legs.

Tony inched closer to Jason so he could put a hand between Jason's thighs. Jason acted nonchalant, sipping his drink, while Tony began to unbutton Jason's fly. Jason wasn't wearing any underwear, so his proud cock suddenly burst into view.

The shaft of his ivory-pinkish cock was heavy, fat at the crown, and covered with thick, blue veins. Tony boldly began to work his fingers up and down Jason's cock, which gradually swelled larger until it filled Tony's fist.

Smiling confidently, Jason leaned over and whispered something in Tony's ear. Then Jason got up and went into the toilet at the back of the bar. Tony waited a few seconds, finished his drink, and followed him in. Curiosity got the better of me, so I followed them.

While I washed my hands, I could see the stall behind me reflected in the mirror. Underneath the door, I saw Tony's toes hugging Jason's sandal-clad feet. When I went into the adjoining stall, I noticed that a large glory hole had been bored through the metal.

I peeped through the hole only to see Tony fondling Jason's big, throbbing cock. Jason tilted his head back, placing his hands on Tony's head. He was guiding his roaring hard-on down Tony's throat. Tony's mouth yawned open, and Jason slipped his cock between the horny cocksucker's lips.

Tony's feverish mouth was glued to Jason's pubes. He was sucking hard as his hands cupped Jason's hard, muscular butt. Jason mashed his groin against Tony's face. He forced his cock all the way down Tony's throat.

Pure ecstasy gleamed on Jason's face. I'd never seen a guy get blown before. The raw, animal sounds of cock sucking were sexually arousing. Before I knew it, I was rubbing my crotch. I could feel my cock rise and swell as Tony's busy tongue rattled noisily over Jason's thick piece.

I wanted to suck Jason's cock more than anything else in the world. Yeah! I'd make Jason groan with pleasure. I'd blow him good, just like Tony. I got a full, raging hard-on when I saw Tony whacking off. So I began jacking my cock too.

Jason whispered harshly, "Yeah, suck it! Suck it hard, you queer." Jason pushed forward, grabbing Tony by the hair, mashing his face into his groin. Tony was choking on Jason's spasming cock!

Suddenly, Jason cried out, "Unngh, unngh, unngh! Awwwwwww fuuuuuuuuuuckkkk yeah, yeah, yeaahhhhhhh!!!!" as he blasted a potent come-load into Tony's eager, slurping mouth.

Jason quickly pulled Tony off his cock, grabbed a hankie from his back pocket, and wiped the come off his cock.

I saw Tony pull two ten-dollar bills from his wallet. "You're worth a hundred, stud!" he said. I had to agree.

"Yeah," Jason said with a shit-eating grin. Tony just laughed good-naturedly, zipped up, and left.

I stayed on the toilet waiting for Jason to leave. Suddenly the door flew open. Jason stood there with his hands in his pockets.

"You watched us?" he asked. His knees rubbed against mine. I could still smell the fresh semen staining his cutoffs. I looked into his beautiful blue eyes.

"Yes," I stammered. "Yes, I did."

Jason grinned. "Did you like it?" I gulped. Jason's semi-hard cock was dangling just an inch from my mouth.

"Yes," I replied.

Jason brushed his cock against my lips.

"Go ahead," he said. "Suck it!"

Jason's hot man-smell rushed up my nostrils as I took his sweet cock all the way down my throat. His plump balls bounced against my chin.

I tugged hard on Jason's nipples. He began moaning again, just as he had for Tony. His body trembled, so I knew he was ready to come. I started jacking off my own cock. My mind was agog, my heart was beating like mad. I couldn't fucking believe that I was blowing Jason in a public toilet.

"Unngh, unngh, unngh," he gasped. "Aww, fuck! Gonna come. Gonna fuckin' come!" Jason's hot come just blasted between my hollowed cheeks, flowed over my waggling tongue, and splashed against the back of my throat. That's when I shot my own hot load all over the floor.

Without a moment's hesitation, I gave him a hundred bucks and my business card.

"Wow!" Jason exclaimed. "You'll be hearing from me."

But I didn't hear from Jason for several weeks. I couldn't keep my mind on my work. Day and night I was obsessed with the blond hustler. I wanted him to ram his big pork-sword down my throat and up my ass and fuck me to death!

A month later, I was about to leave for the day when my secretary told me there was an urgent call. My heart leaped when I heard Jason's smooth, deep voice.

He wanted to see me again. Could he drop by? I was hornier than hell, but still I hesitated. I knew guys who'd been victimized by hustlers. Jason seemed a cool dude, but I didn't want to take any chances. I told Jason that maybe we could meet somewhere else. Jason mentioned a bathhouse where it cost twenty bucks for a room. I said okay, so he gave me the address.

Fifteen minutes later, I was there. Jason was standing by the door clad in cutoffs, baseball cap turned backwards, and his Hawaiian shirt flying wide open, exposing his thick, juicy muscles. He was always smiling. I guess such confidence was justifiable. With a body like that, he'd never be lonely, that's for sure!

After we got inside our cubicle, we both stripped. Jason started to flex and pose for me. He had just come from a gym, so his muscles were thick, pumped up, and wonderfully sweaty.

Then he started to suck on my tits. First he'd bite into one nipple and twist the other one so fucking hard I thought he'd rip it off. He made me so horny that I wanted to scream and fall on my knees and eat his asshole forever!

Jason's ripe manly smell was exhilarating. I'd bury my face in his sweaty, hairy armpits so that I could inhale his fantastic manly odors while I fisted my cock. All the time he would work on my nipples. And after that hot tit workout, I couldn't help but shoot my wad.

"Suck my cock, man," Jason said. The head was shiny, and when a big gob of pre-come appeared at the tip, I quickly dipped my tongue into his slit to lick it off. I told him to lie down on his right side. He lifted up his left leg and propped it on my back and I grabbed his meaty butt to push his groin against my face. I relaxed my throat as much as possible so his beautiful cock could slide all the way down my throat. Jason moaned lustily while I sucked his cock.

I fondled his balls, which resembled two baseballs inside a soft leather pouch. Jason moaned lustily as I sucked them good and hard. Then I pulled my mouth off his cock and began sucking his balls. As I sucked I began stroking his cock to full, ripe hardness. "Oh yeah, man, feels so fuckin' good!" Jason moaned lustily.

Jason suddenly yanked me off his balls. "Turn around," he said. "I'm gonna fuck ya!"

So I hunched over the little bed in the cubicle and stuck my ass out into the air waiting for his glorious cock. Jason lubricated my hole and then shoved his hard, spasming cock right up my asshole.

After about five or six short, brutal strokes, he laughed harshly and then began shooting his wad up my aching hole. He even pulled his cock out and shot come all over my back. The come dripped down, filled my cleft, and puddled in my open hole.

I saw Jason three times a week, paying him a hundred bucks a throw. He was worth it. I still didn't want to bring him home, so we'd go back to the bathhouse, where I'd lick his muscles, his smelly armpits, and chow down on cock and balls.

Jason worked on my tits and I'd shoot my load, and then he'd butt-fuck me. As always, he just shoved his cock right up my hole. He'd pump it hard a few times, and then splatter his load up my ass or all over my back.

One day Jason surprised me. He let me rim him. He squatted over my bobbing face, and I rimmed him for about ten minutes. His sweet butt hole was covered with sweaty little golden blond butt hairs that sprouted from his tight, pink butt bud. Jason thrashed about, moaning and groaning. I dug my tongue deeper inside him.

"Yeah, yeah, yeah! Fuck my ass with your tongue," he cried.

Jason pounded his fists on the bed. He mashed his asshole against my fluttering tongue. He really got off on my rimming his butt.

Afterwards, Jason straddled my chest and jacked off. His face contorted with lust, his eyes clenched, he gasped lustfully, "Unngh, unngh, unngh! Oh yeah, oh yeah, oh yeah! Unngh, unngh, unngh! *Fuuuuuck, yeaaaaaaaaaah! Awwwwwwwww fuuuuuuck!!!!!*"

He opened his eyes, grinning savagely at me when he aimed the tip of his cock right between my eyes. Within seconds, my face was completely covered with his sizzling come.

"Lie down," Jason barked. He hammered his fists into my sweaty buttocks. He was using me like a punching bag. When he got too rough, I told him to stop. "Just fuckin' around," he said. Then he closed his eyes and whacked off for about three minutes. Afterwards, he shoved his cock up my ass and fucked me again.

When he pulled out his cock, he shot a boiling hot load all over my sore butt.

Then all of a sudden I stopped hearing from Jason. I figured that maybe he had lost my number. There was no way for me to get in touch with him. Many times I went back to Dusties, but Jason never showed up.

One afternoon I was driving near the beach when I saw Jason. He was standing on the corner, talking to a couple of his buddies. His faded cutoffs hugged his bulging basket and luscious bubble butt. He wasn't wearing a shirt, and I could see the hot sweat streaming down his awesomely bronzed body. When I honked my horn, Jason turned around and waved.

That gorgeous, toothy grin was spread on his handsome face again. He said good-bye to his buds and sprinted toward my car.

He jumped right in, and the first thing he did was squeeze my crotch. "Hey, dude. Where you been? I lost your number. Glad to see you again!"

I fished in my wallet and pulled out a hundred. "Got time for me today?" I asked him.

"Plenty of time, dude," he said, whipping the bill from my hand and sticking it into his jeans. So we sped off to the bathhouse for a hot fuck.

MY FIRST PROFESSIONAL ENGAGEMENT

BILL DORSETT

FOR A SHORT period of time in the early eighties I peddled my twenty-year-old ass out of a bar in southern California. It started out innocently. I was out cruising for cock one night, and an older guy started hitting on me.

He must have been in his early forties, but then it seemed like he was so old. He was my father's age. He was about five-six—real short for me, but he had an incredibly hard, muscled body. I was twenty, five-ten, 150 pounds, on the wispy side. He bought me a drink and sat next to me at the bar. At that time I had no facial hair and very little body hair.

We talked for a while, and I knew that he had a bone for me, but he just didn't blow my skirt up. He was actually a little older than my father. He kept asking me to go home with him, but I wouldn't commit. He was not unattractive, but I liked them my age. Finally after a while he asked:

"What would it take to get me in your pants?"

"Two hundred and fifty dollars," I replied right off the top of my head. I have no idea why I said it. Remember, this was the early eighties, and $250 was much more than it is today.

"I assume you want cash."

I turned and looked at him harder than before. He was

suddenly more attractive to me.

"What would you want to do? For two hundred and fifty dollars?"

"Take you home, strip you naked, and suck your cock, then you suck me and I fuck you."

"You've given this a lot of thought—to answer so quickly." I was a little shaken. Me—who blew a lifeguard at the beach in his watch shack on Labor Day with throngs of people all around who couldn't see anything but were within earshot.

"Well, I am getting up there, and if I see something I want, I don't mind paying for it. Are you serious?"

"Are you?"

"Well. We'd have to stop at an ATM, but yes."

"Should I follow you?" ATMs were new to me; they had only been in operation for a couple of months.

"No, come with me. You'll have enough money to take a cab back to your car—I'm not that far," he said, getting up and collecting his keys and cigarettes from the bar. "Shall we?"

So I got up and followed him out of the bar—much to the surprise of the bartender, whom I had dated once, and a couple of friends at the bar. So much for my reputation.

We got to his car, a convertible—a red one.

"Up or down?" he said, opening my door for me.

"What?"

"The top. Do you want it up or down?"

"Oh, down, of course," I replied as I slid into the passenger seat.

He quickly put the top down, got in, and drove a short distance to an ATM machine. He parked, took the keys, and said, "I'll be right back."

As I watched him at the ATM, I thought, this isn't going to be so bad. He isn't *that* old. He does have a great body, if a small one, and he hasn't treated me like a whore yet, which apparently I was.

"Got it," he said as he patted his wallet and got back in the car.

"Where to now?" I asked.

"My hotel. Right off the Redondo Pier."

I was excited now. I had always dreamed of the beach but had always lived on the wrong side of Pacific Coast Highway. This was getting better and better. The hotel right off the pier was a Hilton. Fuck me.

"Where you from?" I asked.

"New York. I'm here on business, but I bet you hear that a lot."

"From who?"

"Your other johns … is that what you call them?" he said, looking at me slyly.

"You know, I think you have more experience at this than I do."

"I know," he answered, pulling into the hotel parking lot valet station.

When we got to the room, he opened his wallet and put two hundred-dollar bills, two twenty-dollar bills, and two five-dollar bills on the nightstand, turned to me, and said:

"Come over here and let me inspect the merchandise."

I walked over to him. He put both hands on my hips and pulled me into him and kissed me deeply on the mouth as he unbuttoned my shirt.

He had his tongue in my mouth as he pulled my shirt open and ran his rough, calloused hands over my chest and down my stomach until he was cupping my balls in one hand and holding an ass cheek in the other. He held me closer.

I could feel his cock swelling up against me as he gently squeezed my ass; he released my balls and put his other hand on my ass, grinding his hips into me as his tongue explored my mouth.

My cock was swollen to its full fat nine inches, and I felt my pants fall down around my ankles as he pushed me into a nearby armchair.

Once seated, he ran his mouth down over my chin and down my smooth chest until he reached the thin trail of hair that ran from my belly button, pointing the way to my cock. He slowly tongued my navel as he grabbed my cock in one hand and guided it into his open mouth.

Man, it was hot in there. I looked down to see his dark-haired head bobbing up and down in my lap, his hands on my hips as he kneeled at my feet and began picking up speed, sucking my cock.

"Hot mouth," I said as I relaxed a little more.

"What?" he said, stopping for a minute.

Now, I am going to stop this here for a little speech about something I feel strongly about. When you are having sex with someone and they murmur something that you don't quite hear, don't say, "What?" It completely breaks the mood. You should just know that if it were something important like "I can't breathe" or "I smell smoke," it would be spoken in a loud voice. But soft murmuring? It's encouragement, so say something like "Yes, yes," or even "Yes, baby." There isn't going to be a test later, and chances are it will be repeated when your heads are closer together. Now back to the blow job already in progress.

"You have a hot mouth," I said, pushing my cock back in his mouth. "But this isn't fair. I want some cock too. Let's go over on the bed."

He stood up and slowly removed his clothes. He was short, but he was packed pretty tight. His pecs were hard and square and flat and covered in dark fur. His arms were muscular and also hairy. In fact, this man was hairy all over. Very hairy. Grab-a-fistful hairy. He had an anchor tattooed on his left forearm.

He pulled me over to the bed, pushed me gently down, and then lay down in the time-honored 69 position. Suddenly, I had a face full of cock and pubic hair. His cock was about six inches long, but it was fatter than I had ever seen. This is gonna hurt going into my ass, was all I could think of.

But then I just opened my mouth over the head of his thick,

hard cock and took as much of it as I could into my mouth. He moaned as he felt my tongue on his cock shaft and took my cock even deeper into his silky mouth.

In any good 69 session, there is a point of total connection. Cock to mouth and cock to mouth. We continued this way for quite a while. Then he sat up slowly and pulled my head off his cock and into an open-mouthed kiss. Our tongues slowly intertwined, and I felt his calloused hand grasping my cock as his tongue went deeper into my mouth.

His mouth moved from my mouth to my ear, and he whispered, "I want to fuck you now. Get on your hands and knees at the edge of the bed."

I did as I was told and noticed him hunting for something in the nightstand drawer.

This was a bit before safe sex, so condom usage was not as prevalent as it was to become shortly. He said:

"Don't take this the wrong way, but I am going to use a rubber. I am married and I'm not taking any chances. I always do this."

I didn't say anything, but I did reach down and pull my ass cheeks apart.

He got behind me and rubbed his cock up against my tight hole. Then he put his finger there instead, rubbing lube over the hole and putting his finger inside me, slightly. I squirmed; things are larger than they appear when they are actually up your ass.

He positioned himself right behind me and started gently to push his fat cock through my ring. There was a pop as the thick cock head poked inside me, and I yelped, 'cause hell, I was twenty. I had only been fucked a couple of times by guys my own age. This was the first *man* I had ever been with.

Needless to say, it did not slip right in.

"Fuck, that is the tightest I've had," he said, attempting to push it in further.

Then he reached around me, and his hand closed around my cock shaft. Still lubed, his hands slowly jerked me to a full hard-on, and before I knew it, he was in me to the hilt. I felt his hips against my ass as he slowly rocked his hips into me while he rubbed that calloused hand over my dick, ending with a little polishing gesture at the head. I pushed my ass back a little, fucking back with what little room there was between us.

I was moaning, and he was moaning as he started to pick up speed and fuck me faster.

"Take my fat cock, fucker," he whispered, leaning his body over my back; he released my cock and put both hands on the bed as he humped that meat into my warm hole. Then he started biting the skin on my back, right at the back of my neck.

"Fuck me harder, man," I replied to him as he stuck his tongue in my ear and really started picking up speed. Then he slowed down, biting my ear lobe and whispered to me:

"This is no fair; I'm doing all the work. Let me lie down, and you can sit on it."

He pulled his fat dick out of my ass and stretched out beside me on the bed.

"You want me to drive for a while? Sure," I said as I straddled him, positioning myself so his cock was directly under my asshole, which by now was wide open.

He moaned as I slid my ass down, feeling every one of those six inches, but more the girth. It was so fat, I felt like I was being opened like when you start to peel an orange. Finally, he was completely inside me. I started to bounce slightly up and down as I looked into his eyes. My cock was hard and slapping his belly with each movement.

We went into another time warp. I'm not sure how long we stayed like that, looking into each other's eyes, me rocking back and forth on that fat cock.

Then he said, "I love how you get hard when you're getting fucked."

"That's because your dick feels good," I replied, contracting my ass around his cock.

"I want you to fuck my ass for a while. Can we?"

"Sure." I stopped rocking and raised my ass up and off his dick. There was a slap as his hard dick flopped back down against his body.

He moved over to the bedside table, pulled a condom out of the drawer, handed it to me, and said, "Please."

I took the condom, unwrapped it, and unrolled it over my hard cock.

"How do you want it?"

"I want you to fuck me on my back like a bitch." He flipped onto his back and threw his hairy, thickly muscled legs into the air and pulled his ass open. "Fuck me like a bitch. That is what I am paying you for."

I got on the bed, put his legs on my shoulders, and gently slid my cock toward his asshole. He moaned when it went in and slowly took it inch by inch until I was buried to the base of my cock, my balls hanging down and his legs over my shoulder.

I leaned down and licked his face while I made a particularly hard jab in him.

His hands flew to my ass as he grabbed me to pull me in tighter. "I can feel your heart beating," he moaned.

"I can feel yours too." I ground my cock in deeper.

"Don't come yet, fucker. I have other plans for you."

"Such as?"

"I want my cock inside your ass when you come. I want to feel what your ass muscles do to my cock when you shoot your load on my chest, but let's take a shower first."

"Let's go," I said, pulling out and pulling the rubber off my cock.

We went into the bathroom and ran the shower, standing under the hot spray. Kissing. Soaping up each other's cock. He kissed me while his hand rubbed soap on my ass while he fingered my hole.

He rinsed me off and got down on his knees and started

sucking my cock, which was beginning to swell. When I was fully hard, he turned me around and buried his face between my ass cheeks, his tongue pushing against my hole.

This was a first for me. I was only twenty and had never been rimmed before. Let me tell you, I took right to it. Bent over and spread my legs as wide as I could and still remained standing.

After a while, he stood up and said, "Get me hard."

I immediately dropped to my knees and took his cock into my mouth. When he was fully hard again, he said, "Back to the bed, whore, this is where you earn your money."

I grabbed a towel and started to dry myself. He grabbed it and threw it in a corner and said, "This can't wait." And pushed me toward the bed.

He lay down on the bed, fished another condom out, slipped it on, and shook it at me, saying, "Get over here, slut, and sit on it."

I did as I was told. As I slid my ass down over his fat cock he moaned gruffly and started to growl low.

I looked down at him while riding his pole. That hairy-chested man, moaning and squirming underneath me, his fat cock buried deep in my hole. My dick started to get hard and slap against his stomach.

"You like this, don't you?" (him).

"Yes" (me).

"You're a nasty one, aren't you?"

"Yeah, I'm your nasty whore fucker. You are paying me to ride your cock, and I should be paying you, your fat rod feels so good."

"I bet none of your other tricks makes you come like I am going to, do they?"

"No, stud. No one but you. And I am going to come big, I can feel it building up."

"Me too, fucker, I am getting ready to juice your ass. Ride my cock."

I began to really buck and moan, riding that thick dick.

"Ah ... I'm gonna shoot it!" he said, and I felt his whole body tense up as wave after wave of jizz shot out of him. I could actually feel his dick swell more as he shot out time and again. We slowed down and he said, "Your turn, baby. Jerk it for me. I stay hard."

He was still hard in there, that's for sure. I rocked back and forth, my dick in my hand, stroking myself.

"Look at you. Fucking beautiful. Young man with a hard dick, riding mine while he jerks off. Ride it, fucker."

I was grinding my ass furiously while jerking my cock against his stomach. I could feel it starting in my balls. My legs were shaking, and I could feel the current between my balls and my cock, which was swollen bigger than I had ever seen it.

I leaned back and braced myself with the other hand when the first spasm hit me. I shot a line of jizz out that flew and hit him right on the top of his head. The second one hit his chest, the rest came one after the other, receding until there was a small puddle of come on his stomach over my cock and balls.

He reached up and pulled me down and kissed me. I felt his cock as it popped out of my hole. We were both breathing hard.

"Thanks, man," he said, breaking the kiss. "That was hot. Feel free to take a shower before you go."

"No, that's okay. I can shower when I get home." I got up and walked over to the clothes explosion by the chair. After a quick towel wipedown, I started to get dressed. I dressed quickly. "Thanks, that was great." I said as I made my way to the door.

"Wait. Come here." He motions to the bed beside him. I came to the bed and sat next to him. He pulled me in for a kiss and I felt him put something in my pocket. "What kind of whore are you? You forgot the payoff."

"Oh, I forgot all about the money. Thanks."

"They can call you a cab at the front desk. If you want to leave a card, I'll call you the next time I come to town."

"I don't have a card, but I'll leave you my number." I went

to the desk and wrote a quick note. "Be cool, though, my mom answers that phone too."

"Your mom?"

"Yes, I still live at home."

"Get out of here fast, I'm getting hard again."

I left. I transferred the cash to my wallet in the elevator, and like any good whore, I counted it. He had given me an extra fifty dollars.

I called a cab, went home to my apartment. I had lied about still living at home. The next day I went out and bought two pairs of shoes and a leather jacket. I wore all of them until they were in tatters.

ROBOT SEX IN THE THIRD MILLENNIUM

SETH LEEPER

HE RECOGNIZES THE sex robot by the red ribbon tied to its neck, the universal sign that indicates its status. Up close you can't really tell that the robots aren't authentic humans. Their flesh has natural, inherent warmth to it, and it is just as soft as a human's. In fact, stories are circulating that several humans have met and fallen in love with robots, never knowing the difference until the robot feels obliged to tell them. Robot sex feels the same as sex with a human: they have the same body parts, and they function the same way. The only difference is an ethereal quality to the eye—they almost glow, but they never twinkle. It's possible to be fooled by good lighting, but if you're sitting across from someone and their eyes don't twinkle, they're probably a robot. The only other difference between humans and robots is humans don't cry.

The erection pressing against the zipper of his jeans tells him he's found the right one. The sex robot is on the other side of the street, however, and he has had to wait for the light to change before he can cross. A semi-truck sporting a Pepsi logo passes by, blocking his view of the sex robot. When the truck passes, the sex robot has disappeared. Panicked, his erection growing more urgent, he dashes across the street the moment the pedestrian light comes on and looks around frantically for the robot.

He peers into the Starbucks on the corner, sees only humans, and checks the other stores. He sees no sign of the robot, however, so he continues to walk in the direction he was headed, thinking maybe he'll find another one just as appealing. Several pass by him, all of them with refined features and Adonis bodies, but none of them have the quality he's looking for. He's looking for something very specific.

Thumbs hooked to his jean pockets, head bowed down to the ground, he glances in the window of a sex shop and sees the robot inside. His heart gulps, making him miss a breath, and he pushes through the glass door of the sex shop, a hollow, soulless bell announcing his entry. The sex robot, in cutoffs and a cotton flannel shirt, the sleeves manually removed by cheap scissors, is strumming through a magazine in front of the lubricant shelf. He stops to take in the sight of it, sensual lines outlining muscled calves and thighs, biceps so defined they could have their own dictionary, broad shoulders brushing lightly against the ends of a kiwi brown mane, skin luminescent, a diamond's sparkle white.

He nods. This is the one, he thinks to himself.

He taps its shoulder, and the face turns in his direction, a smoky blue eye glancing over a shoulder and down at him, evaluating him.

"Yes?" a voice says.

"How much for tonight?"

"Five hundred."

"Done. Come with me."

The sex robot closes its magazine, turns around, and reaches for his hand.

"Let's shake on it," the robot says.

This strikes him as a childish and very human thing to do, but he returns the handshake.

He smiles and gestures for the robot to follow him. They walk out of the store, go down the street, and flag a cab. The cab drops them off in the ritzy part of town, where the millionaires who prefer apartments live. He lives in an apartment building twenty stories high and has his own floor. The doorman nods to him as they enter, a smirk on his face.

He takes the sex robot up to the tenth floor, and the doors open on his living room. Lavish furnishings and wood floors, everything he desired growing up. He doesn't like to think of himself as an extravagant man—his furnishings are his only excesses. He invites the robot to sit on his couch while he runs to the kitchen to fetch champagne glasses. He emerges from the kitchen with a bottle in one hand and two glasses in the other.

"So have you had any clients today?" he asks the robot.

"A few," the robot replies.

"Any good?"

"Good money."

He sets the glasses down on the glass table in front of the couch and takes a seat next to the robot, rubbing his leg. The robot looks at him, a puzzle in his eyes, and contorts his mouth into a half-smile, half-inquisitive expression.

"Where are you from?" he asks.

The robot smirks, nods.

"From the factory, of course, where else?"

"Well, where was the factory?"

"I don't know. They shut that part of us down. We never remember where we come from. It's better that way."

"Why do you say that?"

"Think about it," the robot replies. "They turn us on in the real world. We're conditioned to look and act like humans. If our first memory was of being in a box or a processing plant, it would be that much harder to assimilate."

"I didn't realize robots thought of such things," he says.

"You'd be surprised," says the robot.

Silence.

He picks up his champagne glass, lifting it from the middle of its stem, holding it between his index and middle finger, secured by his thumb.

"What's your name?" he asks before sipping.

"Atley," says the robot.

He swallows. "I'm Eric."

Silence. Glass clanks against glass as they set the glasses back onto the table.

"So you want me here for the whole night?"

"Yes."

"What do you want to do with me?"

"I'll tell you in a little while," Eric says. "We have all night."

He doesn't know how to articulate what he desires from the sex robot. This is the first time he's attempted to make his fantasy a reality. Before the New Era, there was a time when humans still cried and felt emotions far deeper than they do in the present day. In the primitive 1900s and 2000s, movies were made that document this, and books and plays were written that explored this. He has in mind a notion, given to him by his obsession with these old eras and taken from a book he read from this time, that suggests that emotions can be pulled from the body while watching a very romantic or dramatic movie. This is one reason he's hired Atley to come here.

"Have you ever seen a movie?" Eric asks him.

Atley shakes its head. "No. What is that?"

"It's an old form of art," Eric replies. "Instead of using the machines to entertain them in various forms, humans used to create entertainment for themselves and other humans long before they made the robot to accomplish the tasks they didn't want to be bothered with. Some of the things they made were called movies, which reflected real life and which appear to have been an excuse for humans to look at themselves. They were very narcissistic back then. A lot of human traits were genetically removed from humans and given to robots later on."

Silence.

"They still have some around, if you look hard enough," Eric continues. "You view them on old machines called VCRs, or DVD players, which are connected to machines called televisions. You can find these at junkyards and thrift stores, which is where I bought mine."

"Does this have to do with why you wanted me to come here?"

"Yes. Back then, in those movies, they felt things, powerful emotions. Humans were passionate and excitable. They cried, and I want to know what that feels like, but I can't, because those kinds of emotions were removed from humans generations ago, so I need to see someone cry, because I can't do it myself, but if I see it happen, then maybe—"

"So you want me to cry for you?"

"Yes."

"I don't know, I mean—I can't just cry on cue."

"You don't have to. I've thought of ways to bring it out of you."

Atley shrugs.

They start with an old Hollywood movie, a romance in which the two lovers are reunited at the end; this kind of story used to cause most women and sensitive men to at least tear up. When this doesn't work, they watch a drama with a devastating ending. Without the context, however, neither one of them feels much of anything, and so Eric decides to move them to the bedroom.

In the bedroom, Eric leans Atley over the bed and massages the seat of its pants, running his hands up its back, then back down to its waist and ass. He slides his hands under Atley's shirt, massaging the muscles in its back. Atley lets out a sigh of relaxation. Eric slides a hand into Atley's shorts and, in one sudden movement, squeezes its ass cheek aggressively. Atley emits a low moan.

Eric rubs Atley's ass cheeks beneath the shorts, massaging and digging, while his dick twitches a little, waking to the realization that his body's engaging in something sexual. The gradual buildup begins. He pulls Atley's body up to his own, clutching it around the middle, rubbing the abdomen, and sliding his hand into the front of its shorts, cupping Atley's erection, pressing against it to create friction.

Atley's back arches, his neck angled over Eric's shoulder; their cheeks brush together, and they share a kiss, tongues battling. In one swift movement, Eric unbuttons Atley's jeans, sending them down its legs, then pins them with his right foot and sends them sliding across the floor behind him. He bends Atley over the bed again.

"Stay there," he says. "I'll be back in a minute."

Atley obeys; when Eric returns to the bedroom with a paddle, Atley is still in the exact same position. The paddle is purple, with a long handle and a wide circular head. Eric wastes no time — he lifts the paddle over his head and smacks Atley's ass with it. The resulting sound is audible through the entire apartment, and the force leaves Atley's ass cheeks bright red in the middle. Atley makes no sound. Eric brings the paddle down again, firm but a little less hard. The next slap is harder, more akin to the first; Eric alternates hard, jarring slaps of the paddle with ones that are less forceful but firm.

Atley's breath can be heard, labored and heavy, shallow and wheezy.

He stops to rub Atley's cheeks, smoothing the blows over with a massage.

He leans over Atley's back, resting his head on its shoulder, and sighs. He looks at Atley's eyes, dry.

"Nothing?"

Atley shakes its head.

Eric picks Atley up at the waist and turns him over on the bed. Atley crawls to the middle of the bed, and Eric moves toward him, erection pressing against the front of his jeans. He stops midway, raises up, and removes his shirt. He unbuttons the top of his jeans, then slides them over his thighs and over his legs, kicking them off the bed. He's risen in front of Atley, cock at full arousal, staring down at the sex robot. He searches the robot's eyes for some kind of emotion. He sees desire and stress, but the eyes are dry. His heart is pounding, desperate for the sight of a tear or a little moistness.

He lowers himself on top of Atley, blanketing the robot in an embrace, laying the side of his head on its shoulder, contemplating his next move. He raises his head, capturing Atley's mouth in his own, sucking on the lower lip. He sucks hard, running his teeth over the robot's lip gently, producing a shudder. He bites down, producing a drop of blood, and slurps it into his mouth, mixing in the bitter potent juice with his own saliva. Atley moans ecstatically and flails its arms out to its sides, in a Christ-Cross pose. Eric pins down Atley's arms at the biceps and presses more of his body weight against the robot, grinding his cock into Atley's abdomen.

Atley rises up with each grinding thrust, and they create a rhythm with their bodies this way. Atley rides each thrust as though there were a tunnel running through his abdomen into some deeper sex chamber.

Eric is on the verge of an orgasm when he stops the motion, reaches over to the night table, and retrieves a box of condoms, a bottle of lubrication, and a small knife. He resumes the rhythmic sex motion as he slides the condom on and lubricates his cock and Atley's ass. He raises Atley's hips and slides his cock in between his spread ass cheeks. He sticks one finger, then two, into the sex hole, breaking it in gradually, before he places his cock at the entrance, and with one heavy sigh from the sex robot, shoves it all the way in. He stops. Waits. The sex tunnel slowly relaxes, slowly making room for further thrusting. He holds it there, waiting for the sex tunnel to adjust fully.

"Now," Atley whispers.

Eric pulls out to the edge of the tunnel, keeping only the head in, before slowly sliding it back in all the way, building the speed and depth of the thrusts each time until the room is filled with vibrato moans and Atley's love tunnel feels like fire. It is in this state of elevating desire and lust that Eric takes hold of the small knife and cuts a small, shallow nip into Atley's bicep, and then its lower arm. He cuts a shallow line down the middle of its abdomen, traveling over its belly button and stopping just above the cock.

A mist emerges in Atley's eyes, a thick moist coating, and the moisture builds, creating pools that ooze over the edges of the eyes. Profuse, copious tracks of water fall from the eyes, making spiderweb trail imprints over the cheeks before dripping from the cliffs of Atley's face onto its shoulders.

Eric, thrusting faster with each in and out motion, loses his breath, his heart pumping too fast for his body to handle. He is overcome with arousal, intrigue, and awe at the sight of Atley crying. With a few more thrusts, he loses control, comes inside the sex robot, and collapses on top of it. He throws the knife across the room, and it hits high up on the wall. The noise of the impact is hollow, and the knife falls to the floor. The edge of the knife leaves a red stain on the wood flooring.

Eric clings to Atley's waist, his back arched, and his head face to face with Atley's. He can't take his eyes away, and his head is pounding in a way it's never felt before. He doesn't know what's happening, and he's convinced his head is about to explode, when he feels a warm wetness trickling down his cheek.

He is overcome. He doesn't understand what is happening to him until his eyes click with Atley's and he understands. He feels his heart tighten, as if being squeezed for juice, like a lemon or a lime or an orange. It's a good squeeze. A fuzzy, grateful sensation.

He smiles down at Atley, the sex robot who has fulfilled him, and smiles.

"You don't have to stay for the whole night if you don't want to," he says.

"What about the money?"

"I'll give you all of it still. What you've given me is worth more than that."

"Whatever," the sex robot says.

Atley rises from the bed, his wounds healed already, as is the nature with robot bodies, and proceeds to put his clothes back on.

"Thank you," Eric says.

Atley holds out a hand for the money. Eric reaches over to the night table, pulls out a wad of bills, and piles the specified amount onto the sex robot's hand. He smiles.

Atley nods, walks into the front room, and shows himself out.

TROUBLE

....

MARK WILDYR

"SETH BAYLESS," THE bailiff called in a monotone.

A slender youth rose from the cluster of prisoners awaiting arraignment in Henry Salman Zamora's Metro Court and shuffled forward uncertainly.

"That one's trouble," predicted the public defender next to me. "He's too pretty."

"What trouble?" another lawyer scoffed. "Must be some mistake. He can't be old enough for Metro."

As if His Honor were privy to the conversation, Zamora peered over his glasses and did a double-take. "What is this, Mr. Prosecutor? This young man belongs in Children's Court."

"I respectfully beg to differ, your honor. The prisoner turned eighteen two months ago."

"I don't believe it. You have proof?"

"Yes, sir," the assistant DA answered promptly, anticipating the challenge.

While the court conferred, I took a look at the youngster under discussion. As a probation and parole officer for the City of Albuquerque, I had a privileged seat with a clear view of Seth Bayless in profile, and I understood the confusion. The face was smooth, unmarked, untroubled by a beard; hell, it didn't even look old enough to have suffered through acne. Tanned, resilient skin was stretched tight with the freshness of youth. High cheekbones balanced the boy's features perfectly. The eyes could have been drawn by a caricaturist: They were huge, brooding, and vulnerable. As he glanced nervously around the small courtroom, I saw the irises were a smoky blue. The blond hair with dark highlights was short in front with some body at the back. A two-hundred-dollar stylist couldn't have improved on it.

It was only when I observed the body that I believed the prosecutor's claim. Although lanky, the torso was defined by a framework of broad shoulders and flaring ribs seldom observed on minors. Even in baggy jailhouse blues, the kid's butt was high and boyish, making me think of the guy in school we called "High-Pockets." But there was nothing adolescent about the mass of muscle swinging behind the jumpsuit's zipper as he shifted restlessly from one foot to the other.

Though he was outwardly cool, the boy's fear was apparent to anyone who cared to look. Probably his first bust. Soliciting, the docket read. Young Seth had propositioned a baby-faced undercover cop. There wasn't a doubt in my mind he'd been entrapped, but that wasn't my call.

Things went about as expected. The kid's public-paid mouthpiece pled him out, anticipating a simple fine. For a while it looked as if Zamora might upset the applecart because Seth Bayless had no family or permanent address in the area. His problem became mine as soon as the jurist's eyes lit on me.

"I see Paul Govan in the courtroom," Zamora announced gravely. I rose grudgingly. "Tell me, Mr. Govan, are you willing to take this young man under your wing and find him a spot in a halfway house somewhere?"

"Uh, my boss usually makes the assignments, your honor."

"So my word carries no weight with you fellows down in Probation and Parole, eh?" There was danger lurking in that question.

"Of course, sir. I'm certain it will be all right for me to accept the assignment."

Yeah, right. Joe Deets would tear me a new one … but he wouldn't take the kid off my shoulders. What was it the public-trough shyster had said? "That one's trouble." You bet! Right from the first time I laid eyes on him.

It took three hours out of my busy day to locate a halfway house with room for Bayless, and another hour to get all of the paperwork done. Finally, I sat across my desk from the probationer, intending to intimidate him with a dead-level stare. I was immediately flummoxed. Some mortals are blessed with either a fine profile or good frontal features; few have both. Seth Bayless was one of the few. His unusual eyebrows, dark and pencil thin, dipped slightly before arching gracefully over his eyes. This fucker was beautiful front, side, and back! If I looked like him, I'd probably be out shagging my ass too, but I'd sell it to the ladies.

"Okay, Bayless," I said with a tired sigh, "you understand what happened, right? Judge Zamora gave you a six-month suspended sentence with supervision. A few ground rules. No drinking of alcoholic beverages and no drugs of any kind. You'll be subjected to random testing for the six months your ass is mine. Got that?"

The solemn, respectful youth nodded. "Yes, sir."

"And stay away from the rabbit run."

"Rabbit run?"

"Yeah. Where you were busted. That area out on East Central where the queers gather to sell their goods. Got it?" A nod this time. I ran down the rest of the list and told him to report tomorrow afternoon to get with the program. "We'll see if we can find you a job of some kind. You got enough money for groceries in the meantime?" He answered with a nod. I hesitated. "You seem like a decent kid. Why are you out peddling your butt to a bunch of fairies anyway?"

"Dunno. They just like me. And they aren't always queer."

My own beetle brows climbed, although I don't know why. After ten years in this business, there should be no more surprises.

"Even that cop had me do him before he busted me."

"Evans? Carlos Evans?" I asked. The old eyebrows really reached for the hairline then. "Come on, he—"

An elaborate shrug. "He said you wouldn't believe me. But he did. He lopped it out in the alley and had me go down on him. He made sure he didn't bust me until after he cracked his balls ... and before he paid me," the kid added bitterly.

"I wouldn't make accusations like that if I were you," I cautioned.

"Not an accusation. It's just the way it was."

"Well, you stay out of trouble until tomorrow. Understand? You need a ride to the halfway house?"

"I can probably hitch one."

"Uh-uh," I came back at him.

He grinned, that wide, mobile mouth curling devilishly at either end and altering his face dramatically. He looked like a heart-wrenching ingénue, except that he was male. "What's the matter, you afraid I'll hit on someone?" he asked.

"Whatever. I'll give you a ride. You're not about to proposition me."

A sudden calculating look sent a shiver up my spine, but I kept my mouth shut.

.   .   .   .   .

IT WAS ALMOST quitting time the next day before I realized that Seth Bayless had not reported in as directed. I was dialing the phone to order a warrant for his arrest when he appeared in front of my desk.

"You're late," I snapped.

"Sorry. But I had a lead on a job to check out. You know, get it without your help. I thought that was important." The kid talked with his hands. His long arms moved as he made his case, the slender fingers curling and uncurling gracefully. His baritone was deep enough to startle; it didn't fit the boy's smooth, slender, sometimes masculine and sometimes androgynous appearance. The kid was a chameleon.

"Let's get our priorities clear. There is only one thing that's important right now, and that's to keep me happy. When I say be here at three o'clock, you better be standing in front of the receptionist at ten till. You got it?"

"Yes, sir. I just thought—"

"Well, you thought wrong." I paused. "Did you get it?"

The head supported by a willowy neck shook slowly. I took another look at the kid. If you considered his individual parts, they weren't that impressive, but when taken altogether ... he was one of the most beautiful humans I had ever seen. Weird!

I gave him a tongue lashing just to get things off on the right foot. I couldn't afford to have him believe the rules didn't apply to him, but in the end I weaseled out and told him I wouldn't enter his tardiness in the record. He gave me a pouty, appreciative look.

Before we were finished, Sheryl, the receptionist, stuck her head in and announced she was leaving. Everyone else had already gone, so I told her to lock the front door and turned back to young Mr. Bayless.

"Where are you from, kid?"

"New York." He anticipated my next question. "Upstate."

"So how did you get out here?"

He gave another of his loose-limbed shrugs as he slouched in the chair, unconsciously thrusting his packed groin at me. At least, I think it was unconsciously. "This is as far as I got." I thought for a minute I would have to drag it out of him piecemeal, but he jiggled his knees a couple of times and gave me his history.

His father died when he was ten, and his mom worked hard to support them. Then she met and married a man where she worked, and young Seth abruptly ran into the stark reality of his new life. Although he was only fourteen at the time, Barnett, his new stepfather, expected him to go to school and pull his own weight. According to the kid, he did just that ... got a box-boy job in a local market and turned over his weekly paycheck to the family.

At sixteen, his life changed again. His mother came down sick and was in and out of the hospital for a few months. Barnett began making new demands on him ... clean up the kitchen ... have something on the table when he got home ... and then the biggie. The man appeared at Seth's bedside in the middle of the night. The boy cried at first, but before it was over decided it wasn't so bad ... if it had been anyone other than the pig who married his mother. Seth claimed Barnett fucked him more than he screwed his wife before she got sick.

His mother returned home, but the middle-of-the-night visits continued. Doubly uncomfortable with his mother in the house, Seth protested and received a fat lip for his trouble. Angry, he spilled the beans to his horrified mother, who demanded to know why her son would make up such outrageous lies about her husband. Rocked back on his heels, Seth lasted another year in the house, even though he now put up a ruckus whenever Barnett approached him.

Finally, Seth delivered an ultimatum to his stepfather: give him enough money to make it to California or he would file a complaint with the police. The man took about thirty seconds to agree. Unfortunately, Seth detoured to New York City before starting west. He learned a little about the tea trade in public toilets, but the city overpowered him, draining his slender resources, so he finally headed into the sunset. His money ran out in Chicago, but he hitched a ride with a long-haul trucker who had a weakness for boy cock. He arrived in Albuquerque on his eighteenth birthday and was enchanted. It was different from any place he had ever been ... part town, part city, an amalgam of Anglo, Hispanic, and Native American cultures. He quickly found the area where the gay hustlers hung out and went into business. Two months later he ran afoul of Officer Evans.

It was twilight before our interview concluded, by which time I had worked up some empathy for my charge. The kid got a raw deal, but the law is the law. Seth got caught ... and now he was mine.

At last, I stood and stretched my back. The keen eyes watching my every move made me slightly uncomfortable. "Well, that's all we can do today. I want you here at nine a.m. tomorrow. I've got a lead on a job. It's not much, but it'll keep you in groceries without selling your cock on the street. Nine sharp ... you understand?"

"Yes, sir." The beautiful head nodded once, emphatically.

"I'm going to the men's room, and then I'll give you a ride to the halfway house. Hold on a minute, okay?"

"Sure," he answered, knees jiggling nervously again.

I drained the old pipe, keenly aware of the young man in the other room. The kid had a rare presence for one his age. I was in the act of zipping up when the door opened behind me.

Seth stepped inside the men's room apologetically. "I need to go too."

My heart stuttered. "Okay." Was it my imagination, or was my voice strident?

I lathered and scrubbed my hands, watching him in the mirror and wondering why the kid unsettled me so. His broad back was to me. The Wal-Mart walking shorts fit his trim hips better than yesterday's jailhouse garb. He had a runner's legs, lean-muscled and hard. You could barely see the fine, golden hair on his calves.

A movement caught my attention. The kid was shaking it off vigorously, which made his butt wiggle. Something foreign crawled up my backbone. He turned suddenly as he fed his cock back into his clothing. The shorts had no fly; he had merely pushed them down in front to piss. I glimpsed a monstrous, semi-erect cock and wondered how he peed like that. I couldn't empty the bladder when I was hard. The shock hit me a moment later.

The kid had exposed himself to me. Even now, as he walked

to the sinks, his thrusting prick was clearly outlined against his shorts. Hell, it looked like the top of the damned thing ought to be peeking out from the waistband. What was worse … the kid had caught me looking.

Seth paused a moment before moving up behind me. His troubling eyes caught mine and held. I felt his heat before he touched me. His groin brushed my butt; he leaned into me, his hard-on pressing against my crack.

"You like me, don't you?" he asked huskily.

"Kid, you'd better watch your step."

"I always try to," he said, bending like he was going to kiss the back of my neck, but he didn't. He was studying my basket in the mirror.

In spite of myself, I reacted. My cock stirred in my jockeys, thickening, lengthening, betraying my reaction to him. I watched a slow smile form on that broad, sensuous mouth. His hands came to rest on my shoulders and slid slowly down my arms.

"Seth—"

"No, it's all right," he crooned. His hands explored my chest; my nipples itched beneath his palms. When he moved slowly down my torso, I came alive.

"Stop this right now! You—"

My thought ended in a gasp as his warm hands cupped my genitals. He glanced up to meet my gaze when he found the rigid muscle beneath my trousers. He had the decency to refrain from grinning in triumph; the smile was one of genuine pleasure.

I twisted around to face him. His hardness met my own, robbing me of my righteous indignation. I faltered again. Seth leaned forward and rested his smooth cheek against mine. I wondered if my five-o'clock shadow repulsed him.

This beautiful youth, this incredibly sexy male animal slowly traveled down my body. He kissed my neck, licked my nipples through the shirt, and finally fell to his knees before me. His mouth nuzzled me through the cotton of my trousers. I lost the ability to protest. Instead, I pushed against him, eager for closer contact. I felt his hands on my belt, moaned when he found my fly, and collapsed back against the cold porcelain of the sink as his hands grasped my flesh.

My legs trembled when his tongue curled about the crown of my erection. That handsome head took me, and I groaned aloud. His warm, moist mouth was as welcoming as any woman's vagina. I am neither terribly large nor unusually scrawny, but he took me all the way to the root effortlessly. Indescribable sensations gripped me as he slowly rode my rod back out to the end. Strange, erotic currents radiated from my scrotum into every part of my being.

His busy hands gently caressed my swollen balls, brushed my thighs, played in my pubic bush, tickled my stomach, invaded my navel. Finally, the nimble fingers kneaded my nipples erect. Everything I had was hard for this good-looking bugger. I spread my legs wider. Immediately, one hand reached for my ass. I pushed away from the sink ... coincidentally shoving my cock farther down his throat. He took it easily.

Things became serious as Seth stroked my crack. His fingers parted the flesh in search of my rosebud; he found it. The boy lightly stroked my sphincter while his head bobbed up and down on my engorged cock.

I yelped as a long finger penetrated me, setting off a chain reaction. My bowels clenched. My thighs shook. My belly flattened as I sucked in a sharp breath. And then my balls drew up in an orgasm that left me reeling. He steadied me as electrical circuits short-wired. My muscles contracting involuntarily, I bucked like a stallion studding a proud mare. The kid stayed with me, sucking, swallowing, licking, tonguing as I worked my way through the long explosion.

When I finally collapsed weakly against the sink, his lips were still clamped onto my cock. I watched in amazement as he slowly expelled my semi-hard shaft, sending shivers of delight throughout my spent body. He grasped me by the root, gave the slit a final lick, and looked up at me with the innocence of a small child.

"See," he said gently, "I told you they weren't all queer."

Panting for breath, I gasped, "Hell, kid, you may have just converted me!"

Seth stood, making sure his groin brushed my naked flesh, before turning away to wash up in the sink adjacent to me. With weary arms, I hauled up my trousers and made myself presentable.

"Come on, kid. Let's get you to the halfway house."

His voice stopped me cold. "Haven't you forgotten something?"

"What?" I asked, turning to face him.

"My twenty dollars," he replied, a beatific smile on his lovely devil's face.

HEAT

....

ADAM KOZIK

I HAVE BEEN in L.A. now for about five years. I am twenty-eight and moved here from Brooklyn, New York. I used to compete as an amateur body builder and was training for professional status. But when an exercise company offered me a job in southern California, I couldn't pass it up. They hired me to be their video fitness model. I made the move west about a month later.

The work was steady at first, but the promotions team didn't have their shit together. The whole company went bust, and I found myself without a job. Living out here is expensive. I don't need to tell anyone what they don't already know. Since I had devoted so much time to weight training, followed by the competitions, I'd sacrificed going to college for the life I was living. My options were limited, and I'd already missed half the training season. I didn't have a trade to fall back on, not like I have now. I was frustrated and started to immerse myself in working out. I found a good trainer, at a gym on Melrose. I scraped up enough money for membership and fees. I could rely on my trainer for anything. We worked together four hours a day, five days a week. I have a great body, but a physique like this doesn't just happen overnight. I am not an arrogant guy. It takes a lot of discipline and a strong will to make something happen. I believe if you love yourself, you know what you want and find a way to get it.

My trainer knew how desperate I was for work. He came over

to me one day after training and said, "Rocco, why don't you start hustling? I know you can make an awful lot of dough. With your looks, you could easily ask for two hundred twenty an hour."

He helped me put an ad on a Web site, along with a hot body shot: New in town. Italian/Irish, 23 yo, Very discreet. 5'10", 230TXB, 9x7c. Versatile. Call 24 hrs.

I started to get calls right away. On a good night I could make seven hundred. I did whatever the johns wanted. Most of them were married businessmen. I suppose they just didn't have the time to look for sex. I kept all conversations easy. Constant chatter makes me nervous. Once in a while, I would go meet someone who turned out to be a famous actor or a well-known athlete. After the first month, I got into a comfort zone and my libido soared. I was able to save tons of money. I saw some of the same men two or three times a week. My regulars just wanted to suck me while they jerked off. Other times they wanted to see me jerk off on myself while they watched. But whether it came to being a top, bottom, or into leather, military, fetish, jock, s/m, b/d, or whatever, I liked it all. I was paid by the hour. Rain or shine, 24/7, 365 days a year— the door was always open. I stocked up on jockstraps, lube, and some good vitamins. I even bought one of those cylinder penis pumps and gained over an inch in length and girth.

I respected each john for who he was and not for what we were doing. This was a service, and that's how I still see it. You have to be able to get a solid hard-on all the time. And you have to expect the unexpected. You're dealing with a lot of energy and a fairly broad range of personalities. There are also some strange requests. I do have nice, cut abs, and some guys paid extra to come over them. I heard it's good for the skin! I know a famous film director who is into raunch: dirty jockstraps, sweaty armpits, and smelly feet. I would work out before I went to see him. He had a spare room converted into a play area, with a sling, toys, chains, and the whole works. I can't get into too much detail about who these men are. If I betray them, I end up betraying myself. But not all of them are famous people. I see this one guy once every month. Always polite, punctual, and he tips too. He has this thing for bathroom sex in public spaces. I heard it's called tea-rooms. He gives me the name of some place, and we arrange to meet. He likes me to bend over a urinal, and he slips it to me from behind.

I think hustling has enlightened me as a human being. I enjoy its power rush. I am a lot more tolerant of other people's feelings now. But you never know what may happen. I found this out for myself when I got caught off guard. Like they say, it only takes once!

It was a Monday morning, very early, when the telephone started ringing. I can still remember the conversation:

"I liked your ad. I bet you're popular. Get a lot of business?"

"Well, I haven't been doing this for very long. But, yeah actually, I couldn't believe the response, and the money that I am making. Wouldn't you like to see me naked and helpless in front of you? Then you could make me do whatever you want."

"That sounds hot. What do you have in mind?" he said.

"You can order me to lick your asshole. If you ordered me, I would have to do it. What choice would I have?"

I sensed an intense and domineering personality. He told me he used to be a Marine. Then he gave me his stats: he stood six-foot-four and weighed in at 220 pounds. The gym near his place was his favorite hangout. He called himself a real exhibitionist and said he couldn't wait to show off his credentials and his beer-can-thick cock. He said he got off three times a day and was "mostly straight." How bad could that be? Or so I had thought.

He asked if he could come right over, because he had to go to work. I said that would be fine. I was just getting out of the shower when the doorbell rang. I put on a pair of jeans to let him in.

I never expected to see a cop standing in the doorway.

His description was accurate enough, though he was older than me. He was probably in his thirties or forties. I was speechless. At first I thought he was putting me on. Then I heard the muffled voice of a dispatcher over his receiver. This was no joke. I had been busted. I may be smiling now, but it wasn't so funny then.

He stood in my apartment, wearing his uniform and leather jacket. His hair was buzzed close to his head. From what I was able to see at the time, he had an impressive bulge in his blue pants. His finger pointed at my face, and he told me to get against the wall. He had to search for concealed weapons. I stayed calm. I had to maintain from one second to the next. But then his hands started to slide up the inseam on my pants. I had on a pair of well-worn jeans. His hands were rough, just like the expression on his face. They pressed against the inside of my thighs, and over my crotch. He grabbed at my ass through my back pockets.

"What is your dick getting hard for? I can feel it through your pants. Does it turn you on to get a police search?"

I suppose it must have. He told me to stand still. He groped the bulge inside my pants, squeezing my dick and balls, until I was hard. I asked him to be careful. I didn't want to see either one of us get hurt.

"Is that right? It would probably make you feel pretty good to overpower me, right? I wonder what that would feel like? Making a deputy do whatever you want, I bet you'd like that. Maybe you can take control and persuade me not to take you downtown."

Without hearing another word, I turned to him and grabbed his enormous balls. I had them cupped in my hand through his pants. I worked my fingers around the loose sack that held them between his legs. I felt his hot breath on my neck. His cock dangled tantalizingly in his blue pants. I could see he was getting excited, as his dick's curved indent was exposed for my view.

"Are you hot from peeking at my dick? You like watching a cop's bulge in his pants?"

His hand held my own swelling crotch. I knew he wanted it, I could tell by his mannerism. He came on so forceful in the

situation. I was thinking the whole time before, how could I be
busted when he came on to me?

I looked at his strong face, swarthy and macho, with dancing
blue-gray eyes. He was a hot man. I took off his jacket and
unbuttoned his shirt, sliding it over his muscular shoulders and
off his sweaty back. Both of our dicks were hard and throbbing. I
bent over and nibbled on his oversized nipples lurking in the furry
triangle. It made him grunt involuntarily. And that made my mouth
water all the more. I was determined to give him the best I had to
offer. And then there was the ever-tempting bulge inside the blue
pants. He was obviously not wearing underwear. His thick cock
and balls announced themselves to anyone who wanted to look. I
think that kind of sublime exhibitionism is exciting. Even though
he was bigger than me, I took him in my arms for a long, soulful
kiss, with a bear hug. I felt the rise and fall of his big balls and his
stiff cock. I can't remember the last time I got hard so fast. His hand
slid down my bare abs to my crotch. He rubbed my stiff rod, but I
felt impatient and overwhelmed. He buried his face between my
legs as I held his buzzed head in place. He pulled at my fly, and I
felt each button come loose with growing anticipation. The tight
denim gave way, until nothing was between him and my cock. I felt
his hot breath on my trimmed pubes, arousing me even more.

Then he took hold of my balls and sucked my cock. His
warm, wet mouth engulfed my thick rod and sent delicious waves
through my whole body. It felt so fucking incredible I couldn't
believe it. Nothing else seemed to exist at the moment, but just
this hot man kneeling in front of me and the amazing dick-suck
that he was giving to me. I thought maybe he was a hustler too,
because his tongue and lips were so skilled. He slid my tool in
and out of his mouth, slurping and salivating over it. The bursts
of pleasure were coming on fast and intense, but I wasn't ready to
shoot my load just yet and let the cocksucker off so easy. He did
just what I wanted him to, sucked and slobbered, getting my cock
slippery and ready for its next adventure. I called him a suck pig,

and I could tell by his reaction, sucking me harder and deeper, that he liked being used this way.

His hands wandered to my backside. His tongue was teasing my cockhead, and he was rewarded with a slippery wad of pre-come. I shifted my weight, turned around, and bent over. I told him to lick my asshole. His expert tongue and talented mouth played on the rim of my ass, each sensual move probing my demanding hole. His hot tongue lashed at my asshole, licking deeper, wanting to get as much inside as possible. My eyes watered from the tongue-fucking. I lifted my butt into the air, but he took it like a man, as I grunted and growled. I turned around and told him to stand up. Kneeling down, I traced the swell of his cock down his left leg.

"Take it out," he begged.

I unzipped his trousers and reached inside the fly. I closed my fingers around the cock shaft. What a huge fucking dick he had. My eyes widened as some nine inches of thick, clipped cock swung from his fly. I could tell he was proud of his monster, especially when it was being appreciated by another man. I grabbed the cop's hard meat, wrapping my lips around it, and sucked it deep inside my throat. I reached down and gave my cock a few quick jerks.

His dick was stiff as a board, with a helmet head almost as thick as my wrist. I peeled off his trousers. He moaned, almost a growl really. And I sucked in response. I swallowed his dick from head to balls, and back again, without ever taking it out of my mouth. I worked the monster prong down the back of my throat. I was groping at his ass, stroking his asshole with my fingers, probing it gently to loosen it up.

Taking a final slurp on his cock, I stood up. Grabbing him by the shoulders, I spun him around, so his back was facing me. My cock was right up against his ass. I reached inside a drawer and pulled out a condom. I slid the lubed latex over my swollen dick. Pressing down on the cocksucker's back, I told him what I wanted, and he obediently bent forward from his waist. I plunged my entire cock inside of him, knowing the pain it caused him, and got off on it. He grunted in pain but didn't try to get away. Commanding him to pay attention, I told him I was going to show him how to fuck a cocksucker. I fucked him hard and deep, slapping my balls against his ass, as I drove us both to home. He put his weight behind each of my thrusts, riding my cock until he sucked every inch inside him.

"Shit," he groaned. "I want you to fuck my brains out, man!"

I told him he better hold on for dear life, flexing his sphincter, and driving my dick at him from all angles. Every thrust released a new rush of pleasure, and I wanted it to be the strongest, hardest, wildest fuck he ever had. He brought one hand up to his crotch, and I could see him jerking himself off while I was fucking him. He loved it, as I listened to him grunt and growl. I could see by the tremors from his body he was ready to come. His ecstasy pushed me to ram it in him faster.

"Do it, man!" he cried. "Fuck the come out of me!"

One, two, three more strokes, and we were both over the top. I used my cock as a crowbar to open up his tight butt-lips. I felt him at the point of no return. He reached his climax and moaned in carnal pleasure. I could feel his anus begin to contract, and I knew he was shooting his load of come on the floor. Then my own orgasm exploded as this incredible pleasure rocketed through me, signaling its intense power, fantastically wonderful and erotic. My cock emptied its load of sperm in the latex covering it. After a few moments, I slowly pulled my cock from his tender asshole. I peeled off the condom and let it fall to the ground beneath us.

He stood up and turned to face me. His face was flushed, and beads of sweat coursed down his forehead. Then he leaned in and kissed me long and tender. He looked at me with his soft eyes, and I smiled. Our time together had come to an end. But I knew it wouldn't be an adventure either of us would forget. We picked up our scattered clothing and got dressed. Then he set down three crisp one-hundred-dollar bills on the table and walked out the door.

A FOOL AND HIS MONEY

MICHAEL MURPHY

THE DUFF WAS packed that Friday night. It was a seedy pub, deep in the heart of downtown and several blocks off the main strip of nightclubs and restaurants. It had a loyal clientele, and that night they all seemed to be there.

My buddy Ted had dragged me out. I was horny and wanted to jerk off with a dildo up my ass in peace at home. Going out and trolling for sex seemed like a lot of work. Not that I'm lazy; I work two jobs and hit the gym regularly. Plus I cycle around town as much as possible. But maybe that's why I'm often too tired to make the effort to get laid.

That particular night the moon was full, which always stirs up my libido, so I agreed to follow Ted on his adventures.

We waited in a line for twenty minutes, during which time I almost called it off. Lining up just to cruise and have a beer? It seemed ridiculous. But lines always fed on themselves, and by the time we'd entered the dank, ill-lit pub, that line was pushing toward the end of the block.

"Those are the hustlers hanging around all the old daddies," Ted pointed out, yelling in my ear over the blaring disco music.

Even the music was lame. But the place really was packed, and men were cruising each other fiercely determined. I noticed about half a dozen smiling come-ons, but my attention was on the gaggle of young whores and their old prey. If you were an old fuck, over fifty, sixty, or even seventy, you could be sure to find some young thing to your liking, for a price.

But I was barely forty, and didn't want to pay for it. As I stared at the slim young men circling the older dudes, I wondered what it would be like to have one of them at my beck and call. In this city, and this pub, they were mainly Latino—dusky, with deep brown eyes and a lusty gaze.

I recognized one of them from my gym. He was short and cute and wearing a tank top even though it wasn't very warm out. His exercise-sculpted body drew many stares. Worn jeans hugged the rounded cheeks of a very sweet and fuckable ass. I could even make out the dark points of his nipples under his cream-colored top.

He caught me looking and nodded. Those deep brown eyes speared me. I felt myself pushing through the crowd toward him, Ted left behind and practically forgotten. He'd understand. Lust was calling.

"Can I buy you a beer?" I asked him.

"Sure," he replied.

We stared at each other for a few moments while the waiter I'd flagged rushed off for our beers. "How much?" I blurted out, and then I flushed crimson at the obviously rude question. I worried he wasn't actually for sale, though a dozen others just like him hovered nearby.

He was a jewel. His silky black hair was trimmed very close to a neat skull, emphasizing those large brown eyes, with their dark brows and lashes. His nose was blunt and a little large, as were his lips and dimpled chin, but he was actually compact and small when I stood next to him. At six feet tall, I dwarfed him in height and muscular build.

He smiled, straight white teeth flashing in the dim light. At least I hadn't offended him. Could you offend a hustler? Wasn't their trade dependent on ignoring insult or injury? I had no idea actually.

"Depends. Twenty if you just want a quick suck-job in the

alley. I'm cheap for you, just for you." He laughed and moved close to rub his side and thigh against mine. I got hard instantly, as much at the thrill of that easy laugh as the sensation of his firm body touching mine.

"What about a few hours in my bed?" I found myself asking. I could ask at least. It didn't mean I was committed or anything.

He gazed up in my eyes intently, as if gauging the sincerity I wasn't really offering. His smile didn't falter as he nodded and stated his price. "I'll come with you and stay for two hours, tops. One fifty."

A hundred and fifty bucks? It was more, and less, than I'd imagined. Two hours was plenty of time to get my rocks off, though. As I was contemplating, and realizing I actually might be going through with it, he slipped a hand into mine and pulled it behind him to press it along the swelling curve of his ass.

I groped, while men bumped into us and shoved past in their own quest for satisfaction. That ass was so fucking sweet! He rolled his hips into my palm and fingers suggestively while grinning up into my eyes.

He was a good salesman. I had the cash at home, and it wouldn't totally destroy my budget if I splurged. I looked around for Ted. I had to admit I was embarrassed to be picking up a whore. But it didn't matter. That firm ass cheek under my fingers was too tempting to resist. At least I knew this guy from the gym, although his name eluded me. I wasn't expecting to get mugged and robbed like you read about in the papers.

Suddenly I got excited about the prospect of those two hours. My cock jerked against my fly, and then I felt his hand on it, pressing and massaging.

"Okay," I said. "Can we go now?"

I don't know why I was in such a hurry. I already had a hand on his plump can, and he was massaging my dick through my jeans, and I wasn't paying anything for that.

"Absolutely. The sooner the better. That way I'll still have time to come back afterwards and pick up someone else."

That admission only made my cock stiffer. My mind reeled. I imagined being that second guy, getting the boy's just-fucked ass to use, sloppy seconds. My dick was doing all the thinking on that full-moon night.

I lived close by, but we took a cab anyway. While he put his hand in my pants and rubbed my hard rod in the backseat, he said his name was Emilio. I was panting by the time we got to my apartment.

In the elevator, we kissed long and passionately. His mouth opened to mine with total abandon, and I tasted alcohol. I squeezed the taut cheeks of his ass while he rubbed my cock through my jeans with both hands.

We stumbled from the elevator to my apartment door. Inside, he laughed as he asked for his money. "I'll take it now. You can tip me later if I'm good enough."

I had never done this before. I was getting the idea, though. The lure of more money would make my little whore perform with more passion, be more amenable, and be more of a slut for my pleasure.

He stripped seductively while I rummaged through a drawer in the cabinet for his money, condoms, and lube. I glanced at the clock, noting it was eleven. I had until one a.m. to get my fill of Emilio's dusky heat.

Emilio was naked and on his knees. I checked out his cock, fat and full but not hard, dangling down between his creamy brown thighs. He was hairless just about everywhere, even around his dick and balls.

He opened his mouth and licked his lips, sticking out his tongue lewdly. I gasped and stumbled toward him, shedding my clothes in a mad rush. By the time I reached him in the center of my living room, naked, he was ready, mouth open and amber eyes shining.

I thrust my dick at his wet lips, too excited to speak. Emilio lunged forward, slurping up my flared knob with a smack and lick. His lips surrounded it while his tongue lapped at the slit. I shivered, my eyes half-closed as my hustler gave me the most awesome blow job I'd ever received.

Naturally, he was a professional. His goal was my pleasure, and he performed like a well-trained athlete. His tongue tickled my piss slit, milking the oozing pre-come while his satin lips massaged the crown. He made all the nasty sounds that intensified the experience, smacking, slurping, and moaning as if he'd never had such a juicy cock in his mouth before.

How many cocks had he sucked? How many had I? I surrendered to the mouth that roamed over my cock, plunging down to engulf it to the root, then coming back up to tease the aching, sensitive knob. He gurgled and moaned when he had the entire fat thing in his mouth and past his tonsils, then smacked nastily when he held just the cap between his lips.

There were all the extras too. He toyed with my balls with his small, fine-boned hands. He tugged them, rolled them, and massaged them. He ran those hands over my stomach and chest, tickling my nipples and teasing the stiffening nubs. He moved those soft, competent fingers around to my naked ass and cupped the firm cheeks, pulling my dick into his face with them as he took my cock all the way in.

All the while he rolled his own naked ass, his knees wide apart so that I could look down into his open crack and get a look at his puckered, hairless hole. It was as if he were inviting me in down there. His creamy brown hole twitched and convulsed while I leaned over to stare at it. It spoke to me. "Fuck me. Shove your cock up my hot, tight tunnel," it seemed to say.

"I've got to have that ass," I blurted out with a strangled gasp.

Emilio moved back to squat on his knees, letting my cock slide from his suctioning mouth. My purple pole jutted in the air, gooey with spit and twitching between us.

"Si," he breathed in Spanish. He looked up from the big dick in his face and stared into my eyes.

Soft orbs, half-closed with lust, feigned or not, speared me for the second time that night. "My ass is for you. How do you want it? Any way you like it, Mike," he said with a sexy laugh.

I actually hadn't told him my name. He must have remembered it from the gym. It hardly mattered as I thought furiously of exactly how I wanted to drill his sweet, fuckable butt. What was my fantasy? I could have it, right now, no questions asked.

"Just use a condom, please."

Yes, that was a given. But what else? How could I use that tight hole to best get my dick satisfied?

Emilio bent over and got on his hands and knees while I gave thought to how to fuck his sweet butt. He faced away from me and wiggled his plump butt cheeks, spreading his knees far apart and offering me another sight of his puckered asshole.

"Get over the arm of the sofa. Spread your legs and hold open your ass for my dick," I blurted out, wanting him spread-eagled on my fancy living room furniture, his own hands stretching apart his plump ass cheeks and offering his hole to me. The image had my dick jerking and leaking.

Emilio obeyed with alacrity, obviously eager to please. He sprawled over the chocolate-brown sofa, one thigh on either side of the left arm. His creamy brown skin looked pale against that darker background. He reached back and placed both hands on his own ass, pulling open the crack and exposing the crinkled hole.

God! He was so damn hot. Muscular, but plump in the right places. His ass rose in a curving swell from the sides of the sofa's arm. The deep divide was smooth and hairless, the hole in its center puckered open as Emilio pouted it for me.

"Take my asshole, Mike. Take it with your big, juicy cock. I want it bad. I need your big cock so bad, Mike."

The lilting plea was not only nasty, it sounded heartfelt. He wanted my big, fat cock up his tender asshole. I almost laughed at myself. Who was I kidding? He wanted the money and was a good actor.

It hardly mattered. I moved forward, my condom-wrapped dick bobbing with greedy need as I stepped between his plush can. I leaned into his ass, rubbing the stiff shank up and down that parted ass crevice, staring at my huge, purple shank as it thrust between the warm brown cheeks.

He moaned and wiggled his butt against my sticky shaft. I squirted a stream of liquid lube all over my thrusting cock and his naked ass crack. He moaned louder, squirmed more vigorously.

The lube made slurping sounds as my cock rubbed between his plump butt cheeks. I tossed it aside and used my hands to massage the slick stuff into his velvety smooth can and then slid into the crack itself to tease the hole with slick fingers.

"Yes, Mike. Lube up my ass for your cock. Get me all wet for your fat dick."

Emilio's voice was a caressing half-whisper, sending shivers down my spine. I could almost believe him. The way his ass rolled, the way his asshole puckered and pushed out to meet my stroking fingers, the way he crooned his need. I almost believed him.

I pointed the blunt head of my cock at his hole, pushing against the puckered lips. He held himself still, arching his back and waiting. Both his hands still spread his cheeks open for me, while mine were at the base of my cock, aiming.

Slowly I pushed inside him, taking my time as I felt the tight rim part, and open. The lips stretched, the sphincter expanded, and the snug butt tunnel beyond swallowed my aching knob. The huge crown disappeared inside him with a squishy slurp.

"Oh yes, yes! Mike! You're so fucking big in me! I've never had so much cock up my ass! Give me more!"

His voice went up an octave, and he really sounded like he was begging for it now. I was shaking, my cockhead enveloped by pulsing contractions. Heat seared my dickhead. I pushed deeper, not satisfied now until I had all my fat eight inches up his hustler hole. I fed it to him an inch at a time, ever so slowly, while he crooned and begged and sighed, his back arched and his creamy brown buns rolling upward to meet me.

"Take my cock. Take it all. I know you love it. You love dick up the ass as much as you can get it," I snapped out, unable to take the sting out of my voice.

He gasped, my cock sliding home as I spoke. I had all that meat up his ass. He was speared by my dick just like he'd speared me with his look. I felt a searing satisfaction as his ass cheeks trembled and his ass hole quivered around the base of my buried pole.

"Yes. I love it more than anything. Fuck me now, Mike. Fuck me with all that fat dick."

I fucked his ass. I pulled halfway out and then drilled back in. His ass cheeks jiggled as my hips slammed into them. He gasped and groaned. "Yes! Uhhhh! I want it—ugggh—hard—you are so big!"

I pounded his butt with no concern for his pleasure or feelings. The way he grunted and shouted out for more, it seemed that was exactly what he wanted. I'd probably never know the truth. I was certainly enjoying myself, though.

Emilio took cock up the ass in the same way he sucked cock. He was a professional—a real sexual athlete. He rolled his butt, he pushed back to meet my slam drills, he worked his butt hole and tight innards in a squeezing, milking churn that had me on fire every single second.

I dragged him by the shoulders off the couch and onto the floor. I pushed him facedown on the carpet and lay on top of him, kicking his muscular thighs apart and driving into his lubed, stretched asshole. I fucked him like that until I was close to blowing, then pulled out.

"Get up and bend over with your hands around your ankles," I panted out.

He obeyed instantly. Bent over, his ass jutted out in front of me, sweaty-slick and flushed pink over the amber. I spread his ass cheeks with my hands, staring at the swollen hole, the lips pouting out and the center dribbling goo. I'd fucked that tight slot into a loose pit.

I rammed home again, hearing his whooshing groan as all that fat cock gored him. He took it like a champ, managing to remain on his feet as I drilled him from behind while he was bent over and clinging to his own calves.

"Get on your back on the dining room table. Pull up your legs and show me your hole," I gasped out, again when I was just about to blow.

He moved quickly, smiling at me as he crawled up on my dining room table and lifted his legs, grasping his own ankles. That swollen, pouting asshole called to me. I leaned into him and fucked him as hard as I could.

His cock was hard on his belly, dripping pre-come, but neither of us touched it. I wanted him hard and aching for release. It wasn't his satisfaction that mattered, only mine.

And I got that satisfaction. His silky hole swallowed every inch of dick I gave it. He clamped his anal muscles over me and seized my knob whenever it drove into him. He released it when I pulled out, then clamped over the crown at the last moment. He was milking me!

"I'm going to blow!" I shouted.

With him on my dining room table, his feet in the air, I shot my load up his ass. I let it go, the condom covering my cock filling with goo. His asshole pulsed around my throbbing meat.

I pulled out and yanked off the condom. More jizz spurted out, and Emilio rose up to pump me dry with one slender hand.

"Nice load, Mike. Nice fuck. I've never had it so hard, and so good. You're a real stud man."

Emilio grinned and his eyes sparkled. His dick was still ramrod stiff as he pumped my draining dick and gazed up into my eyes.

Where had the time gone? It was almost one a.m. Time was up, and even though I was going limp and feeling totally played out, I had his naked, brown body close to mine, and I realized I wanted more. Much more.

"Can we do this again?" I asked, hating myself for asking.

"Of course. Same price—just for you, though. You know where to find me." Emilio moved into my arms, still seated on the dining room table. He kissed my neck and rubbed his hard cock all over my belly. I gasped and reached out to cradle his plump, hot can. I lifted him off the table and held him, his thighs wrapping around mine.

I wanted him again! But he slid from my grasp and dressed. He didn't mention anything about a tip, but I was so overwhelmed, I found another fifty in my drawer and handed it to him as he slipped out my door.

What the fuck had happened? I'd just had the best sex of my entire life. I wanted more. But was I willing to pay for it?

I was and I did. I did again, and again. Twice more, a hundred fifty bucks and a fifty-dollar tip, and his ass sprawled out in every conceivable manner in every corner of my apartment. After he left, I could still see him there in my mind. I was obsessed with his dusky, fuckable ass.

Obsession, love, whatever. After the sixth time in three weeks, Emilio was an addiction. I had to quit. At the Duff, where I always found him, I asked Emilio if he wanted to do it for free, and he just laughed.

"Maybe when I'm old like you, Mike. But for now I'd like to make some cash while I'm still hot."

In the end, I was just a fool with his money. Love was not for sale, I was just a trick to him. Once every few months I still go to the Duff just to see him there, and he smiles at me and nods, but I'm too afraid to approach. The addiction hasn't gone away, it's just held at bay. Maybe it never goes away.

CONSIDER

TROY STORM

"ARE YOU OUT of your mind, dork?" My straight best buddy, Wilson, almost dropped the bar of weights he was hoisting over his chest before wrestling it onto the stanchion. He slid out from under the weight and off the prone bench to confront me, fists planted solidly on his trim hips, square jaw set. "That is a stupid idea. Selling yourself," he grunted derisively. "Hell, you could get all kinds of … sick or something. Stupid."

I knew Wilson wasn't going to like it, but I had to tell him what I had in mind. We had been buddies since forever and told each other everything. That didn't change even when I told him I worshiped the ground his big feet plodded on and intended to follow him to the ends of the earth—after which he proceeded to wonk his willy into the wonderland of every willing high school pussy he could, just to prove to me there was no way, no hope.

Of course, all that did was keep me boned up imagining how Wilson looked boned to the ready—even if not ready for me.

"Stop watching old black-and-white movies with syrupy sound-tracks," he had snarled, but I also noticed he didn't stop getting naked around me as we both developed into post-teen hormonally raging studs.

He never settled into just one of his ever-ready pussies either, but kept plowing the field. Eventually, in the heat of first love, I figured he would run out of prospects and there I'd be … waiting.

For him to consider the possibilities.

But he didn't and I wasn't—having started work on my own track record. Equally wide-ranging and willing.

Finally, the thought of his ever-developing dick going where no gay man would want to go and my own experiments in the male skin trade dulled my ardor, and we drifted back into the old-sneaker, buddy-buddy relationship we had always had before sex reared its glistening, purple-nosed, drizzling snout.

"I could use the money," I explained practically as we headed for the gym showers. "There are some really classy sites on the Internet. Cyber hustling is not that sleazy. At least, I wouldn't be standing around on corners in sleazy neighborhoods in too-tight cutoffs worried about having my old high school teachers drive up."

"You wear those floppy cargos like they're too-tight shorts anyway," Wilson sniffed, stripping off his gym nylons and thumbing down his straining jock. "You've been sticking your nose in too many of these." He shoved the sweet-scented handful of overstuffed hope in my face and strutted away before turning to pop my crotch with a heavy towel.

"What the fuck does that mean?" I yelped, grabbing my stung dick, causing the other guys in the room to look up and smirk as I dashed after him.

"You've got to switch to jockeys, dude. The way big ole you flops around in those oversize knee-lengths is advertising enough."

"It's a noble profession." I soaped up furiously, knowing it was the only safe way for me to go, paying his dirty mind no mind. "Paid companionship. And you should see the prices they charge. I'm in good shape. I'm companionable. I could make a bundle in a couple of years."

He cut me a look out of the corner of his clear blue eyes. The warm water needled over his chiseled pecs, sending diamond-glinting sprays cascading over and around his thick, upright nipples.

I followed the sudsy streams flowing down his washboard abs
and watched them disappear into the thicket of dark blond dick
fur. They emerged with half the steaming water gushing down to
paint his tightly packed, fist-sized ball sac with a nubby sheen, and
the other half to curl caressingly around his semi-solid downward
arch of succulent flesh before white-watering over the rapid of
the thick flange of his bulbous stalk-end and coalescing off the
twin dips that surrounded his gaping piss slit in a solid stream of
lost hope.

My jealous mouth, my lips, not even my aching fingers had
ever traced that liquid path, and the possible dream had been
pissed away long ago.

But just to be the sexless bosom buddy of such a stud pole
was not enough. I wanted Wilson to understand the path I had
chosen. He was the one who had dragged me through the hell of
creating myself in his own hot, superbly molded physical image.
I, too, was a chiseled pile of seething hormones. But it wasn't just
selling my sex I planned. It was the possibility of finally taking
charge of my life. Making my own decisions. It was now time to
cash in on all the hard work.

And on all the frustration.

A few weeks later, with a suppressed sigh of relief, I let my
first customer out of my small apartment. He beamed: happy and
satisfied. Definitely planning to call again when he was in town.
And to recommend me to his friends.

Wilson was waiting outside. I stared at him, amazed, as the
startled customer eyed the glowering hot shit with a mixture
of confusion and lasciviousness. My straight buddy patted me
tenderly on the cheek and slid between me and the older man
into the apartment.

I forced myself not to slam the door in frustration. "What are
you …?"

"He was fat and forty if he was a day, dorkus. Jeez, man, have
you no standards at all?" Wilson sailed into my small tarted-up

living room.

"He was lonely and misunderstood, and I gave him his money's worth," I announced defensively.

It hadn't been nearly as bad as I had figured it might be. The guy wasn't an Adonis, but he was nice and couldn't have been more appreciative. Once I got past dealing with an older, less well-maintained body, it was a piece of—maybe not cake, but at least a comfort-food bowl of fairly firm Jello.

"He was a slob," Wilson growled. "But I guess if you start at the bottom, there's nowhere to go but up."

"He was nervous—at first—but I got him hard enough to work with, and he had a great set of hairy balls." Wilson was being a snot. "His ass was nice and tight—once I worked my way in—and even if he couldn't take it all—I'm pretty damn well built, you know—he loved every min—"

My buddy flopped his fine fanny on the sofa, his big hands clamped to his ears, shaking his head. His finger threaded through his blond tangle.

He sat up straight. "I've had an idea that just might save your sorry ass. But I don't want you to get your gonads in a knot. It's not going to happen. It'll just be sex. Okay? To check things out."

"What the fuck are you talking about, Wilson?" My gonads were already knotting.

"I got to talking with some of the guys at the office. The career-track straight ones. Bullshitting about sex and/or the lack of it. You know that crap. They're mostly losers—but they're basically okay dudes, and they're in good shape. They just need to get their rocks off. But no broads. Too much baggage. So I told 'em about ... your service, and some of them are willing to give it a try. They're practically coming in their high-end Dockers," he ended ruefully.

"Wilson, are you pimping for me? I can get my own ..."

"Look, little D, I've checked 'em out. I think you should know something about those on whom you're spraying your bodily fluids. Who knows what these old desperate farts might do to you? You might end up with a psycho or something. This way, I can keep an eye on … who you fuck … and who fucks you." He stood up and stuck out his hand. "Deal?"

"Look, wonk, you're not the keeper of my fucking." But the firm grip of his palm, the hot press of flesh, the glinting surety in his steely gaze, did me in. I shrugged and started to agree.

And then I got double done.

Wilson's thick blond eyebrows pulled together with determination. "And I think I oughta know what the fuck is going on."

I stared back at him. He still had hold of my hand, contemplating our grip before raising his blond head and hitting me with a dead-on glare. "I think it's time we did it." He had obviously finally worked it out. A tiny smirk played around his full lips. "I need to know exactly what 'services' you offer so I can do a good job of selling. And I'm taking a cut." The smirk vanished. "But it's not going to mean anything more than just sex. There's no way more is going to happen, and I don't want you to get all uptight and blubbery. Deal?" He tightened his grip.

Nothing but sex with one of the hottest guys in town—my straight buddy? It would be tough. I'm an emotional type guy, but I'd manage. I nodded my head solemnly.

A huge sigh of relief rushed from Wilson's broad chest. He grabbed me around the shoulders, his eyes crinkling and his dimples digging huge gullies beneath his high cheekbones. "Good. I knew you could handle it." He squeezed me hard and noogied my head. "If you're determined to do this stupid thing, we might as well do a good, safe job, right?"

We?

Fine with me.

"How about we get right to it?" he said.

I checked his crotch—he was ready.

"Okay, I've got a couple of hours before my next client."

"You've got another guy coming?"

My lip curled. "Yeah. He'll be doing that too. More than once, if he's lucky. Of course, you dumb ass. I'm in business. And this one's even older. He's near fifty. But loaded, Wilson. He could be my sugar daddy."

Wilson's jaw dropped and then snapped shut. "Okay, then let's get to it. What do you do first?"

"Make the guy comfortable. Take off his clothes." I unbuttoned Wilson's shirt and slowly ran my hand over his chest, gently palming his thick nipples. They stiffened as I stroked. "Nipples are highly sensitive. They're a good place to begin." I pulled off his shirt and lowered my head. My lips o-ringed over an upright nub and suckled.

His breath pulled in. "That's good. Girls don't usually suck guy's nipples. That's a good selling point."

"Girls don't do a good a job at sucking guys' dicks either," I said, unzipping Wilson's chinos and shoving them down to his ankles. His white jockeys were bulging and moist. I stretched the waistband and eased the soft fabric over the huge hard-on. I hadn't seen him fully packed in years. He had developed into a total gut-gouger.

I opened my mouth and gouged. All the way down. The whole nine yards—inches.

Wilson grabbed my shoulders and gasped. "Holy …"

I clamped my throat muscles over his throbbing porker and milked the boiling seed right out of his hard brass knockers.

His powerful body shook as he fired half a dozen bolts of clotted cream straight into my gut. Talk about premature ejaculation. I peeled my lips from around his quivering pole and extracted the column of drained flesh from between my dragging lips.

"Usually," I said, helping him hobble to the bedroom, "guys give me a little more time to work my magic." I laid him down and slowly pulled his clothes off.

"Jeez, man, nobody … I mean, no girl … uh, that was amazing."

I slipped a soft-rock CD onto the player and went around the room lighting candles. "Then they get a general massage—dick and balls and ass included—and usually from that I can tell what really turns them on."

"You mess around with a guy's ass? Yuk."

"I'll check with you later on that yuk, but first I want to mess around with your balls." I crawled up on the bed, pushed Wilson's muscular thighs apart, and started licking up his inner thighs. He giggled.

"That tickles, man."

"Does this tickle too?" I suctioned onto his thick ball sac, chewing on the twin ovals packed inside, popping the whole package in and out of my mouth. My tongue dragged over the damp, nubby surface of the straining flesh, flattening the coating of curling hairs.

Over my head, knocking against my short-cut, his dick was rigid again. Curved rock, thickly dripping pre-come. Wilson's breath came faster. "That's cool. I didn't know balls were so … ballsy." He snickered.

I pushed his ass up and sucked on his perineum, rubbing my chin into the fat mound, nuzzling nearer and nearer his ass hole. Spreading his tight, round butt mounds, I tongued around his forest-protected anal entrance.

"Wh— … what're you planning to do?"

"Shhh. Just relax and go for it, little willie," I murmured, fluttering my tongue over his trembling butt-button. I sucked on my middle finger and screwed it in. Wilson grunted, his ass squirming as I gently reamed his virgin hole while my mouth guzzled at his sphincter.

I pulled out from between his legs. His dick was reaching for his abs. "You want to fuck me, Wilson? You ought to know what it feels like. So the guys will know what kind of tight, hot hole they're getting as a replacement."

"Uh …" Quickly I grabbed an extra large and pulled a rubber

over him, not taking the time to offer flavors or colors or tastes. It was tight. I squirted on a load of lube, smeared it over his stalk, and squatted above his hips.

It took effort to pry his meat from its horizontal position and aim it at my hungry hole. My butt sank down, my sphincter splitting wide and sucking him in. The rectal tissues stretched to their capacity to become engorged with his rampant male fuck prod.

"Aagh. Ungh. Holy batmobile. Fucking awesome." Wilson humped his hips up to drive himself deeper. "Damn. You are hot, man. You are so freaking tight." He grabbed the top of my thighs to lever himself up and pound my ass. Six to eight solid inches of power-packed meat slammed deep inside and ripped almost all the way out, my innards crashing in and then crammed aside by the driving pole. Damn, for a straight boy he sure knew how to make a gay ass sing.

He grabbed my flopping rigid dick and pummeled his fists up and down the length of the raging meat. "Shoot off, man. Shoot off with me. I'm fucking coming. Show me your juice, man. Show me the money!"

I fired and hit him square in the face. He gasped and collapsed backwards. I reached back, circled his nuts with my thumb and forefinger, and jammed my middle finger up his ass, punching his prostate. He yelled and unloaded into the rubber crammed deep in my hole. Over and over. Laughing and snorting and rubbing the come out of his eyes and into his tangle of blond surfer-dude waves.

"You fucking horse," he laughed. "That'll teach me not to aim a loaded gun at my own freaking face."

I lay down on his sweat-drenched front, his dick still curved up my ass, and licked my come off his cheeks and eyebrows. I was pretty damn impressed with myself. Usually I only spray a guy's chest. I didn't want Wilson to think his dick up my ass was something special.

I worked up to his mouth and continued licking. He licked back. Soon we were slobbering and smacking and sucking on each other's tongues. His bobbing sponge turned into a Grade AA well-cooked beef bone up my ass as my own meat, hot-dogged between our grinding bellies, swelled to unload another volley.

Wilson pulled his wet kisser away, chuckling. "That is truly weird, man. Sucking face with a guy. What's it like, sucking on a guy's dick?"

I levered up off him, my ass giving a pop of disapproval, and circled over him in a classic 69, my dick dangling in his face.

"Shit," he muttered. "I could have waited till I'd buzzed your butt again. You are one dangly dude there." He eyed my flopping double four and the twin smooth sacs swaying halfway down its length.

"I don't expect you to be an expert at first," I instructed. "But this might give you some pointers." I licked at his dick and dragged my teeth up the fat underbelly, sucking on the bulging come tube and lapping at the fat, pumping veins.

Sticking it in my mouth, I pulled my lips up its length, thrumming over the packed-to-bursting knob and sucking out the greasy nectar. I pushed my face back down into his matted bush, vacuuming hard on the throbbing manpole.

He sucked on my dick, manfully. He choked. He got the giggles. He licked and slurped and sniggered. I should have been annoyed. I was so turned on I barely had time to warn him before the gush again fired against the side of his face.

When I came, my jaws automatically went to work masticating his deep-throated meat. He came again, squeaking and gasping, bouncing his hips up off the mattress.

We finished, pulled the pieces together, and relaxed, lying reversed on each other. "I want to fuck you," I told his ass as I massaged the thick, hard, round pillows.

"What, doofus?" he asked dreamily at my other end. I realized he had been playing with my nuts.

"I said I want to fuck your ass."

"I don't know, dude, that hole is pretty tight. I thought you were going to lose a finger before. I wouldn't want to do harm to your main asset." He worked his mouth over my dick and sucked on the throbbing glans. Pre-come surged into his mouth. He slurped it down. "I'm getting used to it," he noted to himself. "I could probably get used to swallowing come if I had to."

I hopped up. "Okay, doggie, on your knees. I'm gonna give you a lesson in how to loosen up a guy."

Wilson wasn't convinced, but he did as he was told. I contemplated his ass. It was a beauty. Round and firm and tight, the color of the pale unsunned flesh rosying as it neared his ass hole, the rose-brown cavern canyoned deep between the twin mounds. I pried the hillocks apart and applied my loving lips. He cried out in sweet agony. "Un-fucking-believable."

My tongue and my fingers did their work, pushing, prodding, reaming wide, licking, greasing. When I pushed in two digging digits and stirred them around, he unleashed a load onto the sheets. Four or five healthy globs. The guy seemed to have an unlimited supply of manmilk. Good. I would never go thirsty again.

Still, two fingers is about one-third the circumference of my ready rod. I figured that was enough for the first lesson. And there would be more. And more.

"Wilson, I want you to fuck me, face to face." I pushed myself up and stood over him on the bed, gently bouncing.

"Yeah?" He looked up, his gaze running up the inside of my legs and lingering at my swinging balls and rampant rocking meat before sliding up my flat abs and over my pecs to come to rest on my face.

His look was serene, but not quite satiated. A slight smirk played about his moist, quirked upper lip.

"Yeah. I want to see you while you do it. See how you enjoy it." I pulled him up onto his knees and reached for a condom. "I want you to see me. See the face of a happy man." I flopped onto my back and threw my legs up on his shoulders.

He grinned. The canyons in his cheeks etched deeper. "You are one fucking romantic dude. But I told you, there's no way, it's just sex. Just two guys getting each other off."

"Right." I gasped as he pushed in, ramming past my clutching sphincter and driving into my prostate. The dazed gland buzzed. My whole body zinged as he uppercut his massive meat into my willing, guzzling hole.

"So damned fucking tight," he murmured, the smirk growing wider, as he picked up speed, his pole pistoning in and out of me powerfully. "It's enough to make a guy… consider."

RELIGIOUS AFFLICTION

WILLIAM HOLDEN

NO ONE UNDERSTANDS me. They never have, and probably never will. They don't understand how I can do what I do and wake up every morning with a smile on my face. The best answer that I can give for my choice of career is—I'm an addict. I'm addicted to men. It doesn't matter to me who they are, what their preferences are, or what they look like, it's all the same: hot, naked, sweaty sex, and best of all I get paid for it.

You may have noticed that I mentioned waking up in the mornings. I'm not a night person, never have been. So I've had to adapt my career to fit my lifestyle. I'm not like most hustlers, in that I don't find my clients in dark alleys or on street corners late at night. I've made my turf the local mall. Now, I know what you're thinking, but you'd be surprised how busy my schedule is. Five, six, sometimes up to eight men every day, seven days a week, and at my prices I can easily take home in one week what most people take home in a month. I also get a much better clientele than most of the other boys in town, especially the straight married men who want a lunchtime romp. The way I look at it is that they've got nothing better to spend their money on, so why not me? I'm worth it. Not to brag or sound conceited, but I was blessed with good looks and a perfect body. I've never had to work out in the gym, and you would never know by looking at my firm, tight body. I keep the dark brown hair trimmed on my chest and make sure it's sculptured just so as it trails down my stomach and into my pants. I'm a bit shorter than most of my clients, only five-six, but I think they like it that way, wrapping their hands around my slim waist during the heat of the moment, my dark brown hair damp from perspiration, beads of sweat running down my chiseled face. Oh yeah, they like me a lot and don't mind paying for it.

It was difficult at first—not the job, but finding a place to take my clients. I used whatever resources I could find, including bathrooms, unlocked parked cars, and loading docks, but my clients deserved better; I needed a permanent space to entertain in. One day I happened to be walking through the hotel lobby of the Ritz Carlton on my way to work when I noticed the hotel manager behind the counter. Steve was his name, and he was one of the many straight married men I've serviced during lunch. The blinds flew open in my mind. I could almost see my new place. I approached the desk where he stood. He looked up at me with instant recognition. A nerve twitched near his left eye.

"T.J., what are you doing here?" He looked around nervously.

"It's good to see you again, Steve." I flashed him one of my sincere smiles. "Don't look so worried, I'm not here to blow your cover. Your secret is safe with me. By the way, how is your family?"

"T.J., stop playing around. What do you want—money?"

"Of course not, what type of businessman do you think I am?" I tried to act hurt, but just couldn't manage it. "You always pay me quite well, if I remember correctly. Did I ever tell you what a great fuck you are?" A single bead of sweat ran down his neck and disappeared into the blue color of his shirt. I knew I had gotten his attention. "Okay, I'll get to the point. You see, I need a room, one that I will have complete access to 24/7, and you're going to arrange it. Oh, and all costs and services will, of course, be on the house."

"I can't possibly do that. Why are you doing this?"

"It's simple." I leaned further over the counter to close the gap between us. "I help you with your needs, and you help me with mine. Besides, you wouldn't want your company, or for that matter your wife and kids, to find out about us. Would you?"

Needless to say, I picked up the card key to my new suite the following day. You see, in my world the only person you can count on is yourself. No one else gives a shit. You're just a body, a play toy, and you won't make it in my world if you can't accept that simple fact.

Yet even with the drawbacks, I wouldn't change a thing. You get to meet a lot of interesting people, from those who are seasoned sex addicts to the other extreme: those who have never had sex before with another man. Matthew was in the latter category.

It was a Sunday morning, the mall had just opened, and people were crowding in to get out of the heat of the day. I was in my usual attire: faded denim jean shorts, sandals, and a white T-shirt. The shorts had several strategic tears in the fabric to show off the fact I wasn't wearing any underwear. It wasn't hard to figure out what I was doing there, even for the less adept people.

I could smell the fresh-baked bread coming from the Atlanta Bakery. My stomach grumbled with the scent, so I headed over for a quick bite to eat before my day got started. I placed my order for a sausage, egg, and cheese croissant and a large orange juice and found a table nearby. It was then that I noticed someone eyeing me.

I looked up to meet his eyes. He quickly looked away. He didn't move as I continued to stare. He was attractive, and younger than most of my clients, with almost boyish features. His hair, the color of coal, was styled without a hair out of place. His piercing eyes remained motionless. He was dressed in a pair of khaki-colored Dockers and a black button-down shirt. The shirt was buttoned to the top, giving him an appearance of innocence and reserve.

My order was called. I left the table and walked over to the counter. The smell of the sausage and egg made my stomach grumble again. When I turned around, I caught him once again staring at me. I smiled at him. He shook his head slightly as if disgusted with my flirtatious personality and went back to his laptop.

He intrigued me, I have to admit. I'm usually very good at interpreting people's movements and signals, but his I couldn't quite get a handle on. He stood up and took his half-eaten lunch to the trash. It was then that I understood his interest in me. His shirt was embroidered with the logo of a local right-wing religious group whose mission was to wipe out the gay population, one fag at a time. He wiped his mouth on a napkin and tossed it in after his lunch. I watched as he paused for a moment. His eyes were closed. He was clasping his hands together in front of his crotch, as if praying. He took a deep breath, opened his eyes, and walked toward me. He stopped and stood at my table as if waiting for an invitation to sit down. I decided to play his game.

"Can I help you?" My voice was playful with a slight edge to it. My eyes scanned his body before making contact with his. I made my interest in him obvious. The muscles in his jaw twitched before he spoke.

"I'd like to help you. May I sit down?" He spoke slowly. His alto voice was confident, as if he had practiced his lines. "My name is Matthew."

"Sure, help yourself. I'm T.J. But what makes you think I need any help?" I took a bite of my breakfast, which had already started to cool. I hated cold eggs.

"I can help you overcome your problem." He sat down across from me. His interlocked fingers rested on the table. "It's not too late to ask forgiveness and start a new life. I can help you find God."

The look on his face was sincere. I can't even imagine the look on my own face as he spoke those words. "I don't see it as a problem. This is the career I have chosen." I slipped my foot out of the sandal and caressed his leg. I could feel his calf muscle tighten as he realized what I was doing. He quickly slid his chair back out of my reach. He looked around nervously.

"Career?"

"Yes, I'm a hustler."

"You mean you have sex for money?" He took a deep breath and moved back into the table. "It's worse than I thought. Please, won't you let me help you?" He reached out as if by instinct to grab my hand. His long fingers trembled as they grabbed mine. Small dark hairs covered the knuckles of each finger. His grip was firm, reassuring. "My organization can help. We'll help you give up this life and set you on a new path, one free from sin."

I stared at him. His large, dark eyes were pleading with me. Long strands of hair had fallen out of their holding place and hung across his forehead. He reminded me of the porn star Joey Stefano in the movie *More of a Man*. If he only knew how sexy he was and how ridiculous his beliefs were, he could be having the time of his life. I began to feel sorry for him; it wasn't his fault he believed these things.

"Please, let me help you."

I couldn't take it anymore. I needed to get him alone. My intuition is almost always spot-on, and I could feel that there was more to Matthew than he was ready to accept.

"Perhaps you're right. I've just never had anyone who cared enough about me."

"I promise. I'll help you through it." His face lit up. "Let me get my laptop, and we can go over our program so you'll know what to expect." He turned in his chair, stood up, and walked over to his table. He quickly gathered his papers and placed them on the laptop case along with the computer and managed to make it back to me without spilling anything. "Okay …"

"Wait. Let's not talk about this here. I'm a little uncomfortable talking about this out in the open … can we go someplace else?" I could tell he was a little uneasy at this request, so I quickly added, "Please, I really need your help."

"Well, we could go back to the center; it's not far from here."

"I don't know. I'm a little worried about that." I bent my head down as if embarrassed. "Everyone will be looking at the poor homosexual. I'll feel … I don't know, like I'm a freak show." I raised my head and looked directly at him. "If I'm going to do this, I'd prefer to do it one on one with you. You promised you'd help me."

"And I will." He reached out and grabbed my hand again. "If it will help you, we'll do it where you feel most comfortable."

"Thank you. I know with your help I'll be able to get through this." I stood up and waited for him to follow. "I know a place in the mall where we can go." We walked silently through the mall. The echoes of families laughing filled the space around us. I turned down a small corridor with no storefronts, only service doors where the mall employees came and went from work.

"Where are we going?"

"I know the manager of the new Kenneth Cole store they're putting in. It's still under construction, but I have a key." I stopped at the service door and turned to look at him. "I know this seems strange, but I'll feel much more comfortable away from all the noise and people."

"Isn't this illegal?" He held me back by the arm. "I don't know about this."

"It's not illegal. The manager told me I could use this space anytime I needed to. It's not like we're breaking in." I felt as if I was losing him, and I hate to lose, especially when it comes to getting paid. And he would pay—one way or another. "Matthew, I just need to know I'm doing the right thing. I need your help." I unlocked the door and let him into the hallway.

We were suddenly surrounded by concrete. A dimly lit hallway led to the various doors for the department stores. I stopped at the fourth door to the right and unlocked it. It creaked as I opened it. The noise filtered down the hallway. Matthew walked in behind me. The room was dark, but one could sense the large empty span of the store. I turned the switch, and the room became illuminated with a few service lights. The floor was scattered with pieces of broken drywall. The air was thick with the smell of sawdust.

"There's an outlet against the wall," I pointed in the general direction, "if you need your computer." He stood a few feet away and stared at me, his arms still clutching his laptop and papers. "Is anything wrong?"

"No. I guess not." The words seemed to tremble off his lips. "This just isn't usually how things are done." He walked to the other side of the room and sat his laptop down on a small wooden crate. I soon heard the familiar sounds of Windows booting up and joined him as he sat Indian-style on the floor. "First, I want to give you an overview of our organization and its history." He looked through his case, fingering papers.

"Can I ask you something?" He looked up at me, his fingers still resting inside the files. "Have you been with anyone before… I mean sexually?" He seemed taken aback by my blunt question and hesitated before he answered.

"No. Of course not. Sexual intercourse should only be performed by a married couple, and only for reproducing."

"But don't you ever wonder what it would be like?" I brought my knees up to my chest and wrapped my arms around them. I slowly caressed the hair on my legs. I saw his eyes watching my hands. My legs were spread just far enough apart that my package hidden beneath my shorts would show. "I mean not just the sex, but how it would feel to have someone kiss you or touch you."

"No. Never. I don't allow myself to think of such things." He was becoming flustered. The muscles in his jaw trembled again. He kept trying to locate the papers, but his eyes always returned to the movement of my hands.

"It's okay. It's only us in here." I reached out and rested my hand on his ankle. "If I'm going to be honest with you, you can at least be honest with me." He stared at my hand, then looked up at me. He didn't move away.

"No. Anytime those types of thoughts come to me, I push them away. God would punish me for thinking such things." He started to move. "Perhaps this wasn't a good idea. I should go."

"No, please stay." My grip tightened around his ankle. Gentle, yet firm. I moved closer to him, returning my legs to their earlier position. I could feel his heart beating through the thick air. His eyes were wide, his breathing heavy. I caressed his cheek with my fingers. His eyes closed briefly. A small gasp escaped his lips.

"Please don't." He looked at me with those beautiful dark eyes that seemed to plead with me not to stop. "This is wrong. It's against God's wishes."

I raised myself on my knees and leaned into him. My hands braced against the floor to either side of him. I brought my lips to his ear and whispered, "Does being this close to me feel wrong?" I could feel the heat from his body. His skin was damp with desire. I moved back in front of him, close enough so he could feel my breath on his face. I could tell he was scared, but not of me. I knew he wanted me, and I would make sure he got what he wanted. My lips pressed against his for a brief second, and then I pulled back. His entire body trembled. I leaned in again and kissed him harder. He kissed me back. My mouth left his and moved down to his neck.

"Oh God," he gasped.

"God has nothing to do with this, Matthew. It's just you and me."

I slowly unbuttoned his shirt, exposing the thick, dark hair covering his chest. I moved my face closer—his scent intoxicated me. There was no cologne, no perfumed deodorant, just the purest smell of a man's body. I lightly kissed his skin through the tangle of hair as I undid each button, until I reached the waistband of his pants. I slid his shirt off of each shoulder as I kissed his neck. He fell back against the concrete floor, drywall dust spread into the air.

He didn't touch me or make any advances. He lay there motionless as I began to run my tongue back over his chest. His nipples were erect. I teased them, one, then the other, back and forth till they were wet with my spit. I moved down his chest, following his well-defined abs and the treasure trail that led to secrets only he knew about. My tongue moved along the edge of the waistband of his pants. I could feel him trembling, the muscles contracting as I made my way across his stomach. I sat up, straddled his legs, and began to undo his belt, when he made his first move.

"Wait." He raised himself on his elbows and looked at me. His words were intermittent between breaths. "I've never been naked in front of another man before."

I didn't respond, but slowly moved my hands to my waist and pulled my T-shirt up over my head. The air, though stagnant, felt good against my skin. I watched as his eyes scanned my body, absorbing every inch of me.

My cock began to ache. I could feel the blood pulsing through the veins as I watched Matt watching me. My cock grew longer and thicker in my shorts. This wasn't just another paying client for me anymore. Matt gave off a sexual energy that I could feel through every fiber of my body. He didn't have to touch me — his eyes ripping at my clothes, caressing my body, was enough to set me on fire. I stood up and unbuttoned my fly. Matt licked his dry lips briefly as I exposed the thick, dark patch of pubic hair surrounding my cock. The shorts fell away to my ankles, exposing every inch of my body. A bead of sweat dripped down the side of Matt's face. I could tell he was nervous and a bit ashamed at his obvious desire to be with me. I kicked the shorts off to one side and knelt down next to Matt. His eyes followed my every move.

"Do you want to touch me?"

He didn't respond by voice. He just looked at me as his hand slowly made its way to my chest. The air was getting hot, or perhaps it was our bodies. My chest glistened with perspiration as he reached for me. He paused. His fingers trembled. I took his hand and led it to my body. A small moan escaped Matt as his fingers made contact with my skin. He ran his hand over my chest and stomach, his eyes mesmerized by the sight of what he was doing.

"You feel so good." His voice was faint and far away. "I know I will go to hell for this, but I can't stop, not now." He looked at my solid cock protruding from my body. His finger moved down my stomach and brushed through the tangles of my pubic hair. He jumped slightly as my cock bobbed in response to his touch. His finger made small circular motions over my hairy balls before gliding up the base of my cock. A small drop of pre-come formed at the head. We both watched as it pulled away from my cock and slowly oozed its way to the floor.

I couldn't take it anymore. His fingers were filled with an electric charge that sent bolts of pleasure through my body. I moved down and slowly undid his pants. He leaned back and watched as I removed the rest of his clothes. His hard cock was long and skinny, with a thick layer of skin that covered its head. The bluish-purple veins were swollen with excitement. Long, dark hairs were matted to its wet shaft. I moved over on top of him and braced myself up on my hands. I could feel the heat coming off his body as I lowered my crotch to his.

Our cocks met, pressing against each other, squeezing the pre-come out of each other's shaft. Matt began to moan, and I used my cock to stroke his. My hips moved back and forth, smearing his cock and balls with my pre-come.

I moved down his body, until my face was near his crotch and my legs were at the side of his head. My tongue licked the salty flavor of his damp skin. I moved closer to his cock. His body shook violently as he felt my mouth slip over his foreskin. Bit by bit I took another inch of his cock into my mouth. Each downward movement sent Matt into convulsions of excitement, and more of his juices into my hungry mouth. He gripped my leg and began running his hands over my skin. His moisture was sweet, warm, and fresh. The thought of his beautiful dick, never before being tasted, thrilled me. He never spoke. Moans of pleasure were his voice.

As I reached the full length of his cock, his foreskin molded to the back of my throat. I stopped and enjoyed the pulsing beat of his heart as it echoed through the veins of his cock. I used my tongue to stroke his shaft, while my mouth remained motionless. I could feel his pre-come dripping down the back of my throat. As I swallowed, the muscles in my throat squeezed the loose skin of his cock, releasing what remained in the folds of the skin.

My cock was becoming sore from the pressure. I touched myself and felt the warmth building inside of me. My one hand remained on my own cock, caressing the wet head and spreading the dampness down the shaft. My other hand found its way to the tightness of Matt's virgin ass. I could feel the muscles of his ass tighten as he received my touch. His body trembled again. The soft puckered skin of his hole was dry. I reached down to my cock to wet my fingers before going any further.

I moved upward on his cock. My tongue darted inside his foreskin and found the softness of his cockhead waiting below. His piss slit seemed large. I slipped my tongue into it, feeling the warmth and wetness of the tissue. His moaning became more pronounced. His head moved from side to side. His breathing grew heavier in short, deep pulses. I knew he was getting close to his first orgasm.

I made my movements more forceful. As my mouth continued riding his hot, throbbing cock, my finger continued to work on his hairy ass. Finally it released, almost swallowing my finger.

"Shit!" His sudden voice startled me. "Oh God, that feels amazing!"

I couldn't respond except to continue sucking his cock, faster and harder, until my face was slapping against his stomach. The sweat on my face matted his pubic hair to his stomach. The warmth and dampness with each touch drove me closer to the edge.

My finger moved farther inside of him, then two fingers, then three. His ass was opening up for the first time. He was puffing and panting with desire. I could feel the pressure building inside of him. Suddenly, my hand on my cock was replaced by his. He clumsily pulled and stroked my swollen cock, yet his touch thrilled me like nothing else ever had.

"Oh. Oh. Oh!" He panted. I knew he was getting close. His cock swelled further in my mouth. Spit and pre-come oozed out of my mouth and ran down his shaft. It clung to my lips, my chin, and ran down my neck. My face was covered in his excitement. I felt his ass muscles tighten on my fingers. I knew this was it. The moment he had waited for all his life.

"Holy Mother of God" was all he managed to say before the first wave of his first orgasm took hold. My mouth was instantly filled with the warm sweetness of Matt's come. I continued to suck his cock and work his ass. His groaning picked up, and I braced myself for another round. Jet after jet of hot come flooded my mouth. I tried to hold it all in, to savor it slowly as it made its way down my throat, but the muscles in my mouth let go. It sprayed out of my mouth and covered his stomach and balls. I continued sucking on his cock as it began to soften.

"Yeah, Matt, that's it. Keep stroking my cock," I mumbled while his soft, sticky cock was still in my mouth. His rhythm was off, but I didn't care. "Oh, Matt, I'm going to come!" His eyes widened as I released my load onto his chest. I saw a smile cross his face as he felt the warmth splash across his body. His free hand began rubbing it over his nipples and down his stomach, mixing it with his own.

We lay there for a few moments trying to catch our breath. The air was thick with a mixture of sex and sweat. I stood up, sawdust and dirt covering my body. I looked over at Matt lying on the floor. His eyes were still on me.

"I don't know what to say." His voice was softer than when we first met.

"You don't have to say anything." I squatted down next to him and patted him on his leg. "Usually this is where I collect my money and say good-bye. No emotions. No post-sex conversations, just payment and a thank-you." He looked around for his pants. "Don't bother looking for your wallet. I'm not going to charge you. Consider this one a gift." I started to get up.

"Wait." He sat up, grabbed his laptop case, and opened one of the flaps. "How much do you usually charge for your time?"

"Two hundred and fifty for an hour." I began to feel somewhat sorry for him. "Look, I said not to worry about it."

"I know." He seemed to speak to the case. "Here, there's two thousand. It's money that I collected for our organization. I'm supposed to drop it off tomorrow morning." He stood up and faced me. "Will this be enough for you to spend the night with me?"

"Yeah. I think that should cover it." I couldn't help but smile. "Now get dressed. I have a suite at the Ritz with our name on it."

WILD JACK'S

MARK JAMES

FURIOUS WIND BATTERED the small window of the filthy bathroom.

Cody looked at himself in the grimy, cracked mirror. A blond boy with scared blue eyes looked back at him.

"What are you doing here?" he asked himself.

Cody closed his eyes, leaned his head against the mirror, and wished he was anywhere but where he was. He tried to block out the sounds from the bar. The drunken laughter and hollering sounded like shrieks in some bizarre purgatory for men so mean, hell wouldn't let them in.

Back home he had been one month shy of getting a framed piece of paper after two years of college. But one mistake, one bad decision, and here he was, a fugitive in the land of the unforgiven. Wild Jack's was the only bar around for fifty miles. Hell, it was the only anything for miles and miles. Around here, a waiter earned tips in the bathroom on his knees.

The oil workers who came into Wild Jack's were hard men who braved the lonely northern ends of the world nearly every day. On weekends they lived to have fun with a pretty boy.

Suddenly the bathroom door banged open behind Cody. He whirled, heart hammering, and stared into the angry eyes of Bert, owner of Wild Jack's.

"What the fuck you still doing in here, kid?"

Bert was an ex-Marine, and it showed, from his bristling, black crew cut to his six-foot frame of tightly packed, solid muscle. He covered the space between them in two long strides and grabbed Cody's arm.

"Ain't I told you to come right out when you're done?" he said, giving the slender boy a hard shake.

"Sorry, Bert," Cody said in a low, careful voice. His new boss terrified him.

Bert shoved Cody out into the dark, narrow hallway and headed back to the bar.

"Come on, college boy," he said, walking past Cody. "Alex said table seven asked for you. Bring him a beer and a shot."

Anywhere but here, Cody thought, following after Bert, anywhere but this corner of hell.

Cody worked his way up to the crowded horseshoe bar. On the jukebox, a country and western singer whined about his troubles with love.

"Hey, boy," a big man with two front teeth said to him. "You looking real pretty tonight."

He ran a filthy hand the size of a bear's paw over Cody's ass, outlined in tight denim shorts.

"Yeah," the man next to him said, rubbing the crotch of his work jeans. He was built like a mountain and looked dumb as dirt. "You as pretty as a girl." They both roared in drunken laughter.

Cody took the beer and shot glass full of Yukon Gold that Bert gave him on a small wooden tray. He worked his way through men jammed nearly shoulder to shoulder, heading for table seven. He passed the pool table, where men in flannel shirts and faded jeans pawed at his ass as he squeezed by. Just behind the pool players, a table of men played high-stakes poker, drinking bourbon on ice, gambling away the fortune they made down in the mines.

The man at table seven was the only man in the bar who sat alone. He was big and bulky, like all the men in Wild Jack's. The rolled-up sleeves of his navy flannel shirt showed bulging biceps and thick forearms. Cody set the tray down and put the beer and whiskey on the table.

"Sit with me, kid," he said. His voice rumbled, low and deep.

"Can't," Cody said. "I have to work the bar."

Bert's rule—never sit with a customer, keep circulating.

"I said sit down," the stranger said in a slow, dangerous voice.

The hard edge in his voice cut through the boy. Cody looked at him in the shadows of the corner booth. Something hard and mean glittered in his dark brown eyes. The stranger grabbed Cody's arm and pulled the boy down on the wooden bench next to him.

Cody looked into his weathered face. The man had fought a lot of tough winters here in the land of the midnight sun. There was a coldness about him that was like the land he worked— harsh, unforgiving. Something in Cody was irresistibly drawn to him.

"You're real pretty," the man said, emptying the shot glass into his beer without taking his eyes off Cody. "Pretty blue eyes, pink lips, just like a girl."

The stranger ran his rough hands over Cody's bare chest.

"And you're soft like a girl too. Got a name?"

"Cody."

The man laughed. "And got a girl's name too."

The way the man kept calling Cody a girl pissed him off, but it made his cock hard. He was always drawn to men who treated him like this. He liked getting on his knees and pleasing them.

"You're going home with me tonight," the stranger said, running his hand down Cody's smoothly slender legs.

There was something rough and mean about him that turned Cody on like nothing ever had.

"What the fuck, kid?" Bert said from behind the booth. "I got to beat your ass tonight or what?"

Cody instinctively tried to jump up, but the man at table seven held his arm.

"How you doing, Bert?" he said softly.

The ex-Marine came around so he could see who was sitting in the booth. He blanched at what he saw.

"Trent," Bert said, in a weak voice that was nothing like the bellow Cody was used to hearing. "I didn't know you was out—I mean back. Hey, glad to see you, man."

"Are you?" Trent said, looking up at him with dark, unreadable eyes.

"Sure," Bert said, in a voice that was obviously lying. "It ain't been the same without you."

Trent ran his hands through Cody's silky blond hair.

"I'm taking him home," Trent said. "How much to rent his ass for the night?"

"On the house," Bert said too quickly.

"Why?" Trent said. "Ain't my money good here no more?"

"Sure it is. I ain't disrespecting you," Bert said. "He's like a welcome-home present. Enjoy him. Just bring him back tomorrow."

"What if I don't feel like bringing him back? He's awful pretty," Trent said, stroking Cody's legs.

Bert shrugged. "Then keep him. My gift. I'll find another whore."

The last thing Cody wanted was to go home with this dark stranger. "Bert, it's Friday night, I—"

Trent grabbed the boy's arm hard enough to make him squirm and pulled him real close.

"Shut up, kid," he said, looking into Cody's scared eyes. "Ain't nobody talking to you."

"Trent?" Bert said.

Trent turned his hard eyes on Bert, easing up on Cody, but not letting him go.

"What?"

"I didn't say nothing to nobody. You know that, right?"

Trent's dark eyes bored steadily into Bert, but he spoke to

Cody. "Go put on some clothes, boy. You'll catch your death out there in those shorts."

He let go, and Cody slipped out of the booth, past Bert.

"Hey, kid," Trent said.

Cody looked back at him.

"Bring the shorts. I like how your ass looks in them."

When Cody came back downstairs, in jeans faded nearly to white, a heavy green sweatshirt with "23" on it, and his black knapsack slung over his shoulder, both men were on their feet.

"Hey," the boy said, walking up to them.

"You ready, kid?" Trent said.

Cody nodded.

"Let's go."

Trent headed for the door without so much as a backward glance. Cody took a look back at Bert's scared face, then followed the stranger out into the howling night wind.

The ride up to Trent's cabin took them down a narrow, winding road. Towering, jagged stone surrounded them, and beyond that, dense forest. No gas stations, no cell phone towers, no houses, no people.

Bert's words ran through Cody's mind: *I didn't know you was out.* He was out here alone in the big empty with a man who'd just gotten out of jail. Or maybe he escaped. What the hell did he know?

Cody watched the northern lights chase across the night sky in sheets of blues and greens as Trent followed the headlights of his pickup truck deeper and deeper into shadowless darkness. Finally, they turned down a narrow dirt path that could barely be called a road. Giant trees pressed in on both sides of them as Trent drove through pitch-black darkness. After a while, he pulled into a clearing, in front of a small wooden cabin covered in a fine layer of snow.

Cody stepped out of the truck into the strange softness of freshly fallen snow. This was beyond the middle of nowhere. It was the end of nowhere.

Howling wolves filled the night with their unearthly cries. Out here, with a stranger who frightened Bert, the scariest man he'd ever met, Cody seriously thought of hitching a ride back to Wild Jack's. But there was no way to hitch a ride on the deserted road they'd just left. Besides, the wolves would rip him to shreds if he strayed from here.

Trent had walked on ahead of him and opened the front door.

"Come on, kid," he said. His voice was friendly. But his eyes were full of mystery, dark and unreadable. "It's cold out here."

Trent shut the door behind them and started feeding wood to the smoldering fire that burned low in the fireplace built into one wall of the cabin. There was no other light in the small room. Cody looked around while Trent got the fire going. Eyes in the heads of slaughtered elk, deer, and other animals Cody didn't recognize glittered on the wooden walls.

One wall was given entirely to a collection of hunting rifles. Pictures scattered here and there showed Trent next to his animal trophies. A fishing rod leaned in one corner.

Cody sat in one of the two oversize armchairs that stood on opposite sides of the fireplace. They had a homemade look, with dark pinewood legs and soft cushions.

"Bathroom's around the corner. Put your shorts back on," Trent said, without looking up from what he was doing. "And bring me a beer when you come back."

The bathroom was through a small kitchen. Cody went in and put his shorts on. On the way back he stopped in the small kitchen and grabbed two cans of beer from the small fridge.

When he walked back into the room, the flames were leaping high, filling the dark room with the orange glow of dancing firelight. A low, wooden table sat in front of a couch with deep cushions and mahogany legs. Trent had taken off his work shirt, revealing a broad chest thick with muscle, a flat, ridged belly, and arms thick and hard as tree trunks. He was sitting on the couch with his feet up on the table.

"You like my place, boy?" Trent said, looking at Cody with hungry eyes.

"It's cool," Cody said, giving him a beer.

Trent looked at the other beer in Cody's hand.

"Put that back," he said. A shade of anger came into his eyes. It was gone in a moment, but Cody was sure he'd seen it. "I don't like my girls to drink."

"You serious?" Cody said.

"Don't fuck with me, bitch. Put it back. Now."

The mean edge in his voice made Cody head back to the kitchen in a hurry, wondering what the fuck he'd gotten himself into this time.

Trent watched him go, his eyes fastened to Cody's round little ass. When Cody came back, Trent said, "Take off my boots."

The boy knelt on the soft, thick rug in front of the table and started unlacing the big work boots.

Trent popped the top of his beer and took a long swallow.

"Tell me about yourself, kid," he said, looking at Cody in the firelight. "How'd a city boy like you end up in a place like this?"

"How'd you know I'm a city boy?" Cody said, taking off one boot and setting it aside.

Trent shrugged. "I been up here all my life. You act like a city boy, sound like one, so you must be one. Probably a college boy too. Why ain't you in school?"

Cody didn't like this. Too many questions.

"I'm working my way through school," he said, avoiding Trent's eyes.

"In the middle of winter?"

Cody shrugged. "Yeah, well," he said. "I'm between semesters."

"You're a bad liar, boy," Trent said softly. "Who you running from?"

Cody put the other boot next to its twin.

"Look," the boy said quietly, "what do you want?"

"I wanna make you my girl," Trent said, looking steadily at the boy.

Cody laughed, a low bitter sound. "You're too late. Bert already did that."

"Yeah, but he don't know how to make a slut like you beg for a man's cock, does he?" Trent took his feet down and spread his legs. "Come here."

Cody knelt between his legs, looking up at him.

Trent ran his hands over the boy slowly, enjoying the tender feel of Cody's softly trembling body.

"Listen to me real good, bitch," Trent said, looking down into Cody's scared eyes. "Do what I say, and you'll have a real good time tonight. Fuck with me, and I'll make you sorry."

He ran his hands over Cody's nipples, looking at the boy's face. "You got it?"

Cody nodded.

Trent ran his hands through Cody's silky blond hair.

"You're beautiful," he said.

Cody loved the feel of Trent's rough hands on him, but his mind kept slipping back to what Bert said.

"How come Bert's scared of you?" Cody said. "And where'd you get out from?" He couldn't help himself. He had to know.

Trent shrugged. "I got a past, kid."

"Where? In the penitentiary?" Cody said.

Dark laughter danced in Trent's eyes.

"You don't really want me to answer that, do you, kid?" he said in a soft voice.

Cody swallowed in his suddenly dry throat. He'd heard stories about men who lived in cabins like this one, out in the woods, where no one could hear you scream. They took boys like him and raped them for days, then turned them loose, too scared to go to the police.

Trent saw terror leap into the boy's eyes.

"Do what I say, and I won't hurt you, boy. But don't be asking me questions. You won't like the answers."

Trent ran his hands slowly over Cody's soft, smooth body. His muscled arms pulled the boy close and kissed his neck softly, while one of his hands stole into Cody's crotch. The boy moaned softly and forgot all about Bert.

"You like sucking cock, boy?" Trent said, running his hand lightly through Cody's blond hair.

Cody didn't answer, just dropped his eyes. Men like Trent always made him unbearably hot, but he couldn't bring himself to look into those hard eyes and admit that he liked to serve a man on his knees.

Trent ran a rough hand along Cody's left cheek.

"You want to answer me when I talk to you, boy," he said in a soft voice. "The last thing you want in this wide world is to piss me off tonight."

Suddenly Trent grabbed Cody's hair and pulled cruelly hard.

"Answer me, bitch. You like sucking cock?"

"Yes," Cody said, gasping in pain.

Trent grinned down into his face, letting go of his hair. He ran his fingers slowly along Cody's soft pink lips.

"You know what I'm gonna do to you tonight, boy?" Trent said quietly. "First I'm gonna shoot a load down your throat. Then you're gonna get on that table on all fours for me, and I'm gonna fuck you real hard."

Cody looked up at him with scared, helpless eyes.

"You're my bitch tonight, you hear?" Trent said.

Cody nodded. He was more scared than he'd ever been, but still, he wanted Trent's hard cock in his mouth, choking him, shooting his load down his throat.

Trent pulled Cody close and rubbed the boy's face against his crotch.

"You need it bad, Cody. You need a man to fuck you and give

you what you need. Don't you?"

He pushed Cody's head back, looking down into the boy's desperate eyes.

"You need a man who'll make you beg for cock, then give it to you hard and make you come like a bitch."

The way Trent talked made Cody unbearably hot. He wanted Trent's cock in his mouth more than he had ever wanted any man.

"Please," he said softly.

Cody watched eagerly as Trent stood up and undid his jeans. He slid them down over his hips and revealed his nakedness underneath. His hard, thick cock stood straight up, reaching past his navel. The thick head was slick with pre-come. Veins grooved the hard flesh.

"You want it, bitch?"

Cody could only nod, looking at his hardness.

"Beg for it," Trent said.

"Please," Cody said. "Let me suck your cock."

Trent moved closer, towering over the boy like a Greek god, and brought his thick cock to Cody's lips.

The boy opened his mouth and took the man's cock deep down his throat, moaning softly. Trent looked down at the boy's pretty pink lips stretched tight around his driving cock, sliding in and out of the boy's hot, wet mouth.

His movements were long and rhythmic as he used Cody's mouth to pleasure his throbbing cock. Trent grabbed the boy's hair with both hands and held him still while he fucked his face. His head rolled back on his shoulders, eyes closed, while he pumped his cock deep down Cody's throat, enjoying every inch of the boy's hot mouth.

"Yeah, bitch. Suck my cock. Take it all," he said, humping the boy's face.

Trent groaned at the hot feel of Cody's spasming throat grabbing the head of his cock as his deep thrusts choked the helpless boy servicing his thick cock. For a long time, the only sounds in the room were Cody's small moans of pain as Trent's cock hit the back of his throat again and again and his grunts of pleasure as he used the boy's hot mouth. Soon Trent's thrusts became more desperate.

"You fucking hot bitch," Trent said in a strangled voice. "Take my load. Swallow every drop," he said and pulled Cody's face down on his cock.

Trent's hips bucked against Cody's lips, and his cock exploded inside the boy's mouth, sending hot loads of come jetting down his throat.

"Oh, fuck, yeah," he said, stroking into Cody's mouth. Come dribbled down Cody's chin.

"Clean me," he said, pulling out of the boy's mouth and pushing his head down onto his sticky cock.

Cody's hot tongue licked up and down Trent's cock and around his balls, licking up his come. Trent felt himself getting hard again.

"You like my cock in your mouth, bitch?" he said and stroked Cody's hair softly while the boy buried his face in his crotch, licking his cock clean.

Cody looked up at him.

"Yeah," he said, unzipping his shorts. He was desperate to jack off and shoot his load.

"What the fuck you think you're doing, bitch?" Trent said.

"Please," Cody said. "I gotta come."

Trent slapped him, but not too hard. The bitch had sucked him off good.

"You come when I say so," he said and pushed Cody's face back down onto his cock.

Cody went back to licking him, his hard cock throbbing desperately between his legs.

"That's it. Get me hard again so I can fuck your bitch ass and make you my girl," Trent said, running his hands gently over

Cody's soft face.

The boy ran his smooth tongue around the thick shaft of Trent's rising cock, licking up the sticky mess of his come. He slid his tongue to Trent's balls and licked the underside of his cock, now nearly fully hard again, then slid his tongue back to the sensitive skin just behind the balls.

"Oh fuck," Trent said, gasping in pleasure. "Get up here, bitch."

Trent pulled the frightened boy to his feet and slid Cody's shorts down and made the boy step out of them.

"I'm gonna fuck you real hard, bitch," he said, running his hands over Cody's tight, round ass.

Trent suddenly grabbed both of Cody's arms roughly and pulled the boy close until they were only inches apart.

"You're gonna get on that table on all fours," Trent said, gripping the boy's arms tight. "If you take my cock like a good girl, I'll make it nice for you. Fuck with me, and I'll make you scream. You got me?"

The boy nodded, scared that Trent might hurt him anyway, just for kicks.

Trent shoved Cody toward the table, and the boy knelt on all fours, his ass facing Trent.

Trent grabbed the KY from the couch and lubed his thick cock, looking at Cody's ass in the soft firelight. He loved the sight of the boy on all fours, afraid, waiting to take his cock.

"That's nice, bitch," Trent said, lubing his cock, "real nice."

He ran his finger slowly around the outside of the boy's hole. Cody whimpered in fear, sure that Trent would rip into him with his thick cock.

Trent pressed one long finger against the boy's hole until he gave way and let him slip inside his delicious tightness. Cody tensed up as soon as Trent's finger invaded his hole.

"Relax, bitch," Trent said. "I'm taking this ass one way or the other. Don't make it hard for yourself."

"I'm sorry," Cody said quickly.

The boy's voice, trembling on the edge of tears, made Trent's cock throb with hunger.

Trent slid his finger slowly in and out of Cody's hot hole, getting his ass ready for his thick cock. He could tell by the way the boy tensed at his touch that Cody was the kind of bitch who was scared to get it up the ass. The boy would panic the minute he felt Trent's thick cock pressing into his ass. He'd probably have to take him by force.

"You like that, bitch?" Trent said, easing his finger in and out of Cody.

Cody moaned softly, writhing on Trent's finger inside him.

Trent smiled. "I'm gonna fuck this boy pussy real good. That's what girls like you need. A fat cock up their ass."

Trent put two fingers up against Cody's hot hole. "Push that ass back," he said. "Show me how good you're gonna take my cock."

Cody inched back onto his fingers slowly, moaning softly.

"You want my cock up your ass, boy?" Trent said. He slid his fingers out of Cody and pushed against his hole again.

"Yeah," Cody said, pushing his ass back against Trent.

Trent couldn't wait anymore. He guided his throbbing cock to Cody's ass. The boy pushed back against him, hungry for Trent inside him.

Trent grabbed Cody's hips and pressed into him with steady pressure. The boy moaned softly as he felt the pain of his hole opening to Trent's thick cock.

Slowly, the head of Trent's fat cock slid into Cody's ass. The boy gasped in pain and bucked in the man's grip.

"Easy, bitch," Trent said, holding Cody's hips tight. "Don't make me hurt you."

Cody's breath came in little moans of pain as Trent sank his cock slowly into the boy's hot tightness. Cody's ass grasped his cock in a hot massage of tight, pulsing flesh. Trent went as slow as he could, giving Cody a chance. But the boy's nerve broke.

"No," Cody cried out. "Stop. Please. I can't," he said, struggling against Trent. "Take it out. It hurts."

Trent clamped down on Cody's hips, holding him in an iron grip.

"Told you not to fuck with me, bitch," he said.

Trent grabbed Cody's hips even tighter and rammed his cock deep inside the boy's ass while he pulled him onto his cock at the same time.

Cody cried out and struggled wildly, but Trent was much too strong for him. He sank into the boy's hot tightness again and again, driving his cock deep into him. The boy's cries flowed over Trent, echoing in his ears, making his cock throb deep inside him.

"Shut the fuck up and take my cock, you bitch," Trent said, fucking the boy's ass hard.

Soon the skin around Cody's hole turned red from the friction of Trent slamming into him. Every hard thrust rocked the boy's whole body and made him whimper and moan in pain.

"You're my girl now," Trent said, thrusting into Cody. "You'll take my cock, even if it hurts."

Every stroke into the boy's tight hotness was paradise. The sound of his whimpers drove Trent wild, making him groan deep in his throat, but he forced himself to pull out of the boy's ass. He wanted to see Cody's face when he shot his load up his bitch ass.

"Come here, bitch," Trent said, pulling the unresisting boy off the table.

He dragged the scared boy to the thick rug that lay between the table and the fireplace and made him lie down. Trent lay on top of him, looking down into Cody's frightened eyes.

"Told you not to fuck with me, bitch," he said.

He ran his hands over Cody's smooth body, then reached between them and found Cody's swollen cock.

"Look at this, bitch," he whispered, kissing and licking Cody's

"You like getting fucked like a girl?"

"God," Cody said, "yes."

Trent stroked slowly in and out of the boy, using his ass in long, deep strokes.

"Say it," Trent said. "Tell me how you're my girl."

Trent fucked faster into the boy, following the natural rhythm of his hungry, grasping ass. Cody's tight flesh grabbed him in hot wetness on every stroke. The bitch was close to coming.

"Come on, bitch, say it. Or I'll pull out and come in your mouth again."

"No," Cody cried out. "Don't."

"Then say it," Trent said, stroking into him.

"I'm your girl. I'll take your cock even if it hurts."

"Good bitch," Trent said.

He humped the boy's tight ass, fucking him in a hard, primitive rhythm, grunting and groaning in the back of his throat.

"I'm gonna make you come so good," he said into Cody's ear.

He thrust into Cody's hot, throbbing hole again and again, grinding his hips into him, fucking the boy hard and deep.

Cody bucked and moaned under him, gasping in pleasure. He was so close. Trent saw it on his face.

"What are you, bitch?" he said, driving his cock deep into Cody's ass.

"Oh God," Cody said, moaning. "I'm your girl."

Trent pumped the boy's hungry ass, shoving his thick cock hard into him, groaning in pleasure.

Cody squeezed his eyes shut and cried out—then his cock exploded in pleasure. He bucked hard under Trent, grunting with the force of his orgasm.

His ass grabbed at Trent's cock rhythmically, driving the man over the edge.

"Here I come, bitch," Trent said between clenched teeth. He threw his head back and tensed against the boy, driving his cock deep one last time.

"Take my load," Trent said in a low, harsh voice and pumped the boy's wildly pulsing ass full of his come.

Trent pumped into Cody's sweet ass a few more times, then rolled off him. Cody curled into his arms and lay against him.

"No one ever made me come like that," the boy said, almost shyly.

"That's 'cause you never had a real man to give you what you need," Trent said quietly.

He had his arm wrapped around Cody. The boy's head lay on his strong chest.

"Don't take me back, Trent," Cody said in a low voice. "Please. I'll be your girl, if that's what you want."

"You ain't going back there, boy. You can count on it."

Trent kissed the top of Cody's head gently and pulled him closer into his arms. They lay together in the warmth of the crackling firelight, listening to the cold wind rattle the cabin's small window.

ABOUT THE
CONTRIBUTORS

SHANE ALLISON has been called a fag, a nigger, and a genius. He is the author of four chapbooks of poetry. *Ceiling of Mirrors* (Cynic Press), *Black Vaseline* (Blaze Vox Books), *Cock and Balls* (Feel Free Press), and most recently *Black Fag* (Future Tense Books). His fifth book of naughty verse, *I Want to Fuck a Redneck*, is forthcoming from Scintillating Publications. His stories and poems have graced the pages of *Velvet Mafia, Suspect Thoughts, Outsider Ink, Best Black Gay Erotica, I Do/I Don't: Queers on Marriage, Chiron Review, Coal City Review, Mississippi Review, New Delta Review*, and others. Sloppy wet kisses with tongue go out to Jesse Grant and the stars and co-stars at Alyson Books for all their hard work. Shane can be reached at starsissy42@hotmail.com.

A native Californian, BEARMUFFIN lives in San Diego with two leatherbears in a stimulating ménage à trois. He has written gay erotica for *Honcho, Torso, Manscape, In Touch*, and *Hot Shots*.

WHIZZER CRAFTON played minor league baseball for two years and was recruited by the Minnesota Twins before suffering an elbow injury, forcing him to become a hooker. That didn't work out either. Luckily, he has also been writing his whole life. His poems, fiction, and essays have recently appeared in many literary magazines. He used to teach kindergarten at the Little

Red Schoolhouse, but now only teaches bowling, creative writing, government, and modern dance at the Spence School for Girls.

BILL DORSETT is a freelance writer living in the Pacific Northwest. Bill returns here to writing after a twenty-year absence. He wrote theater reviews for the *South Bay Daily Breeze* and had a monthly column in San Pedro's *Random Lengths Community News*. He lives with his partner and two cats.

WILLIAM HOLDEN lives in Atlanta with his partner of eight years. He works full-time as a librarian on LGBT issues. He has eleven other published short stories and one unpublished novel. He welcomes any comments and can be contacted at Srholdbill@aol.com.

MARK JAMES is a writer of male erotica whose writing explores the relationships between men whose love falls beyond the boundaries of society. His stories deny the idea that love is always sweetness and light and take the reader to a place where love lies in the darkness beyond the realms of tradition.

JASON KIMBLE escaped the arctic climes of Michigan winters for welcoming, sultry Florida. That is, if by "welcoming" you mean "full of retirees who ooze a sense of entitlement" and by "sultry" you mean "grotesquely humid and prone to hurricanes." But it's definitely Florida. Plus: no snow to shovel.

ADAM KOZIK is a poet, writer, and photographer. His erotic fiction has appeared in *Honcho*. He is currently making photographs of the male nude accompanied by narrative poems. A native of Chicago, he has lived and worked in New York City and Paris, France. He has been guest poet at the St. Mark's Poetry Project in New York, and at the People's Poetry Gathering at Cooper Union. His poetry has appeared in *Songs of Innocence and Experience*.

SETH LEEPER writes fiction and poetry. He lives in San Francisco where he is currently working toward a B.A. in creative writing at San Francisco State Univeristy. This is his first published story and he looks forward to publishing many, many more.

A published poet and a professional steelworker from southern Illinois, JORDAN LEWIS has a view of life from the labored to the emotional. He exercises his passion for writing every chance he gets.

MICHAEL MURPHY lives in Vancouver, Canada, where he is an actor and personal trainer, dabbling in writing on the side. His erotic stories have been published in the anthology *Ultimate Gay Erotica 2005* and the magazine *Bear*.

AARON NIELSEN holds a B.A. in English Literature from San Francisco State University, where he is currently pursuing an MFA in creative writing. His fiction and poetry have previously appeared in *Velvet Mafia, Outsider Ink, Suspect Thought, The Chabot Review, Mirage, Instant City,* and *Fresh Men 2: New Voices in Gay Fiction* (2005). Aaron is the 2001 recipient of the Fredrick C. Fallon award for poetry. He lives in San Francisco.

MARK ORANJE is a thirty-five-year-old Brit who has only just started writing gay fiction. "San Sebastian" is his third published story.

STEPHEN OSBORNE is a former improvisational comedian who now toils away in the world of retail management. He lives in Indianapolis with two cats and Jadzia, the wonder dog. He is single, but taking applications.

KIRK READ, a freelance writer, is the author of *How I Learned to Snap*, a memoir about being openly gay in a small southern high school during the late 1980s. His work has appeared in *Out, Genre,*

Christopher Street, *QSF*, and a host of alt-weeklies, websites, and LGBT newspapers. He currently lives in San Francisco, where he is working on a second book.

SIMON SHEPPARD is the author of *Sex Parties 101*, *In Deep: Erotic Stories*, *Kinkorama: Dispatches from the Front Lines of Perversion*, and *Hotter Than Hell* and co-editor of *Rough Stuff* and *Roughed Up: More Tales of Gay Men, Sex, and Power*. His work has appeared in over 125 anthologies, including *The Best American Erotica 2005* and *Best Gay Erotica 2005*.

BRAD STEVENS is a gay freelance writer and sex worker living in the Washington, D.C., area. He has been writing stories for twenty years and has only recently begun to write stories that combine his own real-life experiences with imagination, resulting in a unique blend of heartfelt truth and fiction.

TROY STORM has had several hundred sexy short stories published under an equal number of catchy sexy names, covering most shades of the sexual spectrum. He also has had a romantic intrigue novel published and a collection of short stories and is busy hustling, uh, a new, mainstream coming-of-age.

ANDREW WARBURTON enjoys writing erotic fiction as well as experimental prose. He lives in the U. K.

Born an Okie, MARK WILDYR presently resides in New Mexico, the setting of many of his stories, which explore developing sexual awareness and intercultural relationships. Over thirty of his short stories and novellas have been acquired by Alyson Publications, Arsenal Pulp, Companion Press, Southern Tier/Haworth Press, and STARbooks Press.